The Framed Father

The Father Tom Mysteries, Book 2
By
J. R. Mathis and Susan Mathis

D1518213

Mercy and Justice Mysteries, 2021

Fourth Printing, October 2021

Contact: mercyandjusticemysteries@gmail.com

Cover Photo: Adobe Stock Photos

Cover: Millie Godwin

Editing: Anna Palmer Darkes

Also by J. R. Mathis and Susan Mathis

Prologue

Dear Tom, I hope you are well and still enjoying your life behind monastic walls. Sometimes I envy the quiet you must enjoy there, but just as often, I wonder how you stand it. Not that life in Myerton is anything like walking a beat in DC, but at least I get the occasional robbery to keep me busy.

Parish life at St. Clare's is also pretty interesting. I have not yet followed your suggestion to join the Ladies of Charity, but I do attend parish functions occasionally. Most of the time I'm working so Dan can attend with his family. It makes a lot more sense for him to be there with Miriam and the kids than it does for an old widow like me to go. I've only met Miriam once or twice, but I admire how devoted she is to her family.

Oh, Gladys wants me to be sure to tell you 'Hi.' She still has a huge crush on you, so watch your back if you come into town. I'm not sure what she might try if she caught you in a dark corner, and she's pretty fast in that wheelchair. I admit I'm a bit worried about her. She seems to have a very active social life—a little too active, if you know what I mean. As her supervisor, it's none of my business, but as a friend, I wonder if I should say something to her. Another thing you can pray for me over: discernment.

Speaking of social lives and discernment, this thing with Brian is beginning to get out of hand. He just won't leave me alone. In fact, I'm about to the point of saying I'll go out with him once just to prove that it won't work out. I mean, I don't think he's a bad guy, but he's very ambitious politically and as you may remember, that is something I do not care for at all.

So, is there anything new at Our Lady of the Mount? I saw something in a supermarket tabloid about a secret Vatican takeover. Do you know anything about that? I suppose you couldn't tell me if you did. Anyway, please write back when you get a chance. I do look forward to hearing from you.

Helen

One

I begin to reply to Helen's latest email when there's a knock on the door of my cell.

"Come in," I say, quickly closing my laptop.

"Excuse me, Father Tom," a young brother says.

"Yes, Brother Thomas?"

"There's a call for you on the main line," he replies, somewhat out of breath. "The Archbishop."

"Did he say what he wanted?"

Brother Thomas shakes his head. "No, he didn't say. He just told me to get you as quickly as possible. Apparently, he's been trying to call you."

A summons like this is not to be disobeyed and I follow Brother Thomas quickly down the dimly lit hallway to the office. The blinking hold light shows the line the Archbishop is waiting on.

Lifting the receiver, I begin, "Hello, Your Eminence what—"

"Father Tom, I need you to go to Saint Clare's immediately," he orders before I can finish my sentence.

"Excuse me?"

"How soon can you leave?" he asks.

"Well, I don't know," I reply. "I have several—"

"Let me clarify," the Archbishop interrupts. "When I say immediately, I mean today. When I ask how soon can you leave, I mean how long will it take you to pack?"

"I don't understand," I say. "Why the urgency?"

He hesitates. "A . . . A situation has arisen that needs to be addressed quickly and quietly."

"What kind of situation?"

The Archbishop sighs. "One involving Father McCoy."

I furrow my brow. "What kind of situation could Father McCoy be involved in?" Having met the young priest, I have a hard time coming up with one that would agitate the Archbishop so much. I like Father Leonard McCoy, but he seems too scared of his own shadow to be involved in anything that might be termed "a situation."

2

"Something has come to my attention," the Archbishop continues. "I need you to look into it."

"With all due respect, Your Eminence, you haven't answered my question. Are you going to tell me what you want me to look into?"

Silence. "Hello, are you still there, sir?" I ask.

"Yes," he says. "I'm here." A pause. A sigh. "We've received an anonymous allegation of misconduct against Father McCoy."

"What kind of misconduct?"

"Father Greer, are you being obtuse on purpose? What kind of misconduct do you think? All right, I'll come right out and say it. We've gotten an anonymous allegation of sexual misconduct involving Father McCoy and an adult member of the parish."

I pause, then burst out laughing. "You're joking!"

"Do I sound like I'm joking?"

"But really, Your Eminence. We're talking about Father McCoy. Leonard McCoy? The same Father McCoy who is pastor of Saint Clare's Parish in Myerton? That Father McCoy?"

"Yes, Father, the one and only."

"But have you met Father McCoy? I mean, it's absurd! He's the walking definition of milquetoast. This has to be a joke."

"I do not find it the least bit funny."

I pull myself together. "No, sir, of course not. We need to take the allegation seriously."

"We can't afford not to," the Archbishop says. "We're still trying to recover from our past behavior and we can't discount something like this or sweep it under the rug."

"I agree," I say. "So, who is he alleged to have . . . committed this misconduct with?"

I hear papers rustling. "The parish secretary."

I burst out laughing again. "But I know the parish secretary," I say. "She's my mother-in-law. Anna's an attractive woman for being in her early sixties, but she's—"

"I am certainly not talking about Anna—Mrs. Luckgold, Father," Archbishop Knowland says.

"But she was serving as parish secretary when I left Myerton four months ago."

I can hear the Archbishop shuffling papers. "According to the allegation, the parish secretary's name is Rachel Watson."

"Before I left Myerton," I say, "Anna told me they were interviewing for the position but I hadn't heard that Saint Clare's had hired one."

"Is there any reason why you would have heard, Father?"

I think of my weekly emails from Helen Parr, an old friend whose acquaintance I had renewed during my brief time as Rector of Saint Clare's parish in Myreton last year. In keeping with our commitment to avoid personal entanglements, her emails typically concern goings-on in the parish and in the town of Myerton itself. She has not mentioned the parish hiring a new secretary, but then again, I guess she might not have noticed unless she had to go into the office for some reason.

"No, sir. There really is no reason." I answer.

"This says that Ms. Watson," the Archbishop continues, "is a single woman in her late 20s."

"Hmm," I say. "Not your typical parish secretary. Not like the last one."

"Exactly, which is why we have to get on top of this," the Archbishop says. "I need you to go to Myerton to sort this out."

"What do you—"

"Talk to Father McCoy, get his side of the story. Interview this Watson woman, see if anything alleged is true."

I hesitate to ask the next question I have, but it needs to be asked. "Have there been any other similar allegations against Father McCoy in the past?"

"No, not one," the Archbishop says. "I had his file pulled the moment I finished reading the letter. He's squeaky clean, not so much as a hint of scandal at his previous assignments."

Considering his last assignment was at the Archdiocese assisted living facility, I'm not surprised.

"What exactly are the allegations?" I ask.

He hesitates. "I don't want to get into them over the phone," he says. "I sent a copy by email to Saint Clare's."

"So Father McCoy knows about the allegations?"

"Yes, I called him last night to tell him."

"I bet he had a restless night."

"He's not the only one!" Archbishop Knowland exclaims. "This hasn't been good for my blood pressure or my ulcer!"

"Does he know I'm coming?"

"He knows someone is coming. Frankly, you were not the first name on my list. You've shown a tendency to, well, get a little too involved."

"I hardly think being involved in one murder investigation—"

"—two, Father, if you include your wife's."

I pause. The Archbishop says, "Sorry, Tom. I shouldn't have said that. It wasn't fair. But you got too involved last time you were at Saint Clare's. Because of that, you weren't my first choice. But I got to thinking that your familiarity with the parish, with the town, with the authorities could come in handy."

I furrow my brow. "Are the police involved?"

"No," the Archbishop insists. "No, not yet anyway, since the letter does not imply anything illegal has happened. That's one thing I want you to look at." He paused. "If Father McCoy did something egregious to this woman, something that broke a law, then I want you to find that out, and I want you to report it. You know the Myerton Police's lead detective, correct?"

I'm careful before answering. "Yes, I got to know Detective Parr fairly well. She's a good detective."

"What kind of person is she? In other words, will she give the Church a fair shake?"

"Oh, definitely," I say, remembering our relationship of 20 years ago. "She was raised Catholic and may have stumbled in her faith as a young adult, which most people do, but it's my understanding from her own words that she never stopped attending Mass completely. But she has not been involved in a parish since the death of her husband. Still, last I spoke to her, she had begun attending Saint Clare's."

"Well, hopefully, this will not be an issue. If the police need to be involved, involve her. We're not sweeping another problem under the rug. But don't do it unless you uncover something that is a crime."

"I understand."

"Oh, I should also say you'll be taking over the public ministry of Saint Clare's until this matter is cleared up."

"But what excuse will I give?"

"I'm sure you and Father McCoy will think of something appropriate."

I sigh. "What do I tell Father Abbot? We'll be leaving him in a bit of a lurch."

"That's not my concern," the Archbishop yells. "He'll have to manage for a while. We've got to get this taken care of. Pack up and get on the road to Myerton. I'll be waiting for your call." He hangs up, leaving me looking at the receiver.

I ask Brother Thomas if Father Abbot is free. "I think I saw him go in the Grotto's direction. He'll probably be back soon."

"That's all right," I say quietly. "I'll go to him there."

***

I find Father Abbot at the reproduced Grotto of Lourdes, seated on one of the rough-hewn wood benches. The elder monk looks deep in prayer. I approach him quietly, stepping softly on the warm summer grass. It's just after 9:00 a.m. and the early July sun is already hot. I'm sweating by the time I get to the Grotto. The sun is glistening off the white marble statue. I stand a respectful distance away so as not to disturb him.

After a few moments, he looks at me and smiles. "Come, Father, sit by me," he says, patting the seat next to him."

"Sorry to disturb you, Father Abbot," I say, sitting down. "I wouldn't have if it wasn't important."

He shakes his head. "It's perfectly all right, my son. I just come here to meditate. It's often the quietest place on the property. The enclosure gets too noisy sometimes."

I smile inwardly. The monastery is too quiet for me sometimes, and he finds it noisy.

"Now, what is it you need to say to me?" he says, turning to face me.

I tell him about the Archbishop's call. "So he's taking you away from us?"

"Only temporarily," I say, "only until I can get this situation at Saint Clare's straightened out."

"Temporarily," he repeats. "But he gave you no idea how temporary this would be, did he?"

"No," I say hesitantly, "but I can't imagine it would take very long. It's ridiculous, these allegations, and it should only take a week or so to wind up."

He considers what I say, turning to the statue of the Blessed Mother. "Well, I suppose we have no choice," he sighs. "You're still under the Archbishop's authority, and I think we can manage for a few days without a priest. I can still say Mass; one brother will help me move around."

"I'm sorry," I say. "You, the brothers, everyone has been so good to me since I came. It's been a real blessing to me."

He smiles and places his wrinkled hand over mine. "You've been a blessing to us, Father . . . to me." He pauses. "Have you gotten what you came here for?"

"I came here to serve, to help the monastery, to repay you for what you did for me years ago."

Father Abbot smiles. "Yes, I know that's why you say you came. But that's not why you came. You know that. So, I ask again, have you gotten what you came here for?"

I look at the statue of Mary, then the statue of Saint Bernadette. Often my thoughts have returned to this spot, to this place of prayer and solitude, to the day—the moment—I received the call to the priesthood. Out of the depths of my despair over my wife's murder, out of the depths I had sunk to in trying to numb my pain, I had found myself in the monastery all those years ago, wanting peace. What I found then was peace—and a new life.

What had I come back for? After Helen arrested Joan's murderer, after I saw him convicted and locked away, after all the events of last fall, I needed to find peace again. Have I found it? Maybe. But after four months in the quiet and solitude, I am feeling restless and am secretly not sorry to be called to go out again.

"I think so," I reply. "I guess I really won't know until I leave."

"The guilt you once carried, do you still carry it?"

I take time to consider this before I can admit the truth. "No," I whisper. "That's gone, but I still grieve for Joan, for what I lost, not just when she died, but when I learned all that I did last year. It still hurts, even after all this time."

"You wouldn't be human if it didn't," Father Abbot says. "We never really get over our losses. A loved one dies. A favorite pet runs away. Our innocence is taken from us." He pauses and smiles wistfully. "Someone you love marries another person."

I look at him, my mouth open to speak. He looks at me and smiles. "I wasn't always a monk, Father Tom. But that was a long time ago. I never—well, rarely—think about it. So when I say we never really get over loss, I know what I'm saying. Loss isn't something we get over. It's just something we learn to live with. Some people suppress it, others replace it, and others allow their losses to consume them. It's those last who have the hardest time."

"What have you done with yours?"

He smiles. "I'm still figuring that out."

***

"It's ridiculous. It's absurd. It's preposterous. It's . . . it's scandalous!"

I watch the agitated, red-headed cleric pace up and down in the Rectory living room. He's been this way since I arrived, only four hours after the Archbishop's conversation with me at the monastery.

He hadn't greeted me when I knocked on the door. Much to my surprise, Anna answered.

"Tom, thank God," she had said. "I can't get him to calm down."

"What's going on? What are you doing here?"

"What am I doing here? He called me," Anna explained. "At six o'clock this morning he called me. Fortunately, I was up. He asked—begged me to come over. He sounded agitated, so I came right away. He's been in the living room the whole time. Sometimes, he'll sit and stare at the wall, then he'll get up and pace back and forth, mumbling to himself, gesturing with his hands. Then he got a call and when he hung up, he looked at me and said, 'Father Greer will be here around noon. Can you make sure the guest room is ready, please?'" She stopped. "What's going on, Tom? Why are you here?"

I'm not sure how much to tell her. "The Archbishop called me. He asked me—ordered me—to come."

"Why?"

I choose my words carefully, admitting, "I can't say, really. He asked me to look into a . . . complaint against Father Leonard."

She looks confused. "Who could have a complaint against Father Leonard? He's the least offensive person I've ever met."

For Anna to call someone the least offensive person she's ever met is high praise. She has firm opinions about most people, many sharp, few incorrect. It is a trait I have found comes in handy.

"That," I say, responding to her question, "is what the Archbishop wants me to look into. He wants me to see if there's any merit to the complaint."

Anna's countenance turns serious. "Is Father Leonard in some kind of trouble?"

I sigh. "I don't know, Anna, that's what I'm here to find out. Listen, I can't say any more, the Archbishop asked me to be discreet."

She puts her hand up and insists, "Say no more, I won't ask anything else. Though," she smiles, "you know I can find out if I want to."

"And I'm asking you, Anna," I say firmly, "not to."

She nods. "Okay, Tom."

The first words out of Father Leonard McCoy's mouth when Anna shows me into the living room are, "Father Greer, I've done nothing inappropriate with Rachel Watson!"

Anna's eyes get big. *So much for discretion*, I think. I glance at Anna and get a look that is a combination of surprise, concern, and assurance. Surprise at the accusation, concern for Father Leonard, and assurance that I can trust her not to say anything.

"Why don't I go make us some coffee," she says. Returning a while later with a tray holding a coffee pot and two cups with a creamer and sugar bowl, she says, "I'll be in the back cleaning if you need anything." A moment later, I hear the door to the kitchen close, music coming from her phone, and the exhaust fan over the oven running. When Anna has to stay out of the loop, she does it, no matter what the temptation.

Father Leonard spends the next half hour continuing to pace up and down the living room, sometimes quietly, sometimes uttering words of protest, all the time agitated, just as Anna had described.

"Please sit down, Leonard," I say finally, exhausted by his exertions. "Calm down. No one is saying you've done anything wrong."

"Then why did the Archbishop send you? Why is he removing me from public ministry?" He runs his fingers through his mop of hair, grabbing a handful and pulling. "Oh, what would my mother say if she were alive to hear about this?"

"The Archbishop," I say, trying to sound as soothing as possible, "sent me to look into the allegations. Discreetly, quietly. He wants me to take over your public duties, well, to give you a break."

"But what will we tell people? You're not supposed to be here. Everyone knows you're at Our Lady of the Mount."

"I don't think we need to make a big deal of it," I tell him. "I'm here in town for two weeks, visiting family and friends, and I'm helping at the parish. A vacation, we'll say."

He slumps back in his chair and I shift on the couch. I'm pleased to see new—or at least newer- furniture in the rectory. Someone has gotten rid of the sixties vintage thrift-store rejects and replaced them with much more comfortable, much less threadbare furnishings. I recognize a couple of pieces as ones from Anna's house. She must have done it when she was parish secretary.

"Why don't I get us a fresh pot of coffee," I say standing up. "Give you a chance to calm down. Take a few minutes and we'll continue talking when I get back. Okay?"

Father Leonard looks at me, his mouth in a firm line, and nods. "I'd prefer tea if you don't mind."

I carry the tray into the kitchen. Anna turns to me, eyes wide, and exhales.

"Well," she says, "that's something."

"Now, Anna," I say as I empty the coffee pot and fill it with water.

"So that's why the Archbishop sent you here," she whispers. "You're replacing Father Leonard?"

"Oh, no, no, not at all," I say, pouring the water into the coffeemaker and scooping coffee grounds into the filter basket. "Can you put on a kettle of water for Leonard? He wants tea."

"Of course he does," she mutters, then fills the kettle. "So if you're not here to replace Father Leonard, what are you here for?"

"To look into it," I say. "To see if there's any merit."

"I can tell you there's no merit," Anna scoffs. "I mean, Father Leonard? Inappropriate? I doubt he's ever done anything inappropriate, or even thought anything inappropriate."

"I told the Archbishop as much, but he insisted I come and investigate immediately. He says the Church can't be seen as taking any accusation lightly, no matter how improbable." I shake my head. "I have to say I agree with him."

"Well, I see his point. But why you?"

I shrug. "Not sure. He said I wasn't his first choice, but decided I was the best person for the job."

"Well," she says as the kettle whistles. "If you can find Joan's killer after fifteen years, you can get to the bottom of this."

"Well, that wasn't me, that was mostly Detective Parr."

Anna looks at me and smiles. "Don't you mean Helen?"

I glance her. "Oh, don't look so surprised," Anna says. "I know there's something there, though I'm not saying you're in any spiritual danger. Still, it's in your eyes when you say her name. It's in her eyes when I mention you."

I open my mouth to speak when Anna goes on, "So who made the allegation?"

"No idea. It was anonymous."

"Well, whoever did it either doesn't know Father Leonard and Rachel, or really has it out for one or both of them." She hands me Father Leonard's mug, a bag of Earl Grey already steeping in it. "You will not find anything."

"I hope not," I say. "I really hope not."

Two

Father Leonard adds three teaspoons of sugar to his tea when I set it in front of him. He seems calmer, but his red hair is all over the place, like he had continued running his fingers through it while I was out.

"Feel better?" I ask.

"How would you feel if you were in my position?" he replies. "I feel attacked. Assaulted. Betrayed."

"Okay, all understandable. But I'm here to figure all this out. Now just calm down, take a deep breath, and let's talk this over."

He does what I ask. "All right. What do you need to know?"

I pull out my phone to take notes. "Why don't we start at the beginning. When did you meet Rachel . . ."

"Watson," he says. "Rachel Watson. I met her back in April, for the first time. Well, I should say that's when I officially met her. She started attending Saint Clare's just after Christmas."

"Okay."

"I noticed her at 10:30 a.m. Mass, I think on Epiphany Sunday it was." He stops then adds quickly, "I don't mean I noticed her-noticed her, like I took any special notice of her, more like I saw her and thought, 'oh, someone new,' not that I really thought of her then or later, I mean—"

"Father McCoy," I say, holding my hand up. "Leonard, please, I'm not here to trap you. Just go on. So Epiphany was the first day you saw her."

He nods. "It's the first time I saw her at Saint Clare's. I had not seen her here before."

"When did you meet her?"

"Well, you know we needed to get a new parish secretary, after everything that happened," he says. "Ms. Luckgold was wonderful, a valuable person. I asked—practically on my hands and knees—if she'd take the position permanently. But she declined. So we advertised." He sighed. "We got two applicants. One was an old widow, a long-time parishioner, a solid person. The other was Rachel."

"Why did you choose Rachel? It seems like an unusual thing for someone her age to apply for the job of parish secretary and housekeeper."

"I thought so too when I first saw her resume—she was the only one to send a resume. The other woman just left a note in the offering basket. College degree in business management, experience in retail and customer service, quite over-qualified. But I interviewed her, anyway."

"What was that like?"

His eyes brighten, and a slight smile appears on his lips. "Wonder—" He obviously catches himself. "Quite good," he replies. "She was very impressive in the interview. She explained that she wanted to work in the parish because she was discerning a vocation."

I raise my eyebrows. "Really? That's good."

"I thought so too. I thought it was a great deal for everyone. She told me she thought working at the parish would give her the opportunity to be closer to our Lord—more time to pray and attend Mass daily. Her current job was at the office park outside town, so she couldn't make daily Mass and she wanted to adopt that discipline."

"So you hired her, but of course she didn't live here in the Rectory."

"Oh, no, Father, no, she rents a townhouse in one of the recent developments on the edge of Myerton."

"Have you been to her home?"

"What—oh, no, certainly not. I just know where she lives because I drove her home when her car was in the shop and I thought it was too late for a single woman to take an Uber."

"She would work late?"

"Occasionally."

"You'd spend time alone with her, here in the Rectory?"

"Yes, of course, she worked here after all. But nothing inappropriate ever happened."

I look at my notes. "I haven't seen the complaint, so I don't know exactly what the accusation is."

"The Archbishop sent it to me by email," Father Leonard says, getting out of the chair. "I'll go get it for you." He leaves the living room and Anna darts in from the kitchen with a plate of sandwiches.

"I thought some food might help," she whispers. "I'm not sure he's eaten today."

"Could you hear anything?" I ask, taking a sandwich off the plate.

"Oh, Tom, I wouldn't listen to a private conversation."

"I didn't ask if you listened. I asked if you could hear anything?"

She hesitates. "These walls are kind of thin, Tom."

I nod. "Any thoughts?"

She leans closer and whispers to me, "There's more here than he's saying."

"Here," Father Leonard says, brandishing a piece of paper as he returns from the office. "This is—oh, Anna! I forgot you were here. Sandwiches. Thank you. They look delicious."

"I'll leave you two," Anna says. "The . . . kitchen floor needs mopping. I'll just go do that." She hurries from the room as Father Leonard resumes his seat.

"This is the allegation?" I say, taking the paper from him. It's the printed scan of a handwritten document. "It wasn't sent by email?"

"Apparently not," Father Leonard says. "It arrived at the Archdiocesan Office late last week by regular mail. No return address, a Myerton postmark. It wasn't signed. It's a tissue of lies and slander!" He's getting agitated again.

"Father Leonard, I very much want to find out the truth in this situation, and if you are as innocent as you say you are, then to prove that. But to do that, I need to see for myself what's in this letter and I cannot do that with you blathering over me," I say as I try to read the letter.

Only when I've read it through twice do I ask, "Is any of this true?"

Father Leonard shakes his head vigorously. "No. Not a jott. Not a tittle."

I roll my eyes slightly. Why he insists on speaking like a character out of a Dickens novel, I don't know. "So nothing in this is factual? Nothing at all?"

"Not a word of it."

"But you told me you'd work late with her here at the Rectory and," I look at the letter, "it says right here, 'Father McCoy and Ms. Watson are often at the Rectory late at night alone.' So this is true, isn't it?"

"Well," he sputters, "well, yes, I suppose if you put it a certain way, that is strictly accurate. But it's the implication that's incorrect."

"I'm not seeing the implication, Father."

"The person who wrote that," Father Leonard explodes, "is clearly implying that Rachel and I are engaged in some kind of inappropriate behavior here late at night. The whole letter is like that, one unfounded accusation after another. Preposterous." He plops in an armchair and brings his clenched fist down on the arm.

"The letter also says, 'Father McCoy engages Ms. Watson in intimate conversations.'"

"I've offered her spiritual direction," he barks. "She's discerning her vocation. We'd pray together. She'd ask for guidance. I'd offer it as best I could."

I look at Father Leonard. Slowly, he's changing from frantic and anxious to visibly angry. I continue reading, "'They've been seen dining alone together.'"

"We've had dinner a few times at The Bistro, the restaurant up the street," he says. "People have to eat."

"'Several people saw them together at the parish Memorial Day picnic.'" I look at him.

His face turns red and sweat beads on his forehead. A look of panic passes across his face. He swallows and clears his throat. He clenches and unclenches his fist, rubbing it with his other hand. "That—" he squeaks, then clears his throat. "There were a lot of people at the picnic."

"'Father and Ms. Watson disappeared for about half an hour, then someone saw them engaged in deep conversation apart from the rest of the group. Father at one point kissed her.'"

"She had gotten something in her eye," he explodes, standing up and beginning to pace again. "Rachel wanted to discuss something with me, so we went off a short way—a very short way, I could still see the games the children were playing—and sat together to get away from the noise. You know how noisy it is here, all the time, with all the children. We sat together under a tree. She got something in her eye, so I was trying to get it out. I got close to her face, you know, to see her eye."

I regret how lame this excuse sounds. One the one hand, most people know that it's the oldest excuse in the book. A sophisticated man would never use it. But Father Leonard is anything but sophisticated, so it's just possible that that's what actually happened. "What did you and she talk about?" I ask.

Father Leonard shakes his head. "No, I can't tell you that. It's under the Seal."

The Seal of Confession. The shield that can be a sword. "In general, then," I continue. "What did you and she discuss?"

He exhales. "She wanted to discuss her call to religious life. She was having doubts, and she talked to me about them."

"Why at the picnic? Seems an odd place for spiritual direction."

"It was my idea," he says. "I noticed her looking distracted, somewhat upset. I asked her if anything was bothering her. She said there wasn't, but I insisted we go off together to talk."

"What did she tell you?"

Leonard shakes his head. "You know I can't tell you that, Father. You must ask her."

There's a soft knock behind us. "Excuse me," Anna says. "Father Leonard, you have sick calls this afternoon."

"Oh! Oh my, I completely forgot," he says. "I suppose I can't do that now, can I, Father?"

I shrug. "I don't see why not, Leonard," I say. "The Archbishop said nothing to me about your visits or hearing confessions, just saying Mass. I'll be glad to go in your place if you don't feel up to it."

"No," he says, squaring his shoulders and straightening his collar. "No, thank you, Father. These scurrilous accusations have deprived me of saying Mass. I will not let them keep me from my flock. No, my mother always told me, 'When people speak ill of you, go out among them with your head held high.' If you'll excuse me." He starts out of the living room, then pauses.

"I was just trying to help Rachel," Father Leonard says. "We became friends. I've never had that many. It's difficult for me to make friends. Rachel, well, she and I are a lot alike." He sighs. "It's just nice to have someone who understands."

"That's all you are. Friends," I say.

Father Leonard looks me in the eye. "Yes. Friends."

***

"There were many people at the picnic, Tom," Anna says. She squeezes the mop out into the bucket, then leans it against the counter. She dries her hands and looks at me. "I was helping with the kids' games so I saw nothing in particular I thought anything about."

"Have you heard anything? I mean, I know you keep your ear to the ground."

Anna wipes the counter with the towel. "Nothing specific. Just murmurings about how close they seem." She looks at me. "I've heard nothing that would warrant someone writing to the Archdiocese."

"Do you have any idea who would write anonymously?"

She shakes her head. "I can't think of a single person, Tom. Everyone in the parish likes Father Leonard. I mean, we all think he's a little odd sometimes—the way he speaks, his homilies can be a bit long-winded, he sometimes lapses into untranslated Greek or Latin, the fact he's named after a science-fiction character, you know the teens call him Father Bones—but he's been good for the parish. The young people like him. He's done a lot of talks to the Catholic student group on campus. Overall, a nice, calming presence."

"Someone doesn't think so," I point out.

Anna sighs. "Well, I'm sure you'll get to the bottom of it."

"That's what the Archbishop wants me to do." I think for a minute. "So tell me about Rachel Watson."

She shrugs. "There's not much to tell about her. Her family has lived in Myerton for years. They're members of the parish, but not active; if they attend more than Christmas and Easter, I'd be surprised."

"She attended Myer College?"

"No, she went to school in Emmitsburg. Got her degree in business, according to her resume, and took a job with a firm in Pittsburgh. Worked there for a few years, then moved back to Myerton. She's been attending Saint Clare's since January."

"How did she come to be interviewed for parish secretary?"

"She applied," Anna says matter-of-factly. "Simple as that. We put a note in the bulletin asking for applicants. She and Fern Grumly were the only two that applied. Fern just didn't cut it; Father McCoy didn't like her, though I think she would have done a good job. But," she adds slowly, "he took to Rachel right away. Came out of the interview having offered her the job. Only took about fifteen minutes."

"You weren't in the interview?"

"Oh, of course I was," she says. "Had an entire list of questions for her. We kept Fern in there for about 45 minutes—may seem like overkill, but parish secretary is a sensitive job. They're privy to all sorts of information about members, and work intimately—" she stops. "Maybe not the best word under the circumstances, but I mean closely with the priest. They need to get along, have discretion and sensitivity."

I chuckle. "The last full-time secretary had none of that," I say.

Anna guffaws. "Yes and look what happened. Anyway, 45 minutes with Fern, about fifteen with Rachel. I got through three or four questions when Father Leonard offered her the job."

"Didn't you think it was strange?"

"At the time I did. When we received Rachel's resume, he had a negative reaction. Nothing specific, mind you, but I could tell from the way he looked and the tone of his voice when he talked about her he wasn't too excited about her interest. So it surprised me when he offered her the job so quickly. But I said nothing. Rachel was much more qualified. And her reason for applying made perfect sense in one respect."

"But not in all respects?"

Anna shakes her head. "In working here, even full time, she's making less than half what she did in her previous job."

"Leonard told me she has her own townhouse," I say. "Does she still have family in town? Why doesn't she live with them?"

"From what she's told me," Anna says, leaning forward, "she's not on great terms with her family. They're not exactly thrilled that she is considering entering religious life."

"So no support, huh?"

She shakes her head. "No. Oh, her mother and father are decent people. Her father is a CPA in town. I think they just had something different in mind for their daughter. Rachel has a twin sister, Rebecca, who is married." She pauses. "Her husband is Winthrop Myer IV."

I whistle. Winthrop Myer was the founder of Myerton, the founder of Myer College. The Myer family is still a prominent family in town, and Myer Holdings owns much of the surrounding mountains. "So Rachel is related by marriage to the Myer family?"

Anna nods. "There is one other thing I should mention about Winthrop Myer. It's probably nothing. But I think you should know."

I lean against the counter. "What is it?"

She looks out the window over the sink, then turns to look at me. "Not long after Rachel's resume came in, Mr. Myer paid Father Leonard a visit. They were in his office for about half an hour." After he left, Father Leonard gave me a check to deposit in the Parish's account. It was for $15,000, signed by Winthrop Myer IV."

I stare at her. "Do you think Myer persuaded Father Leonard to hire his sister-in-law?"

She shakes her head slowly. "I don't know, Tom. It could just be a co-incidence. You know, the Myers have been patrons of the parish for generations. His great-great-grandfather helped pay for rebuilding Saint Clare's after the fire. He's continued to be a frequent donor, though rarely under his own name. Maybe he threatened to turn off the money?"

I exhale. "I'll ask Father Leonard about it. What can you tell me about Rachel and her sister? Do you think the sister would have sent the letter?"

"Rachel and her sister still seem close, from what I've seen and what Rachel's told me. But even her sister doesn't seem to understand her vocation. But to answer your question, I really don't know."

She folds the dish towel and places it on the counter. "So what are you going to do now?"

"Well, I suppose I must interview Rachel. I'll contact her and try to get that done in the next couple of days. First, I'll get settled in here. The Archbishop wanted me to let him know when I arrived, so I guess I'd better call him."

"I've got the guest room all ready for you," Anna says.

"Thanks." I pause. I wonder if I should ask what's on my mind. "How's Helen?"

"I don't really know," she replies. "I have seen little of her lately."

"But I thought she started attending Saint Clare's?"

Anna shrugs. "With three Masses, she's probably just not there at the same time I am. I mean, there hasn't been a murder since you left, and I can't think what else would make her miss Mass."

I note the sarcasm and laugh. "Well, that shouldn't be a problem this time."

Three

After getting my bag out of my car and taking it to the Rectory guest room, I take a walk. It's a beautiful day and I need the time to think about Father Leonard's situation.

I walk along Main Street, enjoying the July warmth. The street is still decorated with the red, white, and blue streamers and American flags the city put up for the annual Fourth of July parade and fireworks extravaganza. Though warm, it's not too humid, one benefit of being in the mountains. Downtown Baltimore would be unbearable, the concrete and asphalt acting to absorb every bit of the heat and magnifying it. Just thinking about it makes me perspire.

Myer College is on summer break, so there are only a few students on the college side of the street. There are quite a few people out, though, a combination of town residents and tourists who enjoy the surrounding mountains for the hiking and the downtown for its quaint shops. The historic railroad offers daily excursions through the mountains, so some are probably here during a layover.

As pleasant as the weather is, I'm getting thirsty as I walk. Up ahead is The Bistro, a charming restaurant very much like a Parisian cafe, right down to the wrought-iron tables and chairs along the sidewalk. The day is so nice that I'm looking forward to sitting outside and having a nice tall lemonade. Up ahead, the place looks crowded, but I think I see an open table. I quicken my steps, hoping to get there before it's taken.

Then I catch sight of dark black hair shining in the sun. My pace slows.

It's Helen. Helen Parr. Detective Helen Parr. The detective who arrested the man who murdered my wife. She is also the woman I was in love with many years ago. The woman I meant to marry until we took different paths. Her path led to law school in North Carolina, mine led to a master's degree in Maryland. She wanted to be a lawyer and became a police detective. I wanted to be an archivist and wound up a priest.

She doesn't see me. I smile and quicken my pace. I'm trying to figure out what I'll say. The last time I saw her, she had whispered in my ear she missed me. Did she still? Will she be happy to see me?

Why do you care? I think to myself. A good question. I realize now that I have thought of her more often than I should and I make a note to discipline myself to stop.

Our weekly emails, by mutual agreement, avoid any talk of the past. Anything that might be considered intimate. On the surface, they are messages between friends.

That's all we are. Friends, the priest inside me says.

Isn't that what Father Leonard just said? the lover counters.

She throws her head back, laughing. She always had a great laugh. Not like Joan's. No one had a laugh like Joan's. Joan's laugh was a ringing bell, clear and melodic. Helen's was boisterous, almost muscular. I smile, then stop when I see her looking in my direction. She sees me and looks surprised.

I walk up to the table. "Hello," I say with a smile. "Fancy meeting you here, Helen."

"Tom?" she says, standing up. We look at each other awkwardly. Do we hug? Do we shake hands? We do neither. We just stand there, looking.

"I didn't know you were back in town," Helen says, sitting back down. "Your emails didn't mention you were coming."

"I just got in a couple of hours ago," I say, avoiding her statement. "I thought I'd go for a walk, such a nice day."

"Are you visiting Anna?" Helen says.

"Yes, but I'm staying at the Rectory. I'll be saying Masses for a week or so, to give Father McCoy a break." I smile. "I hope to see you there."

The waitress interrupts us. "Will you be joining her, sir—Father Tom! What are you doing here?"

The face is familiar. "Visiting," I say.

"Are you going to be celebrating Mass Sunday?" she asks.

"Yes, Father McCoy's taking a break for a couple of Sundays. The Archbishop thought he could use a rest."

"Oh," she replies, a slight frown on her face. "But he'll be back, right?"

"Oh, yes, he's not going anywhere."

"Oh, good!" she says with enthusiasm. "I'll let everyone know. We'd be really upset if Father Leonard was leaving. He's been so good to us."

"Who's we?" I ask.

"We're the Catholic Students Club at Myer College. I'm Vicki. Vicki Morgan."

"Well, while I'm here, I look forward to seeing you and your friends."

She smiles. "Oh, well, thanks." She turns and walks away, then stops and comes back. "I'm sorry, a little scatterbrained. Will you be joining her?"

I look at Helen. "Sure, why not," she shrugs.

"Lemonade and a menu please," I say. "I'm feeling a little hungry."

Vicki goes off. I turn to Helen as she asks, "So why are you really here?"

I am about to repeat the excuse I gave Vicki when I remember that Helen is, after all, a detective and is particularly adept at spotting lies. I also remember that, unfortunately, I've lied to her a few times and so she knows what that looks like, too. So, I decide to tell the truth and say, "I can't really say."

"Is it about Father Leonard and his church secretary?"

I nearly choke at this and sputter, "What do you know about that?"

"Not that much, just that I got a call at the station a couple of weeks ago from some woman who gave her name as Jane Doe and asked me if he could be arrested for seducing her. I said not if she was an adult, and it was consensual, and the woman hung up on me."

"Do you know who it was?"

"I could find out but I won't. It came in on the anonymous crime report line and that's, well, you know, Tom, anonymous." She says the last with a smile made only slightly less attractive by the dripping sarcasm in her voice.

Vicki sets my lemonade down and hands me a menu. I look through it. "I'll have the Monte Cristo," I say, handing her back the menu.

"Right away, Father," she says and practically skips off. I look back at Helen.

"So do you think there's anything to it?"

She pauses and looks away, not meeting my eyes. I sit there, wondering why this seems to bother her so much, when she says, "I don't know."

"Is that why you haven't been to Mass in a while?" I say. Helen looks at me, surprised. "Anna told me she hadn't seen you in Mass."

"Tom, don't lecture me," she says with exasperation. "It's difficult getting back into parish life, and really, it's none of your business. You're not my priest and Father Leonard doesn't seem to care."

I'm about to ask what she means by that when she slumps back and looks at me. "Look at us. Haven't seen each other in four months and we're already bickering."

I smile. "Wanna start over?"

Helen returns my smile. "I'd like that. You're irritating, Father Tom, but," she leans forward, "it's good to see you."

"You, too, Helen," I say.

"When you left, I didn't think I'd see you so soon. You seemed intent on staying at that monastery."

I sigh. "I was."

She looks at me questioningly. "Is it not what you expected?"

"Oh, it's everything I expected. I'd been there before, remember. The brothers' routine, the prayer, the silence. I have plenty of time to pray, to read. I've been doing both a lot. I've been able to deal with some things I've avoided for a while."

"About Joan," Helen says.

"Yes," I say. "And other things." I pause. I'd thought a lot about Joan, about her murder, working through my residual guilt. Also, I came to terms with the things I found out about her mental illness and her first marriage, both of which she had kept secret from me. I also struggled with feelings about Helen, feelings I had buried long ago but that resurfaced during my previous time in Myerton.

"But recently," I continue, "I've been getting a little antsy, I guess you could say. I'm glad to get out of the monastery for a while. Spend time with Anna." I pause. "Visit Joan . . . and others."

We look at each other for a moment. "Well," Helen says to break the silence, "I am glad to see you. Things haven't been the same without you. I haven't had to arrest anyone at the Rectory in months."

"And I hope that doesn't change," I laugh. "You look good."

She smiles and nods. "You, too. So you'll be here for a couple of weeks? Then what?"

I shrug. "The monks still need a priest, so I guess I'll go back there. It really depends on the Archbishop."

"Well," Helen says, standing. "I need to get back. I'm sure I'll be seeing you."

"Yes, Sunday, right?"

She stops and looks at me, hesitating. She nods. "I'll be there." She walks past me. I touch her arm. She stops and looks down at my hand, then into my eyes. A memory passes between us.

"Helen," I say, "I don't think I ever thanked you for that night at the Rectory, getting there when you did."

She moves her arm away from my hand. "Just doing my job, Father. I can't have a dead priest on my record. I think it'd be bad for my career." She moves toward me as if to kiss or hug me, then stops. She straightens up and I turn to find Vicki standing there with my Monte Cristo. Her eyes are enormous.

"I'll see you, Father," Helen blurts, then walks away.

Vicki sets my Monte Cristo in front of me. "Thank you," I say. "Looks delicious."

She flashes a smile and walks away, though at one point she looks over her shoulder in my direction.

I pick up my sandwich. Before I take a bite, I look over my shoulder. I see Helen, about half a block away, also turn to look over her shoulder. Our eyes meet. Quickly, I turn to my sandwich.

I take a bite and a drink of my lemonade. I'm about to take another bite when my phone rings. It's Anna.

"Hello?" I say.

"Tom, I know you just left," she says, "but you better get back here. Father Leonard just got back from his sick calls. He's upset about something, he won't tell me what, but I can't get him to calm down."

"Has he said anything?"

"Only one thing, over and over again." She pauses. "He keeps saying, 'She's ruined me.'"

Four

I hurry back to the Rectory with my partially-eaten Monte Cristo. Father Leonard is exactly as Anna described him. I find him pacing in the living room again, muttering "she's ruined me" repeatedly.

"He got back here quickly, didn't he?" I say. "How many sick calls did he have?"

"Six. Five at the nursing home and one—" she sighs "—one at Gloria MacMillan's."

"Oh," I mouth. I only had the pleasure of visiting Gloria MacMillan once. She spent most of the time berating me about the supposedly crooked bingo game run for years by Father Anthony, the former pastor of Saint Clare's. She was liable to say anything and I'm certain she was the source of Father Leonard's distress.

"You'd better get in there before he has a stroke," Anna says as she shoves me into the living room.

He doesn't see me at first. He's stopped pacing and is leaning with his forehead against the wall, his fists gently tapping the surface. He's still muttering something I can't quite hear, but sounds like, "I'm so sorry, I'm so sorry."

I walk up behind him and touch him gently on the shoulder. He jumps and yells, startling me and causing me to back away from him. His face is contorted with a combination of anger and distress, his red hair is wild, and he's sweating profusely.

"Leonard," I say as I recover myself, "what happened?"

"Have you stopped screwing your secretary!" he yells. "That's what she said to me. Just as matter-of-factly as if she was asking about the weather! Have. You. Stopped. Screwing. Your. Secretary."

"Who?" I said. "Who said this to you?"

"Gloria MacMillan, of course!" He circles the living room. "That senile old hag," he mutters. "She's been a thorn since I got here. Her and her bingo. She's had it in for me since the electric blanket incident."

I groan. "Don't tell me she didn't win it."

"Not the electric blanket, nor the toaster, nor the complementary dinner buffet at the casino off I-70!" he cries. "She's had it in for me the entire time. But I never thought she'd stoop to repeat gossip." Father Leonard stops and looks at me. "You know what this means, don't you Father? I'm finished here. It's all over the parish, this accusation."

"The accusation says nothing about you and Rachel Watson having sexual relations."

"No, no, it doesn't, but someone is spreading a rumor to that effect." He runs his fingers through his hair, gripping a bunch and pulling. "What am I going to do? I need to leave Saint Clare's." He heads to the entrance to the living room. "I need to call the Archbishop."

"Stop, Leonard!" I say, a little loudly. He turns back to me. "Just stop it right now and get a hold of yourself." I approach him and grasp his shoulders. "Do you think you're the first priest in the history of the Church to have rumors spread about him?"

"But, but—," he pleads.

"You can't pay attention to what Gloria MacMillan says. She's a loose cannon who says the first thing on her mind. We don't know what she's heard, or if she's heard anything from anyone else. She's out there on that farm, she doesn't get to town that much, and I doubt she has many people left alive who'll talk to her. Maybe she heard something, maybe it's all in her head. We don't know."

"But it just seems—"

"And if there is such a rumor going around about you and Rachel Watson, what do you think would be worse? Staying, letting me sort this out, seeing it through with courage and dignity? Or leaving? What do you think people will say then?"

He hesitates, then says, "They'll say I left because it's all true."

I nod. "That's right. The last thing you want to do is leave. It fixes nothing and only makes things worse. Trust me. I know."

Leonard looks at me and sighs. He smiles slightly. "Thank you, Tom. I needed that."

"Now," I say, "why don't you go take a shower and rest the remainder of the day. I'll have Anna give me the list of calls and I'll finish them for you." I pause for a moment. "Did you give her communion?"

He closes his eyes. "I just did that before I ran out. I'm sure the family thinks I've gone insane. I didn't even say goodbye, I just ran through their living room and out the door."

I pat him on the shoulder. "They live with her, I'm sure they thought nothing of it."

Anna comes in as Leonard leaves. She hands me a slip of paper. "Here are the remaining calls. They're all at Mountain View Nursing Home. You remember where that is."

"It hasn't been that long," I say, looking at the list. "I'll get right on it."

She looks at me and blows out a breath. "You've got a big problem here, Tom."

I nod. "I know, I know. A huge one."

"You don't really believe she made it up in her head, do you?"

"No, not really," I admit. "She heard something that made her think it. No, Anna," I say, looking at the direction where Leonard went. "There are rumors going around about that young man. I've got to get on top of this, and fast."

"What are you going to do?"

I look at her. "Can you do me a favor and call Rachel Watson for me?"

"Of course," she says.

"See if she can meet with me tomorrow morning, here." I pause. "Are you free? I'll want you nearby."

Anna smiles. "I'll clear my schedule."

***

The next morning I tell Father Leonard to take the day off and drive to Our Lady of the Mount. "Spend the day in prayer," I say. "Ask Our Lady for guidance. Visit her at the grotto." I pause. "I think you may find it helpful."

"You're going to speak to Rachel?" he asks. "What are you going to say?"

I shrug. "Say? Probably not much. I will ask her some questions about the things alleged in the anonymous note to the Archbishop, see if she has any idea who may have sent it."

"How could she when I can't figure out who may have sent it?" he protested.

"She may know something you don't," I point out.

After he leaves, I settle in with a cup of coffee and look over the letter again. Reading carefully, none of the allegations are very specific, just the fact they spent a lot of time alone together and were frequently together at night. The most specific thing mentioned was the Memorial day picnic.

I sit back and think. Father Leonard's explanation for the picnic was plausible, but delivered with a little too much vehemence. He was agitated when we first talked, so that was probably all it was.

Or was it guilt?

I shake my head. The more time I spend with Father McCoy, the harder time I have imagining him doing anything inappropriate, much less breaking his vow of celibacy. It just doesn't fit with the scared, perpetually nervous, and excruciatingly upright prelate I know. I know nothing about Rachel Watson aside from what Father Leonard and Anna have told me, but based on that, I don't think she'd be the type to make accusations out of whole cloth on the one hand or act inappropriately with a priest on the other. A young woman in this day and age wanting to become a nun wasn't likely to do that.

But I have been surprised before.

Right at 10 a.m., there's a knock at the Rectory door. I hear Anna answer the door, then come into my office. She looks perplexed.

"Father Tom," she says, "Your, ah, appointment is here."

"Good," I smile. "Send Rachel in."

She hesitates. "What is it, Anna?" I ask.

"She's not alone," she whispers, moving closer to the desk. "Her mother and sister are with her."

"But I want to talk to her alone," I whisper. "What are they doing here?"

"I guess moral support?"

"Well, can you ask them to wait in the living room while I speak to Rachel?"

Anna nods and goes off. A moment later, I hear a woman say, "No, we will not wait in the living room." A flurry of steps precedes a woman in her late forties, blue dress, blond hair, tall, sweeping into my office.

"Father Greer," she says with calm authority, "I'm Marjorie Watson, Rachel's mother, and I will be right here while you speak to my daughter."

I stand. "Nice to meet you, Mrs. Watson. I understand your desire to be supportive. I just think it would be better if I spoke to her alone. These are serious allegations, and I think Rachel might be more comfortable—"

"Father," she sighs. "For obvious reasons—of the Church's own making, let me point out—I don't trust you not to manipulate her into saying they're all a bunch of lies." She pauses. "I mean nothing personal by that, Father. I'm sure you're a decent enough man, but you are here because the Archbishop sent you, am I right?"

"Yes, that's correct," I say, "and he told me to—"

"Get this to end quietly? Sweep it under the rug? Make it go away so the Church doesn't have another black mark?"

"No, Mrs. Watson," I say firmly. "He told me to look into these allegations thoroughly and follow the evidence no matter where it leads. And that's what I intend to do."

She regards me with scepticism. "Do you think they're lies?"

Before I can answer, a voice behind her says, "But Mama, they are."

For the first time, I notice three other people in my office. Aside from an apologetic-looking Anna are two young women with the same height, same blond hair, and same face. Twins. In fact, from their height and blond hair, mother and daughters could be triplets. But beyond that the similarities end. One twin outweighs the other by a good 10 pounds, has her shoulder-length hair in a short ponytail, and wears a grey cotton jumper that practically brushes the floor. The other's blond hair is styled, also cut shoulder length; she wears a red dress that goes just below her knees. In contrast to her sister, who wears no makeup, she is well made-up and sports well-manicured nails. Even the shoes are different; one sister wears simple comfortable flats, the other, strappy heels. Two more different people I cannot imagine. But I see the red-dress sister place a comforting hand on the grey-jumper sister and pat her gently. A genuine expression of care and concern.

"Rachel, let me handle this," Mrs. Watson says. She gently takes her daughter's hand. "You've shown you don't know what's best for you."

"Mama," the woman in the red dress, "that's not fair. Rachel just—"

Mrs. Watson is about to speak, then stops herself. She smiles. "You're right, Rebecca," she says, though I'm not sure what Rebecca was right about since she didn't finish what she was going to say. Mrs. Watson turns to me, a smile on her lips.

"My apologies, Father Greer," she says, her voice dripping with graciousness. "I didn't mean to question your integrity. I'm just concerned about my daughter, you understand. This is all so distressing for our entire family. "

"I assure you," I say, "it is for all of us."

"This is our parish and has been for years. I know my husband and I don't attend as often as we should, but we have great affection for Saint Clare's. Both Rachel and Rebecca were baptized and received their sacraments here. Rebecca was married in this church. The thought of a priest, especially here, taking advantage of my daughter is just more than I can stand to think about." Her eyes well up with tears.

Rachel pats her mother's shoulder. "I've told you, Mama, Father Leonard never took advantage of me." She looks at me earnestly. "Father, he did nothing wrong!"

"Why don't we let Father Greer ask his questions, my dear," Mrs. Watson says quietly to her daughter, then sits down in one of the two chairs.

"Mama," Rebecca says, "I think Father Greer wants us to wait outside." When Mrs. Watson doesn't move, the sister looks at me. "If it's all right with Rachel," Rebecca says to me, "can we stay? We'll be quiet. We won't say anything. Right, Mama?"

Marjorie Watson looks at Rebecca and smiles. "Of course, dear." Turning back to me, she says. "May we, Father, if Rachel doesn't object?"

"Is it okay with you, Rachel, if your mother and sister say?" I say to Rachel.

She looks at me and nods. "Yes, it's fine, Father," she whispers, "they can stay."

I nod and look at Anna. "Let's get some more chairs." I excuse myself and leave my office. I hurry to the kitchen and grab a chair. Anna is on my heels.

"I don't think it's a good idea to have them in there, Tom," she whispers.

"I don't either, Anna. But I don't see that I have a choice," I say as I walk with the chair back to my office. Anna nods her head to indicate she'll be at her desk if I need her. I nod discreetly.

I close the door. The three women follow me with their eyes as I go around the desk to sit down. "Now," I say, folding my hands together and leaning forward, "Rachel, thank you for being here."

Rachel starts to speak but her mother says, "I'm just thankful the Archdiocese is not just sweeping things under the rug like it did in the past."

I try to look reassuring. "We've made mistakes in the past in dealing with situations of wrongdoing. We're trying to rectify that. That's why the Archbishop sent me here, to look into what's been alleged and see if there's any merit to these allegations and take steps if necessary. However, there will be no rush to judgement."

Rachel starts to speak again when Mrs. Watson says, "Father Greer. If there was nothing to these allegations, do you think they would have been made? I mean, my daughter's seen her good name dragged through the mud. Not to mention the reputation of Father McCoy. Why would someone do that if there was nothing to this?"

"That's why I'm here, as I say, to look into these allegations, to see if there is anything to them, and," I add slowly, "if there is nothing to them, try to figure out why they were made." I pause. "Making false allegations, bearing false witness is a sin. If they made it up for reasons of spite, for any reason whatsoever, your daughter and a good priest have had their reputations besmirched."

"Father," Rachel finally says, "I'm so glad you're here. Leon—Father McCoy's always been perfectly proper with me."

Mrs. Watson opens her mouth to speak again. Rebecca places a hand on her knee. Mrs. Watson closes her mouth and settles back.

"Well, let's just begin at the beginning," I say. "The letter is anonymous, and there's nothing very specific in here—nothing alleging Father McCoy took advantage of you or assaulted you in any way—but there are allusions to inappropriate behavior. I want to ask you about a few of the things in here. Is that all right?"

She nods, but her mother says, "She'll answer your questions. I'm sure she's eager to get this matter taken care of." Mrs. Watson pauses. "What will happen to Father McCoy, if you find out it's true?"

"I don't think we're anywhere near that yet," I say. "But if there's no criminal activity, they will transfer the priest out of the parish, have to undergo counseling and a period of penance, and then the decision will be made about whether to put him in another local parish. But if a priest commits a crime—in this case, a sexual crime like rape or assault—then, well, we'll let the state take over."

A slight smile plays on her lips. "So either way, he'll be gone?"

"Only if he did something wrong."

"He didn't!" Rachel protests.

"Now, Rachel," Mrs. Watson says.

Rachel opens her mouth to retort, but Rebecca says. "Mama, let's let Father Greer do what he's here to do, and let Rachel answer the questions." She turns to me. "Sorry, Father. This has been very upsetting for everyone, especially Mama. Rachel's the baby of the family, so someone taking advantage of her—well, it's just upsetting."

"I'm not a child!" Rachel says to Rebecca. "I wish everyone would stop treating me like one!"

"Maybe if you'd stop acting like one," Mrs. Watson says. "Fantasies, always fantasies with you."

I hold up my hand, desperate to get the conversation back on track. "Ladies, please." Looking at Mrs. Watson, I say. "I have let you and Rebecca stay here because I thought you were here to support Rachel, that she wanted you here. But if that's not the case, you must leave. I have questions for Rachel, and I want her to answer them without interference or commentary. I have a job to do and I will do it. Am I clear?"

Mrs. Watson looks at me, her eyes betraying a desire to unload on me a stream of invective. Instead, Rebecca says, "Yes, Father Greer. Very clear. We'll just sit quietly while you talk to Rachel. Isn't that right, mother?"

"Yes. Father Greer," she says, "you can ask Rachel any questions you like. I won't say a word."

I incline my head. "Now, Rachel," I say, leaning forward, "how would you describe your relationship with Father Leonard?"

"My relationship?" she says. "He's my boss. I'm the parish secretary, you know, so I work for him. Well, technically, I guess I work for the parish, but he gives me the work to do."

"But beyond that," I say. "How would you characterize him?"

"He's my spiritual director. My confessor." She pauses. "Father Leonard is my friend."

"How did you two meet?"

She looks at me, a flash of panic crossing her face. She recovers quickly and asks, "What do you mean?"

"I think I'm clear," I say. "When did you meet Father Leonard?"

"I met him at Saint Clare's," she says slowly. "One of the first Sundays I started attending Mass here."

"I understand you're discerning a vocation to religious life?"

"Yes," she says. She cuts her eyes to her mother, who looks at her out of the corner of her eye.

"Her father and I," Mrs. Watson says, "have been trying to discourage this. We raised both of them in the Church, made sure they had their Sacraments at the appropriate time and all that. But we want them to make something of themselves. We just don't understand why a young woman as accomplished as Rachel would do something as extreme as becoming a nun."

"I've tried explaining, Mama," Rachel says. "You and Daddy just won't listen."

Mrs. Watson opens her mouth to speak when she sees me shake my head slightly, then closes it and folds her arms.

"I see," I say. To Rachel, I say, "Are you working with a particular order?"

"There's a convent near Emmitsburg," she says. "I've done a few discernment retreats there. I'm hoping to enter as a postulant within the next couple of years. I have some debts to pay off before I can do that."

"I understand from Mrs. Luckgold that you have a background in business?"

"Yes, I got my degree in business management and finance. I had a job at a company just outside town. I quit to take the job at Saint Clare's."

"You took a big pay cut to do that. If you wanted to pay off debt, why would you want to work for less salary?"

She looked at her hands, folded in her lap. "The work environment was . . . difficult. Also, I didn't have the time to pray, and I couldn't attend daily Mass. When I found out about this job, I jumped at the chance. I could work here at the parish, serving God, and I'd have the chance to go to Mass every day and pray." She smiled. "The money wasn't important."

"It was important enough," Mrs. Watson comments, "when you wanted to go to Emmitsburg for college."

"I would have been satisfied," Rachel says, "coming back home after graduating high school and attending Myer." She pauses and looks at Rebecca. "But that was not an option, was it?"

Rebecca puts her hand on Rachel's shoulder. Rachel looks at her hands, but allows Rebecca's hand to stay there.

I sit quietly looking at the three women. So much is going on in front of me, but I don't understand what it is, or what—if anything—it has to do with the issue at hand.

"If we could get back to the reason we're here, please," I say, hoping to steer the conversation back to the allegations against Father Leonard. "Rachel, I will ask you a direct question. Has Father Leonard ever touched you inappropriately?"

She jerks her head up and looks me square in the eyes. "No, Father Greer, absolutely not. Father Leonard never touched me in any way that was inappropriate or unwelcome."

"He never made an unwanted physical advance? Never engaged you in any kind of suggestive conversations? Made no kind of lewd propositions?"

She shook her head. "Absolutely not."

"And the descriptions of you two spending time alone together here at night?"

"We were working," she says. "Sometimes we'd talk." She smiles. "Father Leonard is very easy to talk to."

"What would you talk about?"

"Oh, everything. God, faith, the Church, the Scriptures, theology. Also books—he's one of the most well-read men I've ever met. He's a very interesting person. We'd also talk about . . . " she paused for a moment.

I raise an eyebrow. "Yes?"

She took a deep breath. "Nothing, Father. We'd just talk about many things." Rachel glanced to her right and left. "I'd rather not say."

"Things one might say to a confessor?" I ask.

She hesitates, then nods her head.

"One allegation is very specific," I say. "There's the matter of the Memorial Day picnic?"

"That was nothing!" she blurts. I sit back. She composes herself, then says, "We were just talking, that's all. It was crowded. He doesn't like crowds of people, the children were running around, and he knows I don't like crowds either. He suggested we go off to have some peace and quiet."

"There's a claim that someone saw you two physically close?"

She blushes. "I had stumbled on a root. He caught me, making sure I didn't fall."

I sit quietly. "So you're saying that the allegations are false."

"Absolutely, Father. I don't understand why someone would accuse a man as good and as holy as Father Leonard of something so heinous."

"Do you have any idea who might have sent this letter to the Archbishop?"

Rachel shakes her head. "I don't know who could hate him, or me, that much." She begins to cry.

Mrs. Watson grabs her daughter's hand and pats her on the shoulder. "There, there, dear. It's okay." She looks at me. "You see how upsetting this all is for Rachel. My question to you is, Father, what are you going to do about it?"

I fold my hands. "I don't know if I need to do anything. They both deny the allegations and have offered reasonable explanations for what's described in the letter. Because it was sent anonymously, I can't ask the person who wrote it." I spread my hands. "It looks to me that there's nothing here."

"But Father Greer," Ms. Watson says, "you can see that that priest has a great deal of influence over Rachel. He could have gotten her to say anything. Not to mention this idea about becoming a nun."

"Mama, I've tried to tell you," Rachel says through her tears. "That has nothing to do with Father Leonard. I've felt the call for a long time now."

"But it makes no sense, Rachel," Ms. Watson says. "You've got so much potential, and to throw it all away—"

"I'm not throwing it away!" Rachel stands up and looks down at her mother. "You understand nothing about me! Besides, why do you care what I do? You've got everything you've ever wanted with her." She points to her sister.

"Rachel!" Rebecca says, looking hurt.

Rachel turns to her sister. "It's not your fault," she says. "It's just the way it is. Excuse me, Father," she says, then dashes out of my office. I hear the front door close.

I'm left in my office with Mrs. Watson and Rebecca in an uncomfortable silence. Finally, Mrs. Watson says, "I'm telling you, Father, he needs to leave." She sits back. "Do you know who my son-in-law is?"

I nod slowly. "I understand Rebecca is married to Winthrop Myer."

"That's right. Winthrop Myer. You know, the Myers built this town, the College, owns most of the land around the town. I even believe they built this Church."

"His great-great-grandfather donated to have it rebuilt after a fire, yes, that's true."

"Well, then, I guess you see my meaning," she says with a smile of triumph.

I return the smile. "Thank you, Mrs. Watson, for the history lesson." I stand and say, "But I think we're done here for today. Anna," I call, "please show the Watsons out?"

"But, but what are you going to do?" Mrs. Watson asks.

"Do? I'll keep looking into it, but it seems to me right now that the allegations in the letter are unfounded. However, I am getting more interested in who sent the letter. You wouldn't know anything about that, would you, Mrs. Watson?"

She glares at me. "Are you asking me if I sent that letter to the Archbishop?"

I nod. "Did you?"

"Father Greer," Rebecca says indignantly, "Mama would never do that to Rachel! Make up stories, put them in a letter, send it to the Archbishop."

Mrs. Watson places her hand on Rebecca. "Dear, it's all right."

Rebecca looks at her. "But Mama, you wouldn't do that!" She looks at her. "Would you?"

Mrs. Watson looks at her daughter. "I was worried about your sister."

"Oh, Mama!" she whispers.

"Father Greer," Mrs. Watson says, turning to me. "I admit it. I sent the letter. But I made up nothing I wrote. They were all things that were told to me, based on rumors in the parish."

"Who told you these things?"

"I have friends who still attend here," she says. "They were concerned about some things they heard. Some things they saw themselves. After hearing it, I got concerned about Rachel—she's the baby of the family, after all—so I did something." She paused. "My son-in-law kept an eye on her."

"What?" Rebecca exclaims. "You got Win involved in this?"

"He offered to do it," she says. "Someone needed to look after your sister, and Win was worried about her."

"I just bet he was," Rebecca mutters.

"So, you know who sent the letter," Mrs. Watson says. "Now, what are you going to do?"

I shake my head. "Both Father Leonard and Rachel say nothing improper happened. Until I find evidence to the contrary, I won't be advising the Archbishop to take action."

She stares at me. She's a woman not used to being told "no." Without saying a word, she turns on her heels and marches out of the Rectory.

Five

"He's just so unreasonable," she says from behind the grill. "I can't get him to listen to me. He does whatever he wants to do, he doesn't care about the effect it has on me or the other children. I'm at the end of my rope, Father, I just get so angry with him. I hate the thoughts that go through my head. For these and my other sins, I am very sorry."

"I understand your frustration," I say quietly. "But you need to remember he's only five years old. He won't always be this way. He'll grow out of it. Keep in mind you are the adult and he is the child. You must treat him firmly but kindly. But frustration is a part of being a parent sometimes. Look to the example of Our Lady who, as sinless as she was, expressed frustration at her Son when he went missing. My advice to you is when he is pressing your buttons and you feel your frustration giving way to anger, just look to Our Lady in prayer and ask for her to pray that you'll have the strength to treat your son with love in your frustration. Now for your penance, I want you to say two Our Fathers and two Hail Marys. Now say your act of contrition."

I listen as she says the words of the penitent, then I speak the words of absolution while making the sign of the cross. "Go in peace, your sins are forgiven. Have a pleasant week."

"Thank you, Father," she says. I hear movement, then the door opens. I sit back and exhale, checking the time. Four o'clock. A busy Saturday. Mostly moms talking about their kids. It's the middle of summer, kids are out of school or homeschooling's suspended, children have time on their hands, and the entire under-18 population of Saint Clare's appears determined to drive their mothers crazy.

I don't have that many men so far today. Boat Man, as I call him, came to confess the same sins against his brother over the same boat story he told me about nine months ago. I gave him the same advice then that I gave him today—for his penance, he needed to sell the boat and give his brother the money. And again he left before absolution. I wonder if he'd been to confession with Father Leonard, and what the other priest had given him.

I think about Father Leonard and the reason I'm sitting in the confessional at Saint Clare's. The meeting with Rachel Watson, her mother, and her sister was interesting. I wasn't surprised when Rachel denied that anything inappropriate happened; the letter itself specified nothing in particular, beyond their behavior at the Memorial Day picnic. But her story about the picnic differed from Father Leonard's version; he said she got something in her eye, but she said she stumbled over a root. The more I thought after the meeting, the more that inconsistency troubled me.

Then Miriam Conway stopped by the Rectory.

"Father Greer, we're so glad to have you back," she said breathlessly as Anna showed her into my office. She had stopped by unannounced, but I had almost finished my homily for Sunday, so I was more than glad to talk to her.

"It's good to see you, Miriam. How are you getting along?"

"Well, Catherine's just getting smarter and smarter, the twins are driving me crazy, and Andrew's beginning to walk, so I'm keeping busy."

"And how's Dan?"

Her smile faded a bit. "Fine, fine," she said. "They suspended him for a month after . . . "

I nodded. "He told me about it, how Katherine Shepp manipulated him into giving her my wife's case file."

"After the suspension, things seemed to go fine for a while, but he was just passed over for a promotion. He thinks he's still being punished."

"How d'you take it?"

She shook her head. "Not very well, I'm afraid." Miriam lowered her voice. "His job wasn't the only thing he was suspended from, if you catch my meaning, Father. But we got through it. We're doing fine now."

She sighed and smiled again. "But we—the moms—are just so glad you're back, which is why I'm here. You know Father Leonard cancelled the nativity last year—because of that witch Whitemill—and we've been asking if we could try again this year. He's resisted, but now that you're here—"

"Wait, Miriam, just wait," I held up my hand to stop her. "I think y'all are under a misunderstanding. I'm only here for a very short time."

She looked crestfallen. "Really? How short?"

"Only a couple of weeks," I said. "The Archbishop thought Father Leonard could use some time off." Father Leonard had taken my suggestion and gone to Our Lady of the Mount. He was still there, having stayed through the weekend. "I'll probably be leaving a week from Monday."

"So, asking if we can have a nativity . . ."

I shook my head. "I'm sorry, Miriam. I'll talk to Father Leonard, give him my advice, tell him I think it would be a great thing for the parish, but that's all I can do."

"But when we heard you were back, we thought you were here to replace him because of all the—" she stops and puts her hand to her mouth. "Maybe I shouldn't say anymore. It's gossiping."

I raise my eyebrows. "What's being said, Miriam?" I said, motioning her to sit down. "Why don't you tell me why people think I'm here."

Sighing, she said, "Well, people think you came to replace Father Leonard, that the Archbishop is removing him from Saint Clare's because he found out about him and Rachel Watson."

I tried to look neutral, but I doubt she missed the look of distress that passed over my face. "And what do you know about Father Leonard and Rachel Watson?"

I raised my finger as she opened her mouth to speak. "Now, Miriam, be very careful. Tell me only what you know, what you saw. Not what you heard. Not what you think. Just what you've seen with your own eyes."

"My own eyes," she said. She thought for a minute. "They spend a lot of time together. I mean, I know she's the parish secretary, so it's natural they would work together. But they spend a lot of time together outside of work. I was at the park a few weeks ago and I saw them walking, not quite arm in arm, but close to each other. They were talking and laughing, like . . . oh, I shouldn't."

"Like what, Miriam?"

She sighed. "Like a couple," she said. "Other than not holding hands or anything, and him wearing a collar, they looked no different from any other man and woman their age walking together if they were in a relationship."

I nodded. "Anything else you've seen?"

"She hovers around him after Mass on Sunday," she said. "She's with him at every parish function, always sitting next to him. Sometimes when you want to talk to him about something, she runs interference like—well, like I do sometimes with Dan." She took a deep breath, steeling herself. "Then there was the Memorial Day picnic."

Everything went back to the picnic. "What do you know about that?" I asked, settling back in my chair.

She looked guilty as she said, "Probably more than anyone, since I'm the one who found them."

I sat up. "What did you find them doing?"

"Nothing like that, Father," she blurted. "And I'm sure there's a perfectly innocent explanation."

"Miriam," I said slowly. "It's very important that I'm told what people know for sure—not rumors, not innuendos—actually observed. So I need you to tell me what you saw."

She took a deep breath, then nodded. "Okay. Well, I had just finished with the children's games and everyone was gathering to get the food. We needed Father to lead the blessing, but no one could find him. Someone, I forget who, said they thought they saw him go off. I volunteered to go look for him." She swallowed. "I must have walked about a hundred yards away from the main group when I saw him—saw them, I should say." She paused, an embarrassed look on her face.

"What were they doing?" I asked slowly.

"They were standing together under a tree. They had their arms around each other, it looked like they were dancing." She exhaled quickly. "They were whispering and laughing, he was cradling her, they were rocking back and forth. Then . . . then I saw them kiss."

"Did they see you?"

She shook her head. "Maybe, I'm not sure. When I saw them I ducked behind a tree. I didn't know what to do, Father Tom, I just had seen nothing like that before—well, not with a priest. I couldn't just walk back to the picnic and tell people I couldn't find him. So I had to think fast. I walked about ten yards back in the direction I came from and started calling his name—with my back to where they were, so they wouldn't suspect I'd seen anything. After twice calling him, I heard him say, 'Yes, here I am,' and turned to see him jogging towards me. I said to him, 'Father, it's time for the blessing,' and he said, 'Oh, thank you, I just went off to get away from the noise for a bit'—the man can't stand children, it's a good thing he's a priest, I guess, not being able to have any of his own—then jogged back to the picnic. I turned to where he had come from and saw Rachel standing under the tree." Miriam paused. "I don't think Father Leonard knows I saw them, but Rachel knew. I could tell by the look on her face."

I sat back, leaning my head on the back of the chair and looking at the ceiling. Miriam was a cop's wife and from what I could tell, an honest person. If she said that's what she saw, I had little reason to doubt her veracity, but one thing occurred to me.

I sat up and looked at her. "You were the only one to see this, Miriam?"

She nodded slowly. "Yes, no one was with me."

I smiled at her and gently asked, "How then did a mention of an incident involving Father McCoy and Rachel Watson get around town?" I paused for a moment to see her reaction.

She lowered her eyes. "I told her to keep it quiet. You just can't trust some people, Father, you know?"

"Oh, Miriam," I sighed.

"I'm sorry, Father, I really am, but, well," Miriam sputtered, "I have a weakness."

"How many people did you tell?"

She smiled weakly. "Only one. Jenny Reynolds."

I recognized the name. She was the mother of Benedict James Reynolds, the first baby I baptized during my last stay at Saint Clare's.

"Blabbermouth," Miriam muttered.

"I don't think you're in any position to cast aspersions," I said. "You told one person, she may have told another person. It's a terrible cliché, but it only takes a spark to set a forest fire." I lean back. "That's what's happened here. Somehow it got all over town"

"But I didn't tell Jenny everything I saw," she protested. "I just said I saw them together alone, not that they were doing anything wrong."

"Be that as it may," I say, "your lack of discretion has caused this to go all over the parish, it appears. It's very difficult now for Father McCoy. And for Rachel."

"But Father Greer," Miriam whispered, "it's true. There is something going on between the two of them. What are you going to do?"

I had asked myself that question repeatedly since the conversation. Now, sitting in the confessional, I am still uncertain. Miriam saw them holding each other, whispering, talking, laughing, and kissing. They weren't having sex. They weren't doing anything anyone would consider truly wrong. But for a priest? For a woman who wants to become a nun? Clearly not permissible. But what am I going to do about it?

I know I don't have the full story. There are only two people who do know. Father Leonard and Rachel Watson. And so far, they haven't been completely honest with me. I need to talk to both of them again. I am going to have to get Father Leonard to be honest with me about his behavior—and his feelings. I will have to do the same with Rachel, but I'll have to do it without the presence of her mother and sister. I'll have to tread carefully.

I hear steps on the marble floors approaching the confessional. I collect myself and prepare to meet the penitent on the other side of the grill. But instead, the knob to my door is turned. It opens.

In the doorway is Rachel Watson.

"Father," she says.

"Rachel," I say.

She comes in and closes the door. Taking the seat opposite me, she looks at me expectantly.

I say, "Let us begin this sacrament of God's mercy in the name of the Father, the Son, and the Holy Spirit, Amen."

"Bless me, Father," she whispers, her voice heavy with emotion, a tear snaking its way down her cheek. She lowers her head and continues, "Bless me Father, for I have sinned. It has been a month since my last confession."

I nod. I can feel the emotions, thick in the room. I sense what she's feeling and have a good idea what's coming.

At least I hope I do.

Or do I?

She takes a deep breath. "In the past month, I have lied. To a priest." She looks at me. "To you."

I smile and nod. "I know, Rachel. I know."

She shakes her head. "I didn't mean to. I mean, I did mean to, but I didn't want to. I just couldn't tell you the truth."

"Why don't you tell me now?"

She sobs. I grab a box of tissue and hand it to her. She sobs for several minutes. "I'm sorry," she croaks through her crying.

"It's all right, just take your time."

"I've just felt so guilty since we talked," she says "I haven't been able to sleep, I haven't been able to eat. I knew that I needed to come here today and confess to you, but I've spent the last hour in my car in the parking lot, debating whether or not to come in."

"Why don't we begin at the beginning," I say, leaning forward and taking her hand. "What did you lie about?"

"All of it," Rachel whispers. She looks at me. "No, I don't mean that I lied when I said that Father Leonard did nothing inappropriate or forced himself on me." She smiles, a dreamy look in her eyes. "There was nothing wrong or forced about it. I liked it. I liked every moment we spent together. I liked everything we did."

"What did you do?"

She blushes. "He was tentative, very gentle," she said. "I'll be honest, Father. It was my first time."

Now I blush. I was married at one time, and I wasn't always a priest even when I wasn't. I have a good idea what she's talking about. Frankly, it's the part of confession that leaves me the most squeamish. Sex within marriage is sacred, part of God's plan, nothing to be ashamed of. But even then, I've always been a little uncomfortable talking about it. Outside of marriage, well, it's even worse.

"Neither of us wanted it to happen, we didn't plan it or anything," she continues. "It just happened." Her smile fades. "He was so upset afterwards. He cried. He kept saying he was ruined, that we had sinned, that he had broken his vows. I cried for him. And for myself," she ended with a whisper.

"You want to become a nun," I say. "Or you did."

"I still do," she says firmly.

"When did this happen?"

"The first time was Memorial Day," she said with her eyes downcast. "At the Rectory after the picnic."

"The first—there's been more than once?"

She nods. "Three times. Twice in the Rectory, once at my apartment."

I close my eyes and sigh. "Rachel, how?"

"After the first time," she says, "we were both upset, regretful about what happened. We avoided each other for a week. I called in sick, I just couldn't face him, and I wasn't sure he wanted to see me. I even wrote my resignation;

I decided to leave Myerton and enter the convent. Then on a Friday evening, there was a knock on my door."

"It was Father Leonard," I say.

Rachel nods. "He came, he said, to apologize, to say it was wrong and it must never happen again. It tortured him, I could tell. He was going to leave right after saying that, but he wound up staying. Then we—"

"I get the picture," I say, holding up my hand.

"That just made matters worse," she continued. "We weren't sure what to do after that. But to me, deep inside, it didn't matter. The fact he was a priest. The fact I thought I was being called to religious life. It didn't matter." A tear rolled down her cheek.

I say, slowly, "You were falling in love with him."

"It wasn't that difficult. Leonard is so kind, so gentle, such a sweet man, it's very easy for a woman to fall for him. I'm surprised, frankly, that every woman in the parish doesn't have a crush on him."

This is a woman truly in love, I think.

"So one day I screwed up my courage and went to the Rectory and told him." She paused. "And showed him."

I react with surprise. "I know," she smiled shyly, "I surprised myself, what I did. But I just couldn't help myself." She sighed. "But it didn't help."

"How did Leonard react? What happened afterward?"

She sighed and shook her head. "He said nothing to me. Just got up, dressed, and left me in his room. I thought he'd come back, but he didn't. After a while I got up and dressed myself, went looking for him." She looked down at her hands, twisting in her lap. "I found him here, on his face in front of the altar, crying. He was whispering something over and over that sounded like, 'I'm so sorry, I've let you down again.' "

I sit back. "When did this happen?"

Still looking at her hands, she says, "About three weeks ago."

"Did you tell anyone about this?"

She hesitates. "I . . . told Rebecca what was going on. I had to. I had to tell someone. But she's my sister. She wouldn't do that, betray my confidence."

I sigh. She's told me a lot and is emotionally spent. "What are you going to do now? Are you still intent on entering religious life?"

She takes a deep breath. "After everything that happened, I wondered. I prayed, and I thought about it a lot. But I still feel God pulling me to him. I love Leonard, and I always will, but I have to follow the longing of my heart. Besides, Leonard is a priest and always will be. He can no more give that up than he can cut off his right arm. Mother Superior is expecting me early next week. I'll be leaving Myerton Monday morning." She smiles. "That will put an end to everything."

***

I get through the 4:30 p.m. Mass and retire to the Rectory. I throw myself into a chair, emotionally exhausted. I'm still trying to process what Rachel Watson revealed in confession. She's put me in an unpleasant situation. What she told me in confession, I can't tell anyone. I can't even tell Father Leonard that I know the truth. But Rachel gave me everything I needed to tell the Archbishop that the young priest broke his vows of celibacy and needs to be dealt with.

Leonard can't stay at Saint Clare's. Not because of the rumors, as bad as those are, because if they moved a priest every time there were rumors in a parish about them, there wouldn't be a priest in a parish for more than six months at a time. No, Leonard can't stay for his own sake and the sake of his calling. He needs counseling. He needs to spend time in prayer and penance. He needs time to heal.

If he wants to stay a priest. That is the other thing. Rachel seems determined to follow through on her call to religious life. But is that genuine? I had absolved her because she expressed genuine contrition. I believe she is sorry for what she did, but part of me wonders how sorry she is. I believe she loves Leonard and am concerned that her going into the convent is running from the truth.

Running from the truth is something I know a little about. Eventually you have to stop, turn, and face the truth. What will happen if later in her religious life, she wakes up one day and realizes she made a terrible mistake? What would that do to her spiritual life?

And what about Leonard? Does he still want to be a priest? He had said nothing to Rebecca to indicate anything other than remorse and sorrow for his sins. I needed to speak to him; I needed to get him to admit the truth, and I needed him to do that for the sake of his own soul. Beyond that, there was nothing I could do to help.

But he's at the monastery. I need to talk to him.

Anna comes into the living room with a glass of ice water. "Here," she says, "I bet you're thirsty."

I take it gladly and down it in one gulp. "That's just what I needed," I say, handing it back to her. "Thanks."

She tilts her head to one side. "Rough afternoon?"

"Not one of my better ones."

Anna knows not to ask anymore, so she says, "There was a message for you. From Winthrop Myer."

I sit up, surprised. "Did he say what he wanted?"

Anna shakes her head. "No, he just asked you to call him when you get the chance. I wrote the number on your blotter."

Getting up, I say, "Thanks," and walk out of the room.

"Dinner's in half-an-hour."

I stop. "You didn't have to make me dinner, Anna. I could have just grabbed something at The Bistro."

"Nonsense, you probably haven't had a home-cooked meal since you were last here—actually, you never came for dinner when you were here the last time—so I did some shopping and made your favorite."

I smile. "Lasagna. You remember."

She nods. "Bring your appetite. I made enough for you and Father Leonard, but if he will not be here, I guess I'll have a bit."

I walk to my office and pick up the Rectory phone. The first number I dial, I don't have to look up.

"Our Lady of the Mount, how may I help you?" says the familiar old voice.

"Brother Martin, good evening."

"Good evening, Father Tom," he replies. "How are you?"

"Fine, thank you. I was wondering if it would be possible for me to speak to Father Leonard. Would it be too much trouble if you could see if he's available?"

"I'll check to see if he's in his cabin." He pauses. "He seems very troubled."

"Did he tell you why he was there?"

"He said nothing to me, but he's been talking to Father Abbot. Father Abbot was glad to have him this morning; he said Mass to the community. But I can tell he's carrying a substantial burden."

"That," I say slowly, "he is."

"Hmm," he says. "I won't ask any more. I'll find him and have him call you. It will be about twenty minutes."

After hanging up with Brother Martin, I dial Winthrop Myer's number. A woman answers.

"Hello?" I recognize Rebecca Myer's voice.

"Rebecca?"

"Yes, this is Rebecca."

"Good evening, Rebecca, this is Father Greer at Saint Clare's. Am I calling at a bad time?"

"No, no, we had not sat down for dinner yet. What can I do for you?"

"Well, I'm returning your husband's call."

There is silence at the other end of the phone. "What?"

"Yes, your husband left a message for me at the Rectory and asked me to return his call. Is he available?"

She doesn't answer right away. "Yes, Father Greer. I'll get him." She puts the phone down and I hear her walk away. A few minutes later, I hear quick footsteps. "Hello?" a man's voice says pleasantly.

"Mr. Myer, this is Father—"

"Ah, Father Greer, Rebecca told me you were on the phone. Thanks for calling me back."

"I apologize for the delay," I say, "but I was hearing confessions and then had—"

"Oh, I understand how busy you are," he says. "I just want to talk to you about this situation with Father McCoy and my sister-in-law."

"Well, as I told Marjorie, I am looking into it and will make a recommendation to the Archbishop based on my findings."

"Yes, yes, I understand," he replies. "I just thought you and I could talk, you know, man to man, to clarify things. I just want to make sure things are handled properly. I don't think the Church in this state can handle another scandal, do you?"

"I agree, but if you don't mind my asking, why are you interested?"

"Why, well, why—Rachel's my sister-in-law," Myer says. "I care about her welfare."

"I understand, but what do you want to talk to me about?"

"I just want you to understand where I'm coming from. I find this entire situation very upsetting."

"Understandable. It is for all of us."

"Yes, I'm sure." He pauses, then says. "Why don't you come to our house tomorrow for lunch?"

I sigh. Lunch after two masses on top of what I've already gone through. But I don't have a good excuse to refuse. That they're racing at Michigan doesn't qualify as a good excuse. Anyway, there's a sixty percent chance of rain in the Irish Hills, so it will probably be delayed.

"That would be fine," I say. "I can be over there at about 1:30 p.m., is that too late?"

"No, no, 1:30 p.m. is fine. I look forward to it."

After I hang up, I look at the clock. It is a little after 6:00 p.m., and from the smells coming from the direction of the kitchen, dinner must be about ready. I start to leave my office when the phone rings.

"Father Tom," Brother Martin says, an edge of concern in his voice.

"Brother Martin, is anything wrong?"

"I don't know," he says. "I looked for Father McCoy at his cabin, but he wasn't there. I noticed his car was gone. I asked around and one of the novices said he saw Father McCoy leave about an hour ago. He didn't tell anyone where he was going."

Six

Mass the next day is uneventful. I am distracted. After speaking to Brother Martin, I had tried calling Father Leonard on his phone, but it went straight to voicemail. He was either out of range—not unusual in the mountains—or had turned his phone off. I'm concerned about why he left the monastery without telling anyone he was leaving or where he was going. I have no idea where he is, but he had not returned to the Rectory by morning. Under other circumstances, I wouldn't be concerned.

But circumstances are far from normal.

The crowds at the 8:30 a.m. and 10:30 a.m. Masses are what I had experienced during my last time at Saint Clare's. The former Mass is smaller, older, and quiet; the later is larger, younger, and loud. There seem to be more children than last time; I count at least four new babies and twice that many pregnant moms. Miriam and Dan Conway are in their traditional pew, along with their four children. Anna is where she always is. Helen is there, in the front pew.

After Mass I stand on the steps greeting the parishioners as they filed past me. Anna comes up. "It's like you never left," she says.

"I'm kind of distracted, to be honest. I'm glad it didn't show."

"Still no word from Father Leonard?"

I shake my head. "No. Not a word. I don't mind telling you, I'm getting a little concerned."

"I'm sure he's fine," Anna says. "How about coming over for lunch, something to take your mind off of things? It's just the leftover lasagna from last night."

I shake my head. "Sorry, I'm going over to the Myers' for lunch, remember?"

"Oh, that's right," Anna says. "I forgot. I'm planning to go to see Joan this afternoon."

I smile. "I'll meet you there, about 4:00 p.m.?"

Anna returns the smile. "That sounds fine. See you then."

I watch her walk off. More people file past, shaking my hand and saying how glad they are to see me. Dan, Miriam, and their kids all stop by to say hello. After about twenty minutes, the crowd has thinned out. I turn to go back inside when I see Helen.

"I'm glad you came," I say to her as she walks up to me.

"I told you I'd be here," she says with a smile. "It was good to see you in action again. As a priest, that is."

"What did you think?"

Helen cocks her head to one side. "Honestly, I still have difficulty seeing you on the altar. Too many memories, you know. But . . . it suits you. It's where you belong."

I smile and nod my head. "It's where I'm happiest, honestly. Saying Mass, being close to the Lord. I feel at peace."

She looks at me quizzically. "Are you, Tom?"

I stiffen a little. "What makes you ask that?"

"You seemed distracted today," Helen says. "Like something is bothering you."

"You still know me too well," I sigh. "This situation with Father Leonard has gotten—well, it's more complicated than I thought it would be."

She shakes her head. "I'm not surprised, Tom. Everyone else here may think he's harmless, but there's something about him that's always struck me as a little . . . off."

"Off? How so?"

"Oh, nothing that would hold up in court," she says with a wry smile. "It's just a gut feeling, I guess you'd say?"

"Well," I say with a frown, "I can't go with a gut feeling."

"Sometimes a gut feeling is all a cop has," she says.

"Really? What does your gut say about me?"

No, I don't know what makes me ask that question. Helen seems as surprised to hear it as I am to have said it.

"Hmm," she says, narrowing her brow. "I'm not sure, yet, Tom. I'll let you know."

We just stand there, looking at each other. Finally, Helen says, "It was good to see you, Tom, but I'm meeting someone for lunch."

"Oh? Anybody I know?" I say with a smile.

She hesitates for a moment before saying, "Brian."

My smile fades in spite of myself. "Oh, yeah. I remember your last email."

"It's just lunch, Tom," she says. "I've just got to put a stop to his constantly trying to get back together with me. I have to make him understand I have no interest in him."

I nod. "Of course," I say. "Well, good luck."

"Thanks, I'll probably need it," she says. Then, realizing what she just said, she stammers. "I mean, well, you know men . . . OK, I'll see you around."

She turns and walks off. My eyes linger on her longer than they should.

Then, I retire to the sacristy, take my vestments off, and prepare for my second major meeting of the day.

***

The Myer Estate was once on the outskirts of Myerton when built in the 1800s. Since then, the town had grown around it, but a large expanse of grounds and a stone wall separate the estate from the surrounding homes. The metal gates open as I drive up. I suppose someone is watching my arrival on a camera somewhere. The driveway curves through a tree-lined lawn leading to the entrance.

The Myer home is a sprawling example of pre-Civil War Greek Revival architecture, added on repeatedly through the years as the family's wealth and influence grew. Two stories with two one-story wings on either side, the house is a whitewashed stone and brick edifice that looks like its builders meant for it to stand as long as the mountains surrounding it. But time has taken its toll. Ivy snakes up its walls, with scaffolding showing the house is undergoing some restoration. The worn roof shows evidence of work being done on it. In the bright July sun, the whole place looks vaguely ominous. In the dark, I imagine it looks like something out of Edgar Allan Poe or Stephen King.

I seriously doubt any monsters ever inhabited the house. The Myer family has been known through the decades for their philanthropy and generosity in the town, and throughout the tri-state area, for generations. More than one hospital wing and college building has the name 'Myer' attached to it. It is hardly a family known for evil.

I park my car and walk up. Before I can ring the doorbell, Rebecca Myer opens the door. I wear my clericals with a black suit coat, appropriate, I thought, for lunch with the Myers family. Rebecca herself is much more casually clad, in tight yoga pants and an oversized t-shirt tied at the waist. She wears no makeup and has gathered her shoulder-length hair in a single ponytail. Had I not known better, I would have thought Rachel Watson was standing before me.

"Welcome, Father Greer," she says, appearing genuinely happy to see me. "Come in. Pardon the mess."

I walk into what had once been an elegant entryway, with a wide staircase going up to a landing on the second floor. I can see where a chandelier once hung, there was now only the chain dangling from the ceiling. A paint-splattered drop cloth covers the floor, and ladders are on either side.

"We're renovating the old place," she explains. "Win wanted to restore the house to the way it was when his great-grandfather was here."

"It seems like an extensive project."

"It is," she says, her smile fading a bit. "It's taken a lot more time and a lot more money than he thought it would. But still, it makes him happy. And the house is historically important. Did you know it was the first house in Myerton wired with electricity? Thomas Edison himself came to oversee the project. This was before the town had a power plant, so Edison constructed a small one on the property. There's a photograph, and the building is still there, on the edge of the woods behind the house." She leads me into a side room, a large living room with several comfortable looking couches and armchairs, one wall lined with bookshelves, the other with photographs, with windows overlooking the front lawn.

"Here it is." She points to an old photograph on the wall. There's the famous inventor himself, standing next to an otherwise nondescript building with a wire coming out of the roof. Next to Edison stands a man, slightly taller, with a moustache and wearing round rimmed glasses.

"That's Win's great-grandfather," Rebecca says, pointing to the other man in the picture.

"I see," I say as I walk along the wall of photographs. Most of them are family pictures, a few are of the house or other houses that I assume were owned by the Myers over the years. There are also photos of various buildings, the Myer name prominent on them; these must be the results of the family philanthropy. Interspersed are more personal photos, family gatherings, funerals, and weddings. Near the end, I see color photos of a more re-cent wedding. I stop at one photo. Rebecca is in a white wedding dress, long veil, holding a bouquet of pink flowers. She's standing next to a man wear-ing an Army dress uniform who could have been the twin of the man in the picture standing next to Edison. That man has to be Win Myer. There's lit-tle doubt he's a Myer. On either side are bridesmaids and groomsmen—the party numbers twelve, six of each. Standing next to Rebecca is her maid of honor, Win's best man is to his left. I look at the faces of the bridesmaids; they, along with Rebecca, are smiling, showing the joy typically associated with the day.

At the end of the line of young women is Rachel. She's staring straight ahead at the camera. Her face is expressionless.

Another photograph next to it shows the family, the Watsons, with the radiant bride and groom. I recognize Ms. Watson, beaming with pride at the marriage of one of her daughters. A man who must be Rachel and Rebecca's father is there, smiling like a man not used to smiling, looking uncomfort-able in his tuxedo. And there's Rachel, with the same expression—or lack of expression.

I am about to ask why Rachel looks so unhappy when Win Myer walks into the room. He's not too changed from the picture. Slightly taller than me, muscular, his sandy blond hair beginning to thin, a man in his early thirties who looks like he's carrying the burdens of a man in his late fifties.

"Sorry, I was taking a phone call," he says. He appears agitated.

"I didn't hear the phone ring," Rebecca comments.

"The call was to my cell phone, not the main phone," he responds, a little abruptly. "More problems from those tree-huggers about the Point Arthur project."

"Oh, why can't they see that you're on their side?" She turns to me. "Win's been trying to move Myer Holdings into clean energy projects. He wants to construct a wind farm just north of town to provide electricity to most of the surrounding area."

"But some environmentalists," Win continues, "want the project stopped. Something about disrupting patterns of bird migration. We've told them all the studies we've commissioned show any disruption will be mini-mal. Anyway," he smiles, "nice to meet you, Father Greer."

It's cool inside the house, but I see beads of sweat on his forehead. The phone call must have upset him.

"I'll see to lunch," Rebecca says. "It will still be a few minutes. Win, why don't you show Father to your office."

Win nods as she leaves. "Father," Myer turns to me. "Would you like a drink? I have a well-stocked liquor cabinet," he says as he walks out of the room. I follow him into another room, much more masculine, with shelves lined with books. His home office, I assume, from the desk piled with file folders and other papers. He walks up to his liquor cabinet and pulls out two glasses. He uncorks the crystal decanter and pours an amber liquid. "Want one, Father?" he asks me.

"No, thank you," I say. "I don't really drink, but I'll take a cola if you have one."

He gives me a slightly disdainful look, but he smiles and says, "Of course, Father." He reaches into the mini fridge and pulls out a can. He pours the cola over some ice and walks over, handing me the glass.

"Please," Myer says, showing two chairs. We sit and he leans back, nursing his drink.

"I appreciate you coming over," Myer says.

"Thank you for inviting me," I say. "Lovely room. This is quite a house. Rebecca says you're restoring it."

"Yes, this is my passion project. Getting the family estate back up to snuff. Like it was in great-grandfather's day, back when the Myer name meant something around here."

"Well, I still think it does," I say. "Your family name is on the town, on the college, which I still believe you're on the board of trustees for."

"And a still significant source of donations," Myer adds. "But as the overall percentage, not nearly what it was in the past."

"Where did you get the idea to restore the home?"

"Oh, that was Marjorie's idea."

"Marjorie?"

"Rebecca's mother, Marjorie. Yes, she wanted her daughter to live here after our marriage. You see, Father, the old place had gotten so run-down that we had decided to get another place in the new development on the other side of town—it's really too big for just two people—but Marjorie had her heart set on seeing us live here. So she persuaded me to restore the estate." He sipped his drink. "It's been a haul, and I've spent quite a bit of money, but we're pleased."

"And you're living here during the renovation? That doesn't sound too convenient."

Myer shrugged. "It is what it is. But I didn't have you come here to talk about the house." He puts his drink on the table beside his chair. "What are we going to do about this situation with Father McCoy and Rachel?"

"As I told you on the phone, Mr. Myer—"

"Win," he says. "Call me Win."

I say, "As I told you on the phone, Win, I'm looking into the allegations and will recommend to the Archbishop the appropriate course of action, depending on what I determine."

"And what have you determined?"

I pause before answering, "I will not share that with you. I'm still looking into it." I could not tell him what I had found out, what Rachel had told me, and I needed to talk to Father Leonard again.

"I see," he replies. He sits back in the leather armchair. "So tell me, Father," he says, "What will it take?"

"I don't understand?"

"Oh really, Father Greer. You know what I'm saying. But I'll be a little more explicit. You know my family has been a member of Saint Clare's for generations. I was baptized there and, even though the family's not really been religious, over the years we've donated to the parish. You know, my great-great grandfather oversaw the reconstruction of the church after the original building burned in the 1850s. It's a place of historical importance, you know, one of the oldest in this part of Maryland, one of the few surviving examples of Ionic-style churches."

"I'm aware of both the church's history and your family's relationship with it."

"It's a relationship I've been glad to continue," Win goes on. "You know, Rebecca grew up in Saint Clare's, that's where we were married, so she still has a lot of affection for the place. I've made several sizable donations over the years. Mostly anonymous, mind you." He sipped his drink. "I've been by the church many times and know that the church needs repair. The roof, for example, needs replacing. On a structure that old and that big, that will add up to some money. It would take you years of bingo and rummage sales to raise the amount needed. Now I," he touches his chest, "could write you a check for the full amount today. You'd have no worries."

"I see," I say quietly.

"I think King Henry IV of France said, 'Paris is worth a Mass.' Don't you think a new roof for Saint Clare's is worth one priest? I mean, don't the needs of the many outweigh the needs of the few?"

I smile. "Or the one?"

Win returns my smile and toasts me with his glass. "Very good, Father Greer. Not that many people these days would get the reference."

I fold my hands in front of me. "Can I ask why you're so interested in this? Why are you so eager to see Father McCoy transferred out of Saint Clare's?"

"Ah," he says. He stands and goes to pour himself another drink. "I understand why you would wonder about that. A big part of it is because she's my sister-in-law. I have a great deal of affection for her, always have. She's like the little sister I've never had. That's one reason I agreed to spy on them when Marjorie asked me. But truth be told, Father, there's more to it than that." He sits back down, the ice clinking in his glass as he slowly twirls his drink. "I suppose I feel guilty."

"Guilty?" I say.

"Yes, for my role in this whole thing," Win says, "The fact of the matter is, Father Greer, that I'm responsible for getting Rachel the job."

"I was aware you met with Father McCoy and gave the Church a sizable donation. So it was to persuade him to give Rachel the parish secretary's job?"

"Yes," he replies. "I didn't persuade, really, I just pointed out how qualified Rachel was, given her education and background. And considering she wanted to become a nun."

"I didn't think the family supported that?"

"Oh," he waves his hand, "no, we don't, not at all. But Rachel wanted the job, so I thought—"

"Wait," I interrupt. "Did Rachel ask you to talk to Father Leonard?"

"Ask me? She practically begged me. It was a couple of months after she had moved back to Myerton to take a program manager's job at one of the tech firms outside town. She called me one day saying Saint Clare's was looking for a new parish secretary and asked me to talk to Father Leonard about giving her the job."

"Did she say why she wanted the job?"

"Oh, she said something about wanting more time to pray, to attend daily Mass. I pointed out it'd be a huge pay cut for her, but she said she had more than enough savings to make up for any shortfall. She told me it wouldn't be for very long, anyway."

"What do you think she meant by that?"

He shrugs. "I guess because she'd be entering the convent soon." I saw a touch of sadness enter his eyes.

"So you met with Father Leonard," I say. "And did you mention how much money you'd given in the past?"

"Well," he smiles sheepishly, "I'm afraid I may have alluded to it. Until I mentioned the donation, Father Leonard was very reluctant to say he'd even interview Rachel. I got the impression that he really didn't want her to have the position."

I found that interesting, considering the warmth Father Leonard expressed about Rachel in our first meeting. "I'm sure he appreciated your generosity," I say. "But I doubt he gave Rachel the job because of it."

Win shrugs. "Perhaps, perhaps not. But I feel I contributed to whatever happened and I want to fix it."

"Well," I say, "I can't tell you everything, but let me put your mind at ease. I've found no evidence that Father Leonard abused his position to take advantage of Rachel." I told the strict truth. But not the whole truth.

"I hope he didn't," Win says, his face darkening. "Every time I think about the possibility of that sweet, innocent girl being taken advantage of, I just get so . . . so . . . " He stops and clears his throat. "Anyway, Father, about Father Leonard . . . "

I put my hand up. "I understand your concern, Win, I really do. I can imagine being in your position. But my duty here is to report to the Archbishop whatever I find, good or bad. I won't be persuaded to bend my report towards any particular recommendation."

Win smiles and opens his arms. "You can't blame a guy for trying, Father. No hard feelings, I hope?"

"Not on my part," I say.

"Good, good. I guess I'll just have to trust your integrity." He stands. "Shall we meet Rebecca? I'm sure lunch is ready by now."

***

After a very fine and convivial lunch, I say I have another appointment that afternoon. Win thanks me for coming and says he has some business calls to make. Rebecca walks me to the door.

"Thank you for coming," Rebecca says. "I hope Win didn't press you too much about Father McCoy."

"He was direct about it," I say. "I understand where he's coming from. He cares about your sister very much."

She gives a short laugh. "Oh yes, Win cares about Rachel, that's for sure." At my raised eyebrows, she shakes her head. "Never mind, Father. It's nothing. Thanks for coming."

Seven

"Sounds like you had a pleasant visit," Anna says. "Phew, it's a hot one today!"

We're walking up the hill at the cemetery towards the old oak tree that shades Joan's grave. Anna is carrying a vase; I'm carrying a bunch of peppermint carnations, Joan's favorite flower. The sky is a clear blue, and the sun is beaming down on us, baking us in the still air. I'm glad I changed out of my clericals into shorts and a polo shirt before making the trek.

"Oh, it was. Very nice. Lunch was delicious, and both of them were very pleasant. I'm just trying to get my mind around Win Myer's interest in all of this. I'm not sure Rebecca likes it too much."

"He really must care about Rachel."

"He cares about something, I'm just not sure what. What do you know about their background?"

She stops and turns to me. "Now, Tom, why would you think I'd know anything? I've never even really met them."

"Because, Anna, I know you gather information the way a squirrel gathers nuts for the winter."

"You make me sound like an old gossip," she huffs.

"You're not old, and a gossip talks. You just listen. At least that's what Joan always told me." We get to the grave. Anna leans over and puts the vase down, allowing me to place the flowers inside. She takes a bottle of water out of her bag and pours the contents in. We stand quietly for a few minutes, looking at the marble headstone gleaming in the light. I pull out my prayer book and begin reciting the prayers for visiting a graveside. At the end, we cross ourselves. I bend over and kiss the headstone and say, "I love you, Joan." Anna gently strokes the stone.

Walking back to the car, Anna says, "I don't know that much about the families, other than what everyone knows about the Myers."

"Win Myer is an only child, I take it?"

She nods. "Yes, a later-life one, apparently. Both of his parents are dead; he inherited the entire Myer family business when he was in his mid-twenties. He and Rebecca were high school sweethearts from what I understand."

"He went to school here in Myerton? He didn't go to a fancy prep school in Baltimore or D.C.?"

Anna shakes her head. "Apparently not. He attended Myerton High School. Regular big man on campus, football starter, academic all-star, graduated valedictorian. I think he was in ROTC in college because I heard he served in Afghanistan for a while. He married Rebecca before going overseas. Then his parents died, he left the Army, moved back home, and took over the family businesses."

"Are the Watsons a wealthy family?"

"Hardly," she says. "But from what I understand, Majorie Watson really advocated the two getting married. But it wasn't that hard, as I say, since they had dated in high school."

"Any idea why he'd take such an interest in this situation?"

She shrugs. "Rebecca loves her sister. I guess he's just concerned on his sister's behalf."

I shake my head. "It just seems odd to me. Rebecca and her mother are both concerned, but there's something about Win Myer's interest that strikes me as different." I pause. "He admitted asking Father Leonard to give Rachel the job."

"Well, that explains things, but why did he do that?"

"According to him, Rachel begged him to talk to Father Leonard on her behalf."

She stopped and looked at me. "Really?" Anna thinks for a minute. "There really was no need; she was qualified. She must have wanted the job a lot."

I nod my head. "I accept her explanation why she wanted the job."

"Do I hear a but?"

"But," I continue, "why did she want so desperately to work here that she'd have her very wealthy and successful brother-in-law take time out of his busy schedule to intercede on her behalf? And why would he do it?" I shake my head.

"Tom," Anna says warily. "What are you doing?"

I look at her. "What do you mean?"

"It sounds like you're looking for a complicated explanation when a simple one will do. What do they call it, Occam's Razor?"

I laugh. "Sorry, you're right. I'm overthinking things. It's probably just as everyone has said," I say to her.

But inside, I'm thinking there's something off.

"Well, anyway," I continue, "I need to talk to Father Leonard."

"I'm surprised he's not back by now," Anna comments.

I hesitate. "He's probably just getting some peace and quiet at Our Lady of the Mount. I wasn't expecting him until tomorrow, anyway."

Anna nods. "That's good. If there's one thing that young man needs, it's peace and quiet."

"I just need him to come back so I can put this whole matter to bed," I say before I can think.

"Rather unfortunate choice of words, isn't it?"

I sigh and wipe my sweaty brow. "It's the heat. Anyway, the sooner Father Leonard gets back here, the sooner I can resolve this situation."

We get to the car. Before opening the door, I look at Anna. "What do you think the hardest part of being a priest is?"

Anna looks at me, thinking. "Toddlers rushing the altar during the consecration?"

I laugh. "Believe it or not, that's not at the top of the list." I pause. "It's loneliness."

"What do you mean?" Anna says, getting into the car.

"I mean, it's a very lonely job. After a hard day, I come back to the Rectory and there's no one there to greet me, no one to ask me how my day was, no one who seems happy to see me." I pause. "I guess for me that's been the biggest adjustment. I know what it's like, more than most other priests, to have that."

She pats my hand. "Maybe you should get a dog."

I look at her and chuckle. "No, thank you. I don't like dogs."

Anna looks at me. "What prompted this?"

"Oh, I don't know, just thinking. If Father Leonard and Rachel got too close, too close for a priest, I think I understand how it could happen." I look at her. "Not that it would be right. But, understandable." I sigh and start the car.

"Well, in this case, I think you're on safe ground. If there's one priest I know who would never break his vows, it's Father Leonard McCoy."

***

Loud ringing jars me out of a deep sleep. The time on my phone says it's 11:30 p.m. It's not my cell phone ringing, but the Rectory phone by my bed. I fumble for the receiver.

"Saint Clare's Parish," I yawn, "Father—"

"Father Tom!" says a breathless voice on the other end. It's Father Leonard. "Father Tom! I . . . I . . . oh, Holy Mother of God . . . oh, my dear Jesus . . ."

"Leonard, Leonard!" I say into the phone, fully awake now. "What's wrong, where are you?"

"I'm, I'm here . . . oh, Tom, it's horrible. Something terrible has happened. Oh, Saint Michael, pray for me!"

"Where are you?"

"Where am I? Where am I?" I hear only breathing on the other end of the phone. "I'm, I'm at her townhouse. Oh, dear Jesus!"

"Whose townhouse? Rachel Watson's?"

"Yes, yes! Please hurry? Oh, my Lord!" I hear the phone drop to the floor. He's dissolved into hysterical sobs.

"Leonard! Leonard!" I hang the phone up and throw on my clothes. I'm halfway down the stairs when I realize I have no idea where Rachel Watson lives. I dash into the office. After a five-minute search, I find her address. She's about ten minutes from the Rectory.

I sprint to my car and peel out of the Rectory driveway. I make the ten-minute trip in less than seven owing to the lack of traffic at that time of day. Father Leonard's car is parked outside the address, a small townhouse in a row of townhouses of recent construction. There is no one around.

I walk up to the door and am about to knock when I hear a sound coming from inside. Putting my ear to the door, I hear muffled sobs. The door is not completely shut and opens as I lean against it and step inside.

It's dark in Rachel's home, the only light coming from streetlights filtered by drawn shades. I follow the sound of Father Leonard's crying down the short entry hallway. The way the townhouse is constructed, the main living room area is up a flight of steps. I walk softly up the steps, Father Leonard's sobs getting louder and louder.

I reach the top of the stairs. I see two indistinct forms in the dim light. My hand searches along the wall for a light switch. Finding what I'm looking for, I flick the lights on. They illuminate the room.

What I see chills me to the bone.

Father Leonard is sitting on the floor, his arms wrapped around his legs in a fetal position, his head down, his body wracked with sobs.

Laying on the floor beside him is the lifeless body of Rachel Watson.

Eight

I stand frozen in place, transfixed by the sight. The only sounds in the room are Father Leonard's sobs. Outside I can hear the cacophony of a summer night, crickets chirping along with the other nocturnal creatures.

I move slowly towards Rachel. She's lying on her back, arms down by her side, her lifeless eyes staring into space. Blood has soaked the carpet. Tentatively, I touch the red blot. It's already dried. She's been dead for some time.

I pull out my prayer book and begin to say the necessary prayers over her. After a few minutes, I make the sign of the cross. Then, I go to check on Father Leonard. He's stopped crying, but now he's staring into the distance.

I kneel beside him. "Leonard," I touch his shoulder and whisper his name. He does not respond, doesn't blink. "Leonard," I say louder, shaking him gently. He still doesn't respond.

As I stand and reach in my pocket for my phone, a glint of light catches my sight. It's a kitchen knife, about six inches long, covered in blood. It's on the floor, about a foot from Father Leonard.

I dial 911 and tell them what's happened. They say they'll send the police and an ambulance.

"There's no hurry on the ambulance," I say softly. "It's already too late."

When I finish talking to 911, I make another call.

"Detective Parr," I hear Helen yawn. "Someone had better be dead."

If the sight before me wasn't so horrific, I would laugh. I forgot that Helen wakes up with a disposition somewhere between Godzilla rampaging through Tokyo and a grizzly bear poked with a stick.

"Someone is, Helen, otherwise I wouldn't call you at this hour," I say gravely.

"Tom? What the hell!" she says. "Why are you calling me at . . . do you know what time it is? What is it? Did you say someone's dead?"

"Yes," I say, and describe the situation briefly.

"What's the address?" I hear her writing Rachel's address down. "You've called 911? I'll be there in about twenty minutes. Touch nothing, Tom. And don't move Father Leonard until someone gets there."

I look at the pathetic man, still curled up in a ball. "That'll be no problem. I doubt I could get him to move if the house was on fire."

While I wait, I take the time to look around Rachel's home, being careful not to disturb anything. She is—was—an impeccable housekeeper. There is a place for everything, and everything is in its place. Her place bears no evidence of a violent act having taken place a short while ago. Except, of course, for the dead body and pool of blood.

I walk into the living room. Again, the room is clean, with not a thing out of place. An empty vase sits in the middle of a simple wood coffee table, the table itself flanked by a sofa and a loveseat, with an armchair opposite. There are pictures on the wall, a couple of mountain scenes. There are several photographs. Two are copies of the photos from Rebecca's wedding. Others are of a younger Rachel, obviously in college, with groups of other young women at different parties. Unlike the wedding photographs, she is smiling, even laughing.

I walk from the living room to the kitchen. There is a knife block on the counter, one knife missing. I shudder. Whoever killed her did so with one of her own knives.

Handwritten notes cover the refrigerator. To do lists, the beginnings of a grocery list, a reminder of a doctor's appointment from two weeks before. I study the grocery list. Bread, eggs, milk, assorted fresh vegetables, nothing out of the ordinary.

"Police," I hear from downstairs. "We're coming up. Keep your hands where we can see them." I slowly walk out of the kitchen with my hands out so they're easily seen.

"I'm unarmed," I call. "I'm Father Tom Greer from Saint Clare's Parish. I called 911."

"Father Tom?" a familiar voice says. In a minute, Dan Conway, his sidearm in his hand, comes up the staircase. "It's okay," he calls down the stairs. Holstering his weapons, he approaches me.

"Are you all right, Father?" he asks. Behind him, I see other officers followed by two paramedics. One walks to Rachel, kneels down, and checks for a pulse. "She's gone," she says.

Dan looks at Father Leonard. "Is he hurt?"

I shake my head. "I don't know. He hasn't said a word to me since I got here."

To the paramedics, Dan says, "Check him out."

The other paramedic squats in front of Father Leonard. He says, "Sir, sir, can you hear me? Are you injured?" Father Leonard says nothing. The paramedic checks his eyes with a penlight. "Pupils are equal and reactive. You say he has said nothing?"

"Not since I got here," I answer.

"Julie, help me get him up." The paramedics each take an arm and help Father Leonard to his feet. It's only when Leonard stands that I see he's not wearing his clericals. Instead, he's wearing a white polo shirt and khaki trousers.

The shirt is covered in blood. As are his hands.

***

Red and blue lights flash in the darkness. The normal 3:00 a.m. summer stillness is pierced by the sounds of movement, calls across the parking lot, and uniformed police officers scurrying about, wrapping the area around Rachel Watson's townhouse in yellow crime scene tape. Some of her neighbors, awakened by the commotion, have gathered on the sidewalk. Others stand in their doorways. A few peek out of their windows. All want a glimpse of what's going on. A steady murmur joins the chirping of crickets and the light squeaks of bats flying through the moonlit sky.

I'm sitting next to Father Leonard in the open door of the ambulance. A blanket's around his shoulders. He stares straight ahead into the distance. I see his lips moving, but cannot tell what he's saying. Praying, I suppose.

Close to thirty minutes after I called her, Helen arrives. She looks in my direction before going into the townhouse. The murmur of the crowd dies down. I look up. The technicians from the medical examiner's office are wheeling out a gurney carrying a black bag. I know the bag contains Rachel Watson. Helen is coming out behind it, then walks past it to where I am sitting.

"Do you want to give her last rites before they take her?" she asks.

"I said the prayers before y'all arrived," I reply.

Helen looks at Father Leonard. "How's he doing?"

I shake my head. "I don't know. He hasn't said a word since I got here."

"What was he doing here, Tom?"

I tell her about the phone call, about coming to Rachel's townhouse, and describe the scene that greeted me when I arrived. Helen notes that down in her notebook.

"But what was he doing in her place at 11:30 p.m.?" she says, pointing to Leonard.

"I don't know, he didn't tell me on the phone," I say, telling Helen the exact truth.

Helen fixes me with a look. "Hmm," she says. "Why do I feel there's something you're not telling me?"

"Helen," I say slowly. "I can't tell you some things. But I'm telling you the truth when I say Leonard did not tell me why he was in Rachel Watson's apartment."

She taps her notebook with her pen. "Are we going to go through this again, Tom? If you have information pertinent to this, you need to tell me." She pauses. "Unless—oh, hell!" she yells, causing people to stop and look in her direction. "Get back to work, nothing to see here," she hollers at the officers and technicians, who quickly get back to work.

"He confessed to you, didn't he?" she said, pointing to Leonard.

"No," I shake my head vigorously. "No, Helen, he hasn't told me anything. That, I can assure you."

"But there is something, isn't there?" She looks to that coroner's van as they're loading Rachel. Helen turns back to me. "Her?"

"You know I can't answer that" I say.

"Detective Parr," one of the paramedics interrupts us, "you wanted to know about Father McCoy's condition?"

"Yes," Helen says. Pointing with her pen she says, "Is that blood his?"

"He has no wounds, there's not a mark on him. There doesn't seem to be anything physically wrong with him."

"So why's he like this?"

The paramedic looks at Leonard and shrugs. "Shock, pure and simple. We should take him to the hospital, just to have him checked out."

"Fine," Helen says. Looking at me, she asks, "I assume you'll ride with him?"

"If that's all right?" I say to the paramedic, who nods. The other paramedic joins us, and the two help Leonard into the ambulance. I'm about to climb in when Helen touches me on the shoulder.

"Listen," she whispers. "I understand, Tom. But if you know something, even if it implicates him, I need to know."

I sigh and nod. "I'll tell you what I can, I promise."

The paramedic closes the doors behind me. I sit on a metal box and look out the window to see Helen watching us as we drive off.

***

At Myerton General, the paramedics take Leonard into the Emergency Room, where the doctor examines him. The young priest has no other injuries.

"So there's nothing physical that could cause this?" I say, pointing to Leonard. He's still said nothing, still stares straight ahead except for the occasional blink.

The doctor says, "No, there's nothing physically wrong with him. I'd say this is psychological, a severe emotional shock." She writes something on her tablet. "I will admit him for 24 hours of observation and ask the psychiatrist to have a look." She leaves to put the order in for a room.

When she leaves, a young uniformed officer comes into the room with a paper bag. "Father, we're supposed to get his clothes. They're evidence."

"He's in no condition to help with that," I say. "I must help if that's all right."

He nods and hands me a pair of gloves. Carefully, we remove Leonard's blood-soaked shirt and place it in the bag. He's wearing a brown scapular of Our Lady of Mount Carmel, a sign of his devotion to Mary; it's become stiff with blood. His chest has blood on it. I guess the nurses will wash him later. Next, his shoes and socks, followed by his pants and underwear. Trying to maintain as much of his dignity as possible, the officer and I put a hospital gown around him. During the entire process Leonard says nothing, but responds when we ask him to move.

The officer closes the bag and seals it with red evidence tape. Nodding at me, he leaves, acknowledging the other officer who is now standing outside the examination room.

It's about an hour before they move Leonard to a room. Once there, the nurse fluffs his pillows and tucks him in, Leonard as compliant as a small child. She leaves, then comes back with a tray containing a syringe.

"The doctor ordered a sedative to help him sleep," she explains. I look out the window. The sun is rising over the mountains, the entire sky an orange glow. She jabs Leonard with the needle, and in a few minutes, his eyes close and I hear him snoring quietly.

I sit, watching him sleep, and wonder what I will do next.

Nine

A hand on my shoulder and a familiar whiff of vanilla cause me to open my eyes and sit up. I don't realize where I am for a moment. Then, as the fog lifts, I look around and see the hospital bed containing a still-sleeping Father Leonard. Sun is streaming through the windows. And Helen is looking down at me, holding two cups of coffee.

"Here," she says, handing me one cup. "I thought you could use this."

"Thanks," I say, taking the cup and sipping the coffee. Sweet, strong, and creamy. I close my eyes and feel myself reviving.

"What time is it?" I ask.

"A little after 8:00 a.m.," she says. "I came over after we wrapped up at the scene."

"Find anything?" I ask as I drink.

"Lots of blood. And the murder weapon," she says. "A kitchen knife, from the knife block in her kitchen. Whoever killed her didn't plan it, used what was easily at hand."

I nod. "I saw it on the floor."

"Also," she says, then takes a drink of her coffee, "no signs of forced entry, so whoever it was she let them in." She pauses and looks at me. "Like she knew her killer."

"Not necessarily," I point out. "Her killer could have picked the lock on her door, or maybe she left the door unlocked."

"You're saying a robbery gone wrong?" Helen says. "That's a theory, I suppose. We'll check with her family to see if anything was taken. But I don't think so."

"Why?"

"Three reasons," she holds up a finger. "One, whoever killed her used a knife from her kitchen, which means the killer didn't bring it. Also, for a robber, a knife is a very clumsy weapon to use in the dark. Two, the place is clean. Not just clean—immaculate, like she just finished cleaning it before her murder. And three, it looks like she was expecting someone."

"How can you tell?"

"The two packed suitcases in her bedroom."

I open my mouth to speak. I hadn't gone into her bedroom.

"Was she taking a trip?"

I pause for a moment. "Well," I say slowly, "I may have heard something. Ask her family."

"Wasn't she the parish secretary? She'd have to let you know."

"Well, I'm not—"

"No," Helen says slowly, "but you're at Saint Clare's with some thin excuse about giving him," she points to Father Leonard, still sleeping, "a break. But both you and I know it's something to do with him and the victim."

I nod my head. "I need to speak to the Archbishop before I can say any more."

"Is Father Leonard in some kind of trouble?"

"Honestly, I don't know. He may be. Some things I learned I cannot tell you." Nodding to Leonard. "You'll have to ask him yourself."

Helen nods and looks at Father Leonard. "The nurse told me he's still sedated. Did he say anything to you?"

I shake my head. "He hasn't said a word since he called me, and I told you everything about that."

"So no idea why he was in her townhouse?"

"I didn't even know he was back in Myerton. He had gone to the monastery for a personal retreat." I pause, struggling with what I know. But I can't keep it from her, not this, because I'm concerned about how it looks. "I called the monastery and spoke to Brother Martin. I told him I needed to speak to Father Leonard. He called me back later, saying that one of the other Brothers had seen him leave. He had let no one know where he was going." I pause. "He didn't answer his phone when I tried to call him."

She's been making notes in her notebook. "So the first time you heard from him since—when, Friday?—was when he called you late last night."

"That's right."

At that moment, my phone buzzes. I grab it out of my pocket. It's Anna.

"Good morning," I say, trying to sound as nonchalant as possible.

"What's happened, Tom?" Anna asks.

"What do you mean?"

"What I mean is, one, why is there no priest here to say the 8:00 a.m. Mass?"

I sit up and look at the clock on the wall. It's 8:15 a.m..

"Oh, gosh, Anna, I'm—"

"And two, why are there reporters crawling all over Saint Clare's?"

I look at Helen. "Reporters?"

"Yes, at least three news trucks from Frederick and Baltimore. Nate Rodriguez is here too—wait, he's coming this way. Hold on." Through the phone, I can hear murmuring as Anna speaks with Nate. The next voice I hear is not Anna's, but Nate's.

"Father Tom," he says excitedly, "did you discover Rachel Watson's body? Was Father McCoy found standing over her? Can I get a statement?"

"No, Nate, you cannot get a statement from me," I say firmly. "Now give the phone back to Mrs. Luckgold, please."

"But Father—."

"Now, Nate," I say as Helen rolls her eyes. I give her a questioning look and she mouths, "Pain in the neck."

"Tom," Anna says, "Rachel's dead?"

"Yes, that's true. I'll explain when I get there." I hang up and say to Helen, "There's a circus going on at the Church. I'd better get over there." I look at Father Leonard, who's still sound asleep, then at her.

"I won't question him without you," she says, reading my mind. "But I need to know the background to this, Tom. I need to know exactly what prompted His Eminence to send you here."

"I'll get the Archbishop's okay, I promise. But I'm sure it has nothing to do with this."

But in fact, I'm not at all sure.

***

A circus is an orderly affair compared to what greets me when I arrive at Saint Clare's.

Six news vans, two from Baltimore, one from Frederick, a couple from D.C., and one from a Pennsylvania station have all converged on Myerton like moths drawn to a flame. Reporters are dispersed along the sidewalk in front of the parish grounds, each speaking into their microphones while cameramen transmit their images back to their studios live, providing viewers with their morning mayhem to go with their shredded wheat or avocado toast. Other reporters, probably representing newspapers, mill around with their recorders and notepads.

Among them I see Nate, who has both a camera and a notebook. I wonder again what he's doing there. Last I heard, he was selling the documentary he made about Joan's murder to some online company out of New York, but I don't know if it ever aired. The monastery has Internet, but allows no streaming.

As I pull into the driveway, the gaggle of reporters spot me and run in my direction. The TV reporters all turn and move their cameras towards the Rectory. I'm surrounded by men and women shouting questions and shoving recorders in my face as I try to get out of the car. Nate shoves his way through and pushes the crowd back.

"Let Father Tom get out of his car," he yells, "I'm sure he'll talk to us as soon as he gets out of the car." Everyone moves back enough to allow me to get the door open. I get out and start walking towards the Rectory. The gaggle follows, shouting questions.

"A comment, Father Greer?"

"We understand that the victim was the parish secretary, is that true?"

"Is Father McCoy a suspect?"

"Does the Archdiocese have a statement?"

At the door to the Rectory, I turn a motion for quiet. "I understand you have a job to do," I say. "All I ask is that you keep in mind this is a place of worship, so please be respectful of the property and the people who come here to pray. Please do not ask them questions."

"Is Father McCoy a suspect?"

"You must ask the police about that."

"Is it true you found him sitting beside Rachel Watson's body?"

I look at the reporter who asked the last question. "I have no further comment at this time." I turn to go into the Rectory as the gaggle continues to shout questions at me. Anna closes the door behind me.

With a look of concern she asks, "Are you okay?"

I run a hand through my hair. "About as well as can be expected, I guess. I need a shower and some coffee."

She hands me a cup. "Here, I poured this when I saw you drive up. Do you want me to call the police, to get them off the grounds?"

I look out the window and shake my head. "No, they're back on the sidewalk, and as long as they don't harass any of the parishioners, we'll leave them alone."

"They probably know you don't like reporters," Anna says with a smile, "and don't want their equipment broken."

I forced the last reporter I dealt with off church property and broke her camera. She later wound up dead, but that had nothing to do with me.

"So it's true. Rachel's been murdered."

I walk into the living room with my coffee and plop into an armchair. I lean my head back. "Yes, it's true."

"How's Father Leonard involved?"

"I don't know."

"But you found him sitting next to the body, didn't you?"

I recount the phone call from the hysterical prelate and what I found when I got to her apartment.

"He hasn't said a word to anyone. Doctors say he's in shock. They have him sedated right now."

"And he didn't tell you why he was over there?"

I shake my head. "No. Maybe when he wakes up."

I hear a knock come from the kitchen. Anna and I look at each other.

"I'll go see, maybe it's a parishioner," Anna says getting up. She goes into the kitchen and returns a minute later. "It's Nate," she says with a sigh.

"Just let him in," I say. "By the way, what's he doing now?"

"I think I heard he started a news vlog, focusing on crime and investigations." Anna goes back into the kitchen and returns a minute later, Nate Rodriguez in tow, complete with the familiar frantic excitement.

"Father Tom, thanks for talking to me."

"No, Nate, I'm not talking to you, I just let you in because I want to ask you something."

"Okay, sure, anything."

"How did you find out I found the body?"

Nate shrugs. "The reporter who asked you the question. She's pretty well established with sources, even in Myerton. Probably has a source in the police department or the State Attorney's office."

It really doesn't matter how they found out. The news would have gotten out, eventually. The problem is, I have not had the chance to speak with the Archbishop. He is the one person in Maryland who needs to know the most, and would not appreciate learning the news secondhand.

I excuse myself and go to the office. Picking up the phone, I dial the Archdiocese.

The Archbishop's secretary puts me through right away.

"Hello, Father Tom, I was going to call you later," he says. "Bring me up to speed. What have you found out so far?"

He hasn't heard yet, I think. *Good.*

"Something's come up, Your Eminence," I say slowly. "Something you need to know before you hear about it from someone else."

Silence. "What?" the Archbishop says gravely.

"Rachel Watson. She's been murdered."

I hear nothing but breathing coming from the other end of the phone. "How horrible, just horrible. She was young, wasn't she? Terrible for her family, to lose someone like that, though I suppose you would know better than most, Father."

"Yes," I mumble.

"What was it, a robbery?"

I take a deep breath. "The police don't know yet, but there's more."

He says nothing for a moment, then whispers, "Holy Mother of God. Don't tell me, Tom."

I spend the next fifteen minutes recounting the events of the last twenty-four hours. About Father Leonard's mysterious departure from the monastery. About his frantic call to me. About what I found when I arrived at Rachel Watson's apartment. About Father Leonard's condition.

"As far as I know," I conclude, "he's still asleep."

"And you say he's said nothing since you found him."

"The last time he's spoken a word was on the phone to me."

The Archbishop sighs. "Do you think the police see him as a suspect?"

"I'm not sure. Detective Parr—"

"Is she leading the investigation?" the Archbishop asks.

"She's the lead detective in Myerton—actually, I believe she's the only detective in Myerton—so of course she'd head the investigation."

"She's the one you worked with a few months ago, isn't she?"

"Yes."

"Do you have a good relationship with her?"

I pause before answering. Should I tell him everything, that the reason I know Detective Parr is because I once loved her and was engaged to marry her? Or should I keep that quiet for now. After all, it's not really relevant.

Is it?

"Father Tom? Are you still there?" Archbishop Knowland asks over the phone.

"Yes, yes, I'm still here," I say. "We have a good relationship, yes."

"Didn't you say she attends Saint Clare's?"

"Yes. And to anticipate your next question, she has heard the rumors about Father Leonard and Rachel Watson."

The Archbishop sighs. "Well, she was bound to find out sooner or later. I assume she figured out why you're there?"

"I said nothing to her, and she doesn't know the specifics. But she surmised that my being here has something to do with Father McCoy. She is a detective. An excellent one."

""Do you think she'll give Father Leonard a fair shake?"

"One thing I can assure you about Helen," I say, "is that she's a woman of integrity and strong convictions. She'll follow the evidence no matter where it goes."

He takes a deep breath. "I cannot ask for anything more than that. Tell her I appreciate her work, and that she can expect full cooperation from the Church." He pauses. "Do you think Father Leonard has anything to do with this young woman's murder?"

"No, sir, I really don't."

"So what was he doing over at her apartment at that time of night?"

"I don't know. I won't know until I talk to him." I pause. "The police will talk to him."

"You make sure you're there when Detective Parr questions him. In the meantime, I will contact the lawyers, see what I should do at this point." He pauses a moment. "I'm putting Father Leonard on administrative leave. Tom, you're in charge of Saint Clare's until this whole matter is cleared up."

"I understand, sir." I was about to hang up when the Archbishop says, "What did you find out? About the reason I sent you there in the first place? Was there any truth to the original allegation?"

I think for a moment. Before I can answer, the Archbishop says, 'No, never mind. Forget I asked. It's better if I don't know. God bless."

I hang up the phone and lean in my office chair. There's a painting of Saint John Vianney, the patron saint of priests, on the wall.

"Dear Saint John Vianney," I mutter, "please pray for Father Leonard." Then, "And for me. I need all the help I can get."

Ten

I've just finished saying Noon Mass when Helen calls.

"What are you doing this afternoon?" she asks.

"What did you have in mind? Lunch? I have a hankering for a chilled tomato bisque. I hear The Bistro serves a good one."

"Nothing so enjoyable, though it sounds tempting," she laughs. "I was wondering if you could be there when I talk to the Watsons."

I stop. With all my concerns over Father Leonard, I had completely forgotten about the Watsons. They had lost a daughter, violently, unexpectedly. They were in shock, grieving, possibly despondent.

I knew their feelings all too well. I should go, offer my condolences, give them some spiritual comfort.

"I'm not sure they would enjoy seeing me," I say. "The one time I've talked to Rachel's mother didn't go so well."

"When did you meet her—wait, don't answer that," Helen says. "It's the thing you can't tell me unless the Archbishop gives you permission, isn't it?" She pauses. "Well, did he?"

"He told me to tell you the Archdiocese would cooperate in any way possible"

"So you can tell me?"

"Yes," I say. "I'll get you the document, but I was sent here in response to an anonymous letter that alleged inappropriate behavior on Father Leonard's part with Rachel Watson. You should also know I've learned that it was Rachel's mother, Marjorie Watson, who sent the letter. I cannot tell you anything else I learned."

Helen takes a deep breath. "Whoa," she says. "That's motive, you know?"

"Now, Helen—"

"What else did the Archbishop say?"

"He's appointed me to the parish and placed Father Leonard on administrative leave."

"That shouldn't surprise you, Tom," she says. "The parish can't have a murder suspect saying Mass now, can they?"

"So he is a suspect," I say.

"Of course he's a suspect, the person who finds the body is always the first suspect."

"By that measure," I comment, "I should be a suspect."

"Technically, you didn't find the body, you found Father Leonard with the body, so unless you did it and you staged the scene to frame him, then no, you're not a suspect. You're not that clever."

"I don't know whether or not to be insulted," I say. I put my phone on speaker and continue removing my Mass vestments. "But I'm still not sure my being there is the best idea."

Helen didn't speak for a minute. Then she sighs. "Look, truth is—I want you there. It would help me out. The part of this job I've never been good at is—well, is the first interview with the victim's family. I always send a uniformed officer to do the initial notification, putting it off as much as possible. It brings back too many memories of when someone came and told me John was dead. Honestly, doing it scares me."

"I'm surprised to hear you say that," I say. "When we were together, nothing scared you."

"Well, that was a long time ago," she says quietly. After a pause, she says, "So, anyway, how about it?"

"Okay, Helen, for you, I'll do it. But don't be surprised if they aren't too happy to see me."

"I'll have my gun, I'll protect you," she chuckles. "We'll see you there."

"We?"

"Yeah, I guess I should tell you. Brian will be there, too."

I furrow my brow. "Why is the State Attorney going to be there?"

"You know this is an election year, right?"

"I guess I knew that, but what—"

"You've heard that money is the mother's milk of politics?"

"Yes, but—"

"Well, Winthrop Myer IV is the cow," Helen says. "He's a big donor to Brian's campaign, so Brian thinks it's important that he takes a direct interest in the investigation."

"This isn't going to be a problem for you, is it?"

She's quiet for a moment. "Why would it be?"

"Frankly, your past relationship—"

"Is in the past, Tom," she says firmly. "I made it as clear as I could to him over lunch that I had no interest in him. We're both professionals." She pauses. "Will his being there be a problem for you?"

"Why would it be a problem for me?" I say.

She sighs. "It wouldn't, I guess. Just meet us at the Myer Mansion at 2:00 p.m. I'll text you the address."

"No bother, I already have it."

"Oh?"

"Yes, I was over there yesterday afternoon for lunch. Win Myer invited me to discuss . . . some issues."

"I see," Helen says. "So, how was lunch?"

"Good," I reply. "Rebecca is a gracious host. Win, well . . . he seems like a good guy. But he's slick. I don't think he's used to being told no."

Helen says nothing. "I'll see you at 2:00 p.m.," she finally says before hanging up.

I'm suddenly aware of how tired I am. I've had little sleep in the last 24 hours, only about four hours. It has already been a long day, and it is about to get a lot longer.

***

I pull up to the front entrance of the Myer Mansion. Helen and Brian Dohrmann are already there, standing by a car I take to be his. Unlike Helen's rather sensible sedan, Dohrmann's is a burgundy Dodge Charger, complete with a racing stripe down the side.

"Mid-life crisis," I mutter under my breath. Out of jealousy, to be honest. It is one fantastic car.

You're not just jealous of the car, are you? the lover says. *You're jealous because of HER.*

You have no reason to be jealous of either, the priest says.

While the priest and the lover begin to argue—again—I pull in behind the Charger. Dohrmann turns to Helen when he sees me and says something to her. He doesn't look pleased. Helen shakes her head and walks towards me as I get out of the car.

"Father Tom," she says with a smile, "Thanks for coming."

"Of course, Helen, glad to do it. I don't believe we've met, have we?" I say, turning to the unhappy-looking man next to her. Extending my hand, I say, "Father Tom Greer."

There's a brief flash of recognition when he looks at me—why, I don't know—but he grasps my hand and says, "Brian Dorhmann, Father Greer."

"Father Tom, please," I say with a smile.

He doesn't smile, but says, "Fine. Brian, then. I know about you through your wife's case, of course, and your corrected statement. I could have prosecuted you, you realize that, don't you?"

I struggle to retain my smile as I say, "And I really appreciate you showing me mercy."

"Oh, mercy had nothing to do with it. Detective Parr made an impassioned plea on your behalf." He grins. "Helen and I are . . . friends. Isn't that right, Helen?"

Helen glowers at him. "We have a very good working relationship, Brian," she says with a pleasant enough smile, but a tone that says 'go to hell'.

"I hope Detective Parr did not inconvenience you?"

"Helen, inconvenience me? It's never an inconvenience. I had nothing else to do this afternoon. Besides," I say pointing at the collar I'm wearing, "consoling the grieving comes with the territory."

"Hmm," he says before turning to Helen. "Shall we?" he says and begins walking toward the front door.

Helen looks at me. "Sorry about that," she mutters.

"Did I run over his dog or something?" I whisper.

"I really don't know what his problem with you is," Helen says, "other than the fact that you're a priest."

"He doesn't like priests?"

"Doesn't like religion, doesn't believe in God—take your pick."

This perplexes me. "Why did you go out with him?"

She opens her mouth to answer, then shakes her head. "Never mind."

Dohrmann rings the doorbell. I expect Win Myer or Rebecca Myer to answer. Instead, it's a pudgy, balding man who looks to be in his early fifties. He's about six inches shorter than I am, which makes him about the State Attorney's height. His eyes are red from crying. I recognize him from the wedding picture. He's Rachel's father.

"Hello," Dohrmann says, "I'm Brian Dohrmann with the State Attorney's Office, and this is Detective Parr of the Myerton Police." I see Mr. Watson look over Brian's shoulder at me. Leaning between Brian and Helen, I say, "I'm Father Tom Greer of Saint Clare's Parish."

"Yes," he growls, "I know who you are. You're responsible for all this." He looks at Dohrmann and Helen. "Ed Watson, I am—I was Rachel's daddy," he says, dabbing his eyes with his handkerchief.

"I'm so sorry for your loss," Helen says, "but we need to ask some questions. May we come in?"

"Questions . . . yes, yes, come in," he says, stepping aside to let us in. "Everyone is in the living room this way," Mr. Watson says. We follow him.

The room is brimming with grief. Majorie Watson is sitting on a couch, appearing stoic, staring out a window. Next to her, Rebecca sits patting her mother's hand and wiping her own tears. Thrown down in an armchair, Win Myer is staring at a point in the distance and nursing a drink.

"You!" he says, standing up when he sees me. "How dare you show your face here! This is your fault!"

Ed Watson steps between Win and me. "Now, son, just take it easy," he says, trying to calm Myer down.

"Take it easy? Take it easy!" he mutters. "He's responsible for the death of your daughter, and you're telling me to take it easy?"

"Win, please," Rebecca says. "That's enough."

"Now don't criticize Win like that," Marjorie Watson whispers.

"But Mama, Father Greer is a guest—"

"An unwelcome one," she says.

"Hear that?" Win says. "You're not welcome here. Please leave. Now!"

"Win," Rebecca says, "Stop."

"Rebecca," Majorie says, "I told you—"

Laying her hand on Marjorie's shoulder, Rebecca says gently, "Mama, this is my house. Father Greer came here to offer his respects. He's our priest. He'll stay." Turning to Win, she says less gently, "sit down."

Win looks about to say something. Instead, he goes back to his chair and returns to his drink.

Rebecca walks over to us. "I apologize, Father Greer," she says, "we're all in shock." Turning to Helen and Dohrmann, she introduces herself and motions for them to sit. I go over to one bookcase and lean against it, arms crossed, perusing the contents out of the corner of my eye.

"I want to say, first, Win," Dohrmann says, "that you have my word that we will find the person who committed this heinous crime."

"Oh, I already know who did it," Win says. Draining his glass, he stands up, "What I don't understand," he says, pointing to Helen with the glass, "is why you haven't arrested him yet?"

"Arrested who, Mr. Myer?" Helen asks as she takes out her notebook.

"Who?" Win says incredulously. "Father Leonard McCoy. The priest who was forcing himself on her."

Helen and Brian look at me. I close my eyes. So much for that.

"He knows all about it," Marjorie says, pointing to me. "Did nothing about it, tried to cover it up just like they always do, like they did with those perverts who molested those little boys."

"Mama, Rachel denied anything happened," Rebecca says.

Helen interjects, "I think we need to get to the reason we're here."

"Exactly," Marjorie Watson says. "Why are you here instead of arresting Father McCoy?"

Helen is about to say something when Dohrmann places his hand on her arm, which she discreetly pulls away. "These are routine questions in any investigation, Mrs. Watson," he says. "I assure you that as soon as we have evidence pointing to a suspect, we'll make an arrest. And I assure you that as soon as he can talk, we will interview Father McCoy."

A vague look of irritation passes across Helen's face. I'm forced to suppress a smile. She always hated it when someone spoke for her.

"We understand," Ed Watson says. "Let's let the Detective ask her questions so she can get on her way."

"Thank you," Helen says. "Now, when did anyone last see Rachel alive?"

There's a pause before Marjorie says, "The last I saw of Rachel, she was running out of the Rectory after our meeting with Father Greer."

"We'll get to that later," Helen says. "So that was Friday afternoon?"

"Yes," Marjorie Watson says softly. "Rachel was upset by the whole scene, she ran out of the place, and I didn't see her again." She stares out the window. "Oh, my baby girl," she whispers.

"The scene didn't upset her, Mama," Rebecca says to her mother. "You upset her."

"How did I upset her?"

"Oh, I don't know? How about continuing to disparage her desire to become a nun? Detective Parr," Rebecca says to Helen, "my mother is right. The last time we saw Rachel was that afternoon during our meeting with Father Greer. She got quite upset, and left. She had driven her own car; I had driven Mama."

"I see," Helen says, "so that was the last time you saw or spoke to her?"

"Yes," Marjorie says.

"No," Rebecca replies.

Everyone looks at Rebecca. "You spoke to your sister between Friday afternoon and the time of her murder?" Helen asks.

"Well, not exactly spoke," Rebecca says. "I received an email from her on Sunday morning."

"I didn't receive any email," Marjorie says.

"No, mother, I'm sure you didn't. You wouldn't have liked what it said, anyway."

"What did it say," Dohrmann says, ignoring Helen's look.

"She wrote that she had decided after a lot of prayer and thought to enter the convent. She was going to leave Monday morning," Rebecca said. "She said she loved me, that she would probably never see me again, but she wanted me to know that she would always pray for me and all of us and that she'd hope to see us all together in heaven someday."

"When did she send it?" Helen asks.

"I must double check, but I think it was sometime Saturday night," Rebecca replies.

"But you didn't see her or speak to her otherwise?"

"No, not at all." I can't see her face, but I saw her wipe away a tear from her cheek.

"Did she have any enemies?"

"Enemies? Of course not," Win says. "Rachel was the kindest, gentlest creature you'd ever want to meet. She was just, just such a wonderful person. I can't believe . . ." Overcome with emotion, he stops talking. Rebecca looks to one side.

"So you can't think of anyone who would want to do her harm?" Dohrmann asks.

"Other than that priest," Ed Watson says, "not a soul."

"Wait," Rebecca says. "There was someone at her old job she was afraid of. I think that's one reason she left and took the job at the parish."

Win looks at Rebecca and snaps his fingers. "That's right, she mentioned that to me. He was giving her a hard time, always trying to get her to go out with him."

Rebecca looks at Win. "When did she talk to you about this?" she asks with an even tone.

He looks at his drink. "When she asked me to talk to Father McCoy about hiring her as parish secretary."

"Win!" Marjorie says, "You got her the job at the parish? Why would you do that?"

Win sighs. "Sorry, Marjorie, looking back I shouldn't have, obviously, but she wanted the job, and she asked me to help her."

"And you could never say no to Rachel, could you?" Rebecca says, her sarcasm mixed with a tinge of bitterness.

"Now, Rebecca—"

"If I might ask," Helen interrupts, eager to get the interview back on track, "did she ever mention his name?"

The family thinks. Finally, Rebecca says, "Oh, I'm so bad with names. Richard? Robert? Roger? I really can't remember."

"Don't waste your time with him," Marjorie Watson says, "when you found the murderer next to her body."

Helen makes a note, then asks, "Mrs. Watson, you didn't receive an email from your daughter?"

"No, but then I don't really do email," she says. "But she hasn't sent me a letter, at least that I've received yet."

"She asked me to tell you myself," Rebecca says.

"What about you, Mr. Myer?" Helen says.

"Me? An email from Rachel? No, I don't think so."

Rebecca looks at her husband, a puzzled expression on her face. "Are you sure? I could swear she emailed both of us."

"Really?" Win says. "You know how busy I've been with this whole environmental impact issue. Detective," he says to Helen, "I could have received the email, but I didn't read it if I did." He shakes his head. "But I don't see why you're asking all these questions. We've already told you who you should arrest. I don't know why you don't do it!"

"We have not even spoken to Father McCoy yet," Helen says.

"Well, you need to get up and go do your job then," Marjorie says.

"Father McCoy," I say, "has been in no condition to talk since that night. He's probably still under sedation."

As soon as the words leave my mouth, I know I've overstepped. Helen looks exasperated. Dohrmann looks irritated.

"What Father Greer says is true," Helen says. "Father McCoy is in the hospital under sedation. As soon as the doctors clear him, I will interview him and get his statement."

"And then you'll arrest him," Win says.

"Win, we'll make an arrest as soon as we have evidence that points to a suspect," Dohrmann says. "Detective Parr is still early in her investigation."

Win points at Dohrmann and says, "You just remember which side your bread is buttered on. I've spent a lot of money on your campaign. I expect to get a good return on my investment. I don't want you caving to pressure from the Church."

"I assure you, Mr. Myer, there will be no pressure," I say. "If—if—Detective Parr determines that she has enough evidence to arrest Father McCoy for murdering Rachel, the Church will not stand in her way." I say that, hoping that it was true—for Helen's sake as much as for the sake of the Church.

"And even if it did," Dohrmann adds, "it wouldn't work. I'm only interested in justice."

Win nods. "Good. I'm glad we understand each other."

While Helen asks a few more questions and waits for Rebecca to return with a hard copy of the email from Rachel, I wander around the room, looking at the titles on the shelves and the wall of photographs. Again, I see the photographs from Rebecca and Win Myer's wedding showing a dour Rachel. Why did she look like that? Was she upset that her twin sister was marrying before she was? Did she resent the attention she was getting from her mother, who seemed to prefer one daughter over the other? Was this the reason she had decided on religious life, to escape her family?

I look more closely at one photograph. Rachel was unhappy in this one. But she wasn't the only one who looked out of place. Usually, the two people you can count on being the happiest in a wedding picture are the bride and the groom. And Rebecca was the very stereotype of the radiant bride, her face beaming with joy, and her eyes sparkling.

Win was something else. He was smiling, but it wasn't a joyful smile. Not like I was in my wedding picture with Joan. That was the happiest day of my life, before my ordination, and you could tell from my face in our picture.

Win looked dissatisfied. An odd look for a man on his wedding day.

"When were you two married?" I ask him.

"What?"

"You and Rebecca, when were you two married?"

"We married right before I went to Afghanistan," Win says.

"You were in the Army?"

Win nods and walks up to a picture on the wall. The photograph shows Win in camo fatigues among a group of other men, similarly dressed, in a rocky area. "Special Forces," he says, pointing to a photograph. "One tour in Afghanistan. I had to leave the Army when my parents died. They were both sick for a long time. They couldn't even attend the wedding."

"Win and Rebecca were high school sweethearts," Marjorie interjects with a smile. "Inseparable. Isn't that right, Rebecca?"

Rebecca smiles. "Yes, Mama, that's right. We dated in high school, beginning in my junior year. He took ROTC and went into the Army right after college."

I notice Rebecca. Her smile is strained, as if the memory is tinged with pain.

"You two went to the same high school?" I turn to Win. "I'm surprised your parents didn't send you to a fancy prep school."

"My parents loved this town," he replies. "They saw themselves as the caretakers of the Myer family heritage here. They wanted me to be the same. So, I went to Myerton High School. Just like any other teen boy."

"Hardly like any other teen boy, Win," Marjorie says with pride. "Captain of the football team, class president, valedictorian." She looks at me. "Rebecca was very fortunate Win picked her."

"Oh, Mama," Rebecca says. "I'm not a piece of fruit, for crying out loud!"

"I don't see what these questions have to do with Rachel's death, Father?"

"Oh, they don't," I say, smiling. "I just have a curiosity about people. Occupational hazard, you see."

"Well, Brian," Win says, turning away from me. "Do you have anything else for us?"

"No, not today," Helen says as they stand. "I'll be in touch if I have any more questions." She turns to Rebecca. "You have that email?"

"Here you go, Detective," she says, handing her a single sheet of paper.

Helen studies it. "Mr. Myer," she says, "is this your email address?"

Win takes the paper from Helen and studies it. "Yes, that's my work address. If she sent it there, I wouldn't have seen it, not on a Sunday. It's probably in my inbox right now; obviously I haven't gone through my emails today."

"Of course," Helen says, taking the paper.

We say our goodbyes and follow Win out of the room. Rebecca says, "Oh, when can we have Rachel's body?"

Helen stops and says, "It will be after the post-mortem, which will be in a couple of days. We'll notify you."

"Thank you. Father," Rebecca says to me, "can you help with the arrangements?"

Marjorie interjects, "Why him?"

Rebecca turns to her. "Because Father Greer is our priest, and Rachel would have wanted a funeral Mass." To me she says, "Can you?"

"I'll be honored to," I say. "I'll come over in a few days to discuss the arrangements."

Win Myer shows us out. As we're walking to our cars, Helen's phone rings.

"Hello? Yes, yes. Good. Okay, thanks." Helen hangs up her phone. "Father McCoy is awake. I'm going to talk to him. I assume you want to be there, Father?"

"I would like to, if that's okay. But can't it wait, Detective? I mean, he's been through quite a shock."

Dohrmann starts to speak when Helen says, "Yes, that's fine, but he's your responsibility. Bring him to the police station tomorrow morning at 10:30 a.m. I have quite a few questions for him."

"Believe me, I have questions for him too," I say. "Are you going to look into that man Rachel mentioned was harassing her?"

"I will, Tom."

I nod and turn towards my car.

"Wait a minute, Father," Dohrmann says. "I have a question for you." Placing his hands on his hips, he says, "What were they talking about in there?"

I hesitate before saying, "There was an anonymous complaint received by the Archbishop about Father McCoy last week."

"What were the allegations?" Dohrmann presses.

"The kind you'd imagine," I say, "that Father McCoy was engaged in inappropriate behavior with the parish secretary."

"Rachel Watson."

I nod. "The Archbishop sent me here to talk to Father McCoy and Rachel, to find out if the allegations were true."

"What did you find out?" he asks.

I pause before answering, "I can tell you I found out that Marjorie Watson sent the anonymous complaint , that Win Myer was spying on Father McCoy and Rachel, and that the letter contains insinuations with no explicit events recounted."

"But are the allegations true?" Helen asks.

I look at her. "That, I can't tell you."

"Why," Dohrmann says, "because you don't know if they're true or not?"

"No, Brian. He knows," Helen says, "but he can't tell us. Can you?"

"I can tell you that there was no force or coercion on Father McCoy's part. He didn't threaten Rachel or commit any criminal acts."

"But you can't say exactly what you found. Because of the seal, right, Tom?"

"The seal?" Dohrmann asks.

"The seal of confession, Brian."

He rolls his eyes. "Oh, not this!" he says. "A woman is dead. Murdered."

"I know. But anything anyone tells me in confession, I must keep private."

"But she's dead!"

"That doesn't matter," I say. "Church law is very clear. I cannot violate the seal for any reason."

Dohrmann looks at me incredulously, then at Helen. "Well? What are you going to do?"

"What would you like me to do, Brian?"

"What—" he says pointing at me. "He has material evidence in a murder case that he's withholding. I want to know what he knows."

"He already said—"

"I don't care what he said," he says. "I want that information."

Helen lifts her chin. "But Brian, he's right. I don't like it as a police officer. But as a Catholic . . ." She trails off and looks at me. "If a priest held my deepest darkest secrets, I'd want to know that they were safe."

Dohrmann looks at her incredulously. "Even if it means protecting a murderer."

"We can find the information some other way," Helen says firmly. She crosses her arms. "Or don't you think I'm a good enough detective?"

He opens his mouth to speak, looks back at me, then says to Helen, "Of course I think so." He sighs. "Fine, fine. Okay." He walks to his car and stops in front of me. Pointing his finger at me, he says, "But I promise you Father, I will drag you into the Grand Jury myself if it comes to that. And if you don't answer my questions, I'll throw your butt in jail."

"I'll bring my pillow," I say with a smile. Out of the corner of my eye, I see Helen roll her eyes.

"You smile now, Father," he scowls. "We'll see how you're smiling after a few days in jail." He then turns to walk to the car.

Helen shakes her head. "He's serious, Tom, he'll do it."

"I'm serious too. You know that," I say. "But thank you for backing me up."

She hesitates before saying, "You know my beliefs as a Catholic. But the detective part of me still thinks you need to tell me."

"I understand that," I say. "Look, you're right, you're a good detective. You'll figure it out without me breaking the seal." I stare at her. "Just remember there are two people involved here."

She looks at me and nods. "I'll see you tomorrow, with Father Leonard." She gets in her car and drives off, leaving me standing in the Myer driveway.

I'm about to get in my own car when I look back towards the house. Win Myer's in the window, looking at me..

***

"Well, Father Leonard," the doctor says, looking at her tablet, "there's nothing physically wrong with you. All our tests are normal."

"Then why can't I remember anything?" Father Leonard asks. He's sitting up on the edge of his hospital bed, dressed in a green polo and khaki shorts with tennis shoes.

"I'd say it's psychological trauma, the shock. The brain will block out something that's that traumatic; it's a defense mechanism."

"Do you think he'll remember?" I ask.

"Maybe with time, treatment might help."

"How much time?" Father Leonard asks, clearly worried.

"There's no way to know, Father," the doctor says. "It may be days, it could be months, even years." She smiles and pats his arm. "Now you go home, take it easy for a few days."

"I'll see that he rests. Thank you doctor," I say.

She nods and leaves the room. "Rest," Father Leonard says. "Rest. How can I rest?" He puts his head in his hands.

I pat his back. "It will be okay, Leonard."

"How?" he says, looking at me, stricken. "How is it going to be okay?"

"It will be," I say again.

"I don't see how."

I sigh. "Let's just get you back to the Rectory."

He stands up and takes a step forward. He turns to look at me.

"Was it horrible?" he whispers. "I mean, Rachel."

I pat him on the shoulder and nod.

"Do you think she suffered?"

I answer the question as honestly as I can. "If she did," I say, "she's not suffering anymore."

"No, no, I suppose not," he mutters. "Poor Rachel, my poor, dear Rachel," he adds quietly, a tear snaking its way down his cheek.

My poor dear Rachel.

"Let's go, Leonard. You need to sleep," I say.

"When I get back to Saint Clare's," he says as we walk out of his room, "I will go into the church, spend some time in front of the Tabernacle praying for her soul."

"I'll join you," I say.

"I'd prefer to be alone," he says, stopping in the hallway. I turn to look at him. "I prefer to be alone," he repeats.

I nod. "Of course."

We continue walking. He sighs and says, "I suppose I must talk to the Archbishop."

"Eventually, but not right now."

"And I must get back on top of the parish. I suppose you'll be leaving now."

I stop. Looking at him, I say, "No, no. I'm staying for the time being."

"There's no reason for you to," Father Leonard says. "She's dead. The allegations don't matter now."

It's odd that he would say that, I think. *Very odd.*

"Leonard," I say, "I've already talked to the Archbishop. He's put me in charge of Saint Clare's temporarily. You're on leave until this whole matter is cleared up."

He looks at me, blankly.

He really does not understand what's going on.

"Don't you understand? I found you sitting next to a murdered woman, your clothes covered in blood—not your own, so probably hers. You say you have no memory of what happened. You are linked to the woman. You were her boss. You admit giving her spiritual counsel. And there is an allegation of inappropriate conduct against you." I pause. "Now do you see?"

He looks at me blankly, then I see his face fall. "I see," he sighs. "Well, it's what I deserve. I've lost everything, and now I'm a murder suspect." He closes his eyes and drops his head, muttering something I can barely hear.

"God is punishing me."

Eleven

Something wakes me. Sounds coming from Father Leonard's room. I look at the time. 2:00 am.

As I come to consciousness, I hear slaps, muffled utterances, one after another. I get out of bed and pull on my robe. I walk to Father Leonard's room and knock softly on the door. I can hear the sounds more clearly now. Firm slaps, rhythmic, repeated. Father Leonard is muttering softly to himself. I catch one or two of the words when his voice rises with a slap.

Then I realize what he's doing.

I place my hand on the doorknob, then remove it. He wants his privacy, and I don't want to violate it, not for this. This is too personal. But I want to make sure he's all right. I lightly grip the doorknob and quietly turn until I hear the latch slip. Slowly, I push open the door and peer inside.

What I see confirms what I hear. A shirtless Father Leonard, back to the door, firmly scourging himself, praying the Miserere, David's psalm of penance.

Repeatedly, he brings the seven-cord rope whip down on his back, the three knots tied into the ends of each cord leaving a discernible red mark. A couple look like they're bleeding, but I see no other signs of injury. I quietly exhale, unaware until that second I had been holding my breath. From personal experience, the discipline doesn't draw blood, sensationalistic movies notwithstanding.

Normally, at least, it doesn't draw blood.

On one occasion, in my early days at Our Lady of the Mount, it had. Father Abbot gently but firmly explained to me its proper use, its purpose. Penance, not punishment. Mortification, not mortality.

I stand watching Father Leonard for a minute, then quietly close the door.

***

I say nothing to Father Leonard about the night's events when he sits down for breakfast. Anna is here, having come for 8:00 Mass, then gone into the

Rectory kitchen to prepare food. Before Mass, I only had coffee, observing the Eucharistic fast, so by 9:00, when I sit in front of the scrambled eggs, bacon, toast, orange juice, and coffee, I'm hungry. I normally don't eat a lot for breakfast, but we have a long day ahead and I will need my strength.

Father Leonard comes into the kitchen and sits. Anna smiles and places a plate in front of him. He looks dully at the food.

"No, thank you, Anna," Father Leonard says, pushing the plate away from him. "I won't be eating today. Just coffee, black, please."

"You will need your strength, Leonard," I say. "You have a long day ahead, answering Detective Parr's questions."

"Tom's right, Father," Anna says, pushing the plate back to him. "Just eat some."

"Really, no, thank you, I'm fine," the young priest whispers.

"At least have some—"

"I said no thank you!" Father Leonard yells at Anna. Shocked, Anna takes a jump back. Collecting herself, she picks up the plate and takes it to the counter. She grabs a coffee mug, pours a cup, and returns to the table, placing it in front of the priest with a clunk, sloshing some contents on the table. Fixing him with a glare, she turns and leaves the kitchen.

I look at Father Leonard quietly. He slumps. "I'll go apologize. I shouldn't have raised my voice." He moves to get up.

"No, no, sit," I say, touching his arm. "Anna will be fine. You can apologize later."

He nods and looks at his coffee. He shifts uncomfortably in his chair, gently rubbing his right thigh. I look down and see the impression of a braid under his pants leg.

Father Leonard is wearing a cilice, a spiked metal braid, around his thigh. *The discipline, the cilice, and fasting,* I think. *You're piling on the penances.*

"How are you feeling?" I say.

Father Leonard sighs. "I don't know, honestly. Numb."

I pick up my coffee cup. "How did you sleep?"

"I didn't," he says. "I tossed and turned. At one point I went into the Church and prayed before the Tabernacle."

"I didn't hear you leave."

"No, well, I think you were snoring," he mumbles. His eyes widen. "Not that you snore, Father. I mean, I'm sure—"

I chuckle. "It's all right, Leonard." I know I snore. Joan would sometimes describe me as a car without a muffler, though I don't think I'm that loud. In seminary, I kept having a succession of roommates, so maybe she was right.

"Are you ready for this morning?"

"I've never been questioned by the police before," he says. "What do you think they'll ask me?"

"They'll probably start with why you were at Rachel's apartment in the middle of the night," I say. Looking at him, I ask, "Why *were* you there, Leonard?"

He looks at me, then stares straight ahead.

"Leonard," I press. "Why were you at Rachel's apartment?"

He says nothing. I slump back in my chair and shake my head. *This is going to be a long day*, I think

***

At the police station later that morning, Helen is getting irritable.

"Tom," she says to me in the break room around the corner from the interrogation room, "him not talking only makes him look guilty."

"I know that, but it's his right not to talk to you. You know that."

"Yes, yes, I know, but he hasn't asked for a lawyer yet."

I look towards the interrogation room. "Honestly, I'm not sure he will."

She looks perplexed. "Why?"

I shake my head. "He feels guilty about something. I have a good idea about what, but he has said nothing to me either."

"So," she says slowly, "you haven't heard his confession?"

"No, he hasn't asked me to hear it." I trace the rim of my coffee cup. "He needs to. He knows that. But he's taking his punishment on himself for what he did. Whatever that was."

"But you said you have a good idea what he feels guilty about?"

"Only part of it," I say. "But there's something else. He left Our Lady of the Mount without telling anyone. He didn't contact anyone after he left, and the next I hear from him he's in Rachel's apartment." I shake my head. "There's something else here, and only he knows what it is."

"Well," Helen says, putting her cup down on the counter, "he needs to say something."

We're about to leave when Brian Dohrmann walks into the room. "Well, Hel—what's he doing here?" he points to me.

"Good morning, Brian," I say with a smile. "I'm here with Father Leonard. Offering moral support."

"Huh," he says. "Sure you're not looking out for the Church's interests?"

"As far as I can tell, there is no threat to the Church's interests."

"Well," he says with a dismissive wave of his hand, "I'm not here to argue with you, Father. What has he said, Helen?"

Crossing her arms, she says, "Nothing."

Dohrmann says, "What do you mean, nothing?"

"I mean other than 'Good Morning, Detective', and 'I'd rather not say, Detective,' and 'I remember nothing until I saw her body,' and crying," Helen explains, "he hasn't answered my questions."

"Has he asked for a lawyer?"

"No," I interject. "And before you ask, the Archdiocese hasn't contacted one on his behalf."

Dohrmann looks at me, then back at Helen. "Have you pressed him?"

Putting her hands on her hips, she says, "Are you questioning how I do my job, Brian? Because I don't care who you are, or what our relationship was, I won't take that crap from anyone."

He puts his hands up. "I'm not questioning how you do your job, Helen. But maybe you're just a little too close to this."

"Why? Because I'm a Catholic?"

"Well, it might cause you to go softer on him because he's a priest."

Helen glares at him. I place my hand over my mouth to suppress a smile. The last time I saw that look, she almost had me arrested.

"Okay, fine," she says slowly. "If you think you can get him to talk, be my guest."

"All right, let's go." He turns and walks out of the break room. Helen looks at me and, seeing the smile on my face, spits out, "What?"

"Oh, nothing, nothing," I say, still smiling.

We leave the break room and meet Dohrmann outside the door. "No, not him," he says, pointing at me.

"He won't say anything, Brian." Helen says.

"I don't care, I don't want anyone on Father McCoy's side in there."

Helen sighs. I say, "It's all right."

"You can watch through the two-way mirror in here," Helen says, showing me a room next to the interrogation room. I enter the room and close the door behind me. There's a large window into the next room; from many TV cop shows, I know the other side is a mirror. I also know that because last year, I spent time where Father McCoy is sitting now.

He's slumped in his chair, leaning forward, resting his head on his hands in a rough attitude of prayer. He doesn't even look up when the door opens.

Dohrmann and Helen enter the room and take their seats opposite Father Leonard. He looks up.

"Hello," Father Leonard says.

"Father McCoy," Brian begins, "I'm Brian Dohrmann. I'm the State Attorney for this county. Do you know what that means?"

He nods. "I know who you are, Mr. Dohrmann. I recognize you from the campaign signs around town."

"So you know I'll be prosecuting the person who killed Rachel Watson."

"Yes, I guess that's true."

"Now I'm here because I understand you haven't been answering Detective Parr's questions. That you refuse to answer her questions."

He nods. "Yes, I have not answered her questions about why I was at Rachel's apartment that night."

"Why is that?"

He drops his eyes. "Because I believe it's my right as a citizen not to answer questions. Am I correct?"

"Well, yes, yes, that's true."

"Besides, my being there has nothing to do with her death."

Dohrmann sits back. Helen says, "How can you be sure?"

Father Leonard looks at Helen. "Because I know why I was there," he whispers.

"Why don't you tell us, Father," Helen says softly.

Father Leonard shakes his head. "No."

"Listen, Father—" Dohrmann snaps.

"Father Leonard," Helen says, interrupting. Dohrmann glares at her and slumps back his chair. She continues, "Let's start somewhere else, can we?"

"Okay," Father Leonard says.

Helen pulls out her notebook. "You were at Our Lady of the Mount Monastery from Thursday afternoon onward, is that correct?"

He nods. "I had gone there on a private retreat at the suggestion of Father Greer. I needed time to pray and meditate."

"On anything in particular?" Helen asks.

Father Leonard looks at his hands. "Yes, but I'd . . . "

"That's okay, Father, you don't have to tell us. I'm just trying to get a timeline right now. When did you leave the monastery?"

Helen already knows the answer to that question, because I told her.

"Saturday afternoon," Father Leonard answers.

"Who did you tell you were leaving?"

Another question she knows the answer to.

Father Leonard looks to one side before answering. "I told the extern—I'm sorry, the brother who serves as the Monastery's contact with visitors."

"And what is his name?"

"Brother Martin."

Brother Martin had told me Father Leonard had left without telling anyone. "Why did you lie, Leonard?" I mutter to myself. What is worse, Helen knows he's lying.

"So you left the monastery Saturday afternoon. Where did you go?"

"I don't remember," Father Leonard answers. "Nowhere in particular. I drove around the mountains. I think I stopped for dinner."

"Where did you sleep that night?"

"I didn't," he replies. "At least I don't think I did."

"What did you do the next day, Sunday?"

He hesitates. "I found a Mass and attended. I don't remember the name of the parish, or where it was. It was somewhere south of Frederick, could have been in West Virginia."

Helen sits back. "Aren't you required to say Mass at least once on a Sunday?"

He nods. "I didn't that day. Something I must go to confession for."

"Why didn't you stay at the Monastery, say Mass on Sunday morning, then leave afterwards?"

He shakes his head. "I needed time to think."

"I thought you went to the Monastery to think and pray?"

"I did," he says. "It didn't help. I thought a change of scenery . . ."

Helen looks at him. "Did it?"

He nods slowly. "Yes, at least I thought so."

"So what happened Sunday afternoon after the Mass?"

"I drove to an overlook off of 270, south of Frederick. I sat in my car and stared out, I said a Rosary." He hesitates before going on. "I guess you'll find this out anyway, checking her cell phone records. You do that, don't you? That's what they do on TV."

"Yes, we've requested her records," Helen answers. "Did you call Rachel Watson?"

Father Leonard nods.

"About what time?"

"I honestly don't remember. I can check my phone," he reaches into his coat pocket and pulls it out. A moment later he says, "I called her at 4:30 p.m."

"What did you two talk about?"

I look at Father Leonard. He's struggling with something. I think I know what it is. But I can't say anything.

"Father Leonard?" Helen presses.

"No, no, I'm sorry," Father Leonard says, practically crying. "No, I can't tell you, it doesn't matter, anyway."

Dohrmann leans to Helen, "I've had enough of this. Father McCoy, if—"

A knock at the door interrupts him. Helen says, "Come in?" A young uniformed officer comes in and whispers something in her ear. Helen looks at me, then whispers something to Dohrmann. He throws his hands up and utters an expletive.

The officer opens the door and in walks an African-American woman in her late thirties, dressed in a purple business suit. She looks vaguely familiar.

"Good afternoon, Detective Parr, Brian," she says with a smile.

"What are you doing here, Angela?" Brian says, unhappy to see her.

"The Archdiocese has hired me to represent Father McCoy," she replies. "Father McCoy, don't say another word." Turning to Detective Parr, she says, "Detective, is my client under arrest?"

"No, no, he's down here under his own volition," Helen says.

"Then if you will excuse us, I think we're finished here," the lawyer says. "Come on Father, let's get you back to your church where we can have a nice long talk."

Father Leonard looks thoroughly confused, but does as he's told. His lawyer opens the door and gently guides him out. She's about to leave when Dohrmann steps forward.

"What kind of stunt is this, Angela? What kind of game are you playing?"

"Game, Brian? This is no game," she says with a smile. "I'm looking out for the best interests of my client. Just as you are yours."

"My client is the people of the State of Maryland."

"Brian, you and I both know that your client is Winthrop Myer," she says. "If this were any other case, you wouldn't be here." Angela looks at Helen. "Have a nice day, Detective." She leaves the room, leaving Helen and Dohrmann alone.

He dashes from the interrogation room and the next thing I know, the door to where I am flies open. "So the Archdiocese has hired no lawyers, have they?" Dohrmann yells. "I should have known. You're circling the wagons!"

"Brian, please calm down," Helen says.

"Brian, I knew nothing about this," I say. "When I spoke to the Archbishop—"

"Oh, don't waste my time," he says before flying out of the room, slamming the door.

Helen looks at me with her hands on her hips. "Well, Tom?"

"Helen, I promise you, I don't know who that woman is, and I had no idea the Archdiocese retained her."

Helen exhales. "Okay, Tom." She shakes her head. "This will get bad."

"Why? Who is this Angela?"

"Who is Angela? Angela Jenkins. She's a local defense attorney."

"Okay, but why is Brian so upset?"

Helen looks at me. "You really don't know. Oh, why would you, you've only been back in Myerton a few days. You know, Brian is running for re-election as State Attorney, right?"

I shrug. "Yeah."

"Well, Angela Jenkins is his opponent."

Twelve

"I'm on your side, Father Leonard, I really am," an exasperated Angela Jenkins says, "but I can't help you unless you're honest with me."

"I didn't ask for your help," Father Leonard mutters. "I don't want your help. No one can help me."

She sits back and sighs. We're in my office; she is in the chair next to Father Leonard, I'm behind the desk. We've been at it for an hour. In that entire time, Father Leonard has added almost nothing to his statement at the police station. This, despite repeated assurances from his lawyer that it's necessary for his defense.

Jenkins shakes her head and looks at the legal pad propped on her lap. "Okay, let's go over this again," she says. "You called Rachel Watson at 4:30 p.m."

He nods.

"So where were you when you called?"

"The overlook off of I-270, just south of Frederick, I already told you that."

"Why did you call her?"

He sat quietly and looked at his hands. "I told her I wanted to see her."

"Okay, okay, that's good, now we're getting somewhere. Why did you want to see her?"

"No," he jerks his head up. "No."

Jenkins looks up from her pad. "Father Leonard—"

Shaking his head vigorously, he says, "No, I can't tell you. I won't tell you. Not you, not them, not anybody."

"Leonard," I say gently, "she needs to know."

"No, she doesn't," he says sharply.

"We'll get back to that later," she says. "So what time did you arrive at the apartment?"

"I got there about 7:00 p.m., I think. I don't remember."

"She let you into the apartment?"

He looks off for a moment. He shakes his head. "No," he whispers. "I knocked and rang the doorbell, but there was no answer. I remember knocking and calling her name. I tried the doorknob, and the door was unlocked, so I let myself in."

I think to myself, *he's remembering a lot all of a sudden.*

"So what happened next?"

He hesitates. "I remember stepping inside her apartment. The curtains were closed, so it was dim in the apartment, no lights were on, which I thought was odd. I think I called out for her." He shudders, clears his throat, shakes his head. "Then I felt a presence."

"There was someone else there?" I ask.

"No, not some*one*," Father Leonard says, "some*thing*. A presence. Out of the darkness behind me." I see tears coming from his eyes. "Suddenly, I felt like I was suffocating. Everything went dark. The next thing I know, I'm laying on the floor next to—" He doesn't finish, but collapses in sobs.

Jenkins puts her pen down and reaches out to rub his shoulder. "It's okay, Father, it's okay. That's enough for now." She looks at me and motions with her head to step out of the office with her.

In the hallway, she says to me, "I need more from him. I can't give him an adequate defense unless he explains why he was there."

"I've asked him, and he won't tell me. If he did, maybe I could get him to tell you."

"I also need to know the exact nature of the relationship with Rachel Watson," she says.

"He insists they were just friends," I say.

Jenkins looks at me. "But you know differently, don't you, Father?"

I really need to work on my poker face, I think. To Jenkins, I say, "Anything I know beyond what Father Leonard has said, or Rachel Watson told me, is privileged."

She nods. "I understand. The initial allegation to the Archdiocese was vague and seems innocuous. I'm surprised the Archbishop bothered to send you here."

I had not told her about that. "How did you find that out?"

"The Archbishop told me on the phone when he retained me," she said. "He sent me a copy of the accusation and gave me some information about my client." She looks into the office at Father Leonard, his head bowed in prayer again. "Born in Wisconsin, parents both dead, attended all-boys

Catholic high school there, attended seminary here in Maryland, ordained about three years ago." She looks at me, "He's young to have his own parish, isn't he?"

"Under normal circumstances, yes," I say, "but our Archdiocese, like almost every other one in the country, has a shortage of priests. When circumstances demanded that Saint Clare's have a new priest, the Archbishop assigned Father Leonard."

Jenkins nods and crosses her arms. "Well, if he will not cooperate with me, there isn't a lot I can do for him. Do you think he'll listen to you?"

"I can try, but he hasn't been willing to talk to me yet. I'll give it another shot."

"Thanks." She pauses. "Can I ask you a question, Father?"

"You can ask," I say.

"Were they having a sexual relationship? Father Leonard and Rachel Watson?"

I stare at her, saying nothing.

She looks at me and shakes her head. "You can't say, can you? Well, I'll just have to hope he tells me."

"Can I ask you a question?" I ask.

Jenkins smiles and replies, "You can ask."

"Why did you take this case?"

"In the interest of justice, everyone has the right of legal counsel."

"Yes, yes, I know, but what's your real reason?"

"The real reason? People cannot fool you, can they, Father?"

"Not all the time," I say slowly. "Well?"

"The real reason, besides the reason I just gave you—which I really believe in, otherwise I wouldn't be a criminal defense attorney—is because I don't want to see him railroaded for political reasons."

"By your opponent in the upcoming election for State Attorney, right?"

She nods. "The town is a lot larger, and they're not as in control as they used to be, but the Myer family still has a lot of power in this area. You know he's Brian Dohrmann's biggest contributor, right?"

I nod.

"With money comes influence," Jenkins says. "Oh, I'm not saying Brian will deliberately frame the person Win Myer wants him to for the murder, he has more integrity than that, but he's a human being, and human beings are not always motivated by their better angels. But you would know that better than I would."

"So you think Dohrmann may shape a case to please Win Myer?"

"Please Win Myer, to look tough on crime, even let voters know he will not be intimidated by the Catholic Church, which as you know doesn't have the best reputation in the world right now."

"Well, I don't know about Dohrmann," I say, "But Detective Parr is a woman of integrity. I trust her to do the right thing."

"From everything I've heard around town, I agree with you. Look," Jenkins says, looking at her watch, "I have a meeting with another client." Pointing to Father Leonard, she says, "See if you can get him to talk to me. I'll be in touch."

She goes back into my office to retrieve her briefcase. "Father Leonard," she says, placing her hand gently on his shoulder. He jumps and looks at her, startled.

"I have another client I need to meet with," she says. "I will speak to you later."

"Speak to me later," he repeats. "Got it. Speak to me later."

After she leaves, Father Leonard looks at me. "If it's all the same to you," he says, standing, "I think I'll go on to bed."

I look at the time. "It's only 6:00 p.m."

He shrugs and sticks his hands in his pockets.

"Don't you want something to eat? Anna can get you some soup if you'd—"

"Thank you Father, but I'm not hungry," he says as he starts out of the room.

"Leonard, wait," I stop him, placing my hand on his shoulder. He turns to look at me.

"I want to help you. Your lawyer wants to help you. The only way we can do that is if you talk. Now if you don't want to start by talking to her, I can hear your confession, and by that, I don't mean your confession to the crime, I mean why you were at Rachel's apartment to begin with, and frankly what your relationship with her was." I pause and look in his eyes.

I see a flicker, just a flicker of relief. I sense his shoulder relaxing beneath my hand. He opens his mouth.

Then, he snaps it shut, the tension in his shoulder returns.

He shakes his head. "I don't want help," he mumbles. "No one can help me."

"Leonard," I shout, "for heaven's sake, do you know what kind of trouble you're in?"

With pitiful eyes, he looks at me and answers, "It's what I deserve." With that, he leaves my office and walks upstairs to his room.

A while later, I walk past the closed door and hear the slaps of the discipline against Father Leonard's bare back.

***

Breakfast the next day comprises a cheddar cheese, ham, and mushroom omelet, hash browns, coffee, and orange juice. The smells coming from the kitchen hit me when I enter the Rectory after 8:00 am Mass. Anna had slipped out after communion. I now know where she went.

"Anna," I say, sitting down before the plate she placed on the kitchen table, "you really don't need to keep doing this."

"I enjoy doing it," she says, wiping her hands dry. "Besides, it's not like I have a lot going on."

I take a bite of omelet and chew thoughtfully. Anna pours herself a cup of coffee and sits down. "Father Leonard still asleep?"

I nod as I chew. Swallowing, I wash the breakfast down with some orange juice. "His door was still closed when I went into the church."

"How is he doing?"

I shake my head. "Not good. The poor man is suffering. Problem is, he won't talk. Not to me, not to the police."

"That probably doesn't bother his lawyer," Anna comments, "though I can't imagine Brian Dohrmann is happy with his opponent as Father Leonard's attorney."

I look at her, surprised. She smiles. "I hear things, you know."

"What do you know about Angela Jenkins?"

She sits back. "Not too much," she says. "She's not native to Myerton, I think she's from Philadelphia originally. I'm not sure how she wound up here, but she's been an attorney in town for about five years, mainly criminal work, but she's also done more community advocacy work. You know, pro-environmental work and the like." She snaps her fingers. "Come to think of it, I think she's the lawyer for the group working against Myer Holdings' wind farm."

I raise my eyebrows. "Really? That's very interesting. Why is she running for State Attorney?"

Anna shakes her head. "I guess she wants the job, probably as a stepping stone to something bigger, State Delegate or State Senator. She'd be the first African-American elected to county office. That'd get her a lot of attention."

"I just hope she's not looking at Leonard as one of those stones she's stepping on."

"From what I've heard, she is a talented lawyer with a lot of integrity. I don't think she'd let her ambition affect her defense."

Behind me, I hear shuffling. I turn to see a bedraggled Father Leonard trudge into the kitchen. He pulls out one chair at the kitchen table and drops into it.

I look at him, opening my mouth to speak, when Anna says gently, "Father, can I get you something to eat?"

Father Leonard slowly shakes his head. "No, thank you, Anna."

"Leonard," I say, "you need to eat something. You had no dinner last night."

"Tom's right," Anna says. 'How about toast and coffee, something light?"

"Fine," he says, "fine. Toast and coffee, thank you."

Anna pours him a cup and sets it in front of him. Father Leonard stares at it blankly. I look at him as I finish my breakfast. Standing, I motion to Anna. We walk to the doorway to the kitchen.

"Can you stay and keep an eye on him? I'll be in my office."

"You go work, we'll be fine," Anna says reassuringly.a

In my office, I'm just sitting down when the rectory phone rings.

"Good morning, Father Tom," Rebecca Myer says, "I hope I'm not interrupting you."

"Not at all, Mrs. Myer," I say. "What can I do for you?"

"Well, I was wondering if I could talk to you about the funeral arrangements for Rachel," she answers.

"Absolutely," I say. I pull my appointment calendar to me and flip through the pages. It's a pro-forma flip. I know the pages are blank. "Any day this week would be fine."

"Could we make it early this afternoon?"

"Of course," I say. "I'll come out to your house—"

"I'd like to meet with you at Saint Clare's," she interrupts. "Not here. It will just be me."

"Oh? Your mother—"

"My mother isn't interested in the funeral arrangements," she says carefully. "She's letting me handle all of that. I just want to make sure we do what Rachel would have wanted."

"I understand," I say. "Is 1:30 pm a good time?"

"That will be fine," she answers. "1:30 p.m. I'll meet you there."

As soon as I hang up, my cell phone rings. *It's going to be one of those days, I'm afraid,* I say to myself. I look at the number.

It's Helen.

"Did I catch you in the middle of saving a soul?" she says.

"Not currently, soul saving isn't on my schedule for another hour. Shouldn't you be catching a bike thief?"

"That's not until this afternoon," she says, "This morning I have 'call ex-fiancés who became priests' on my calendar."

"Oh, well, I guess it's a good thing I'm free. What's up?"

She hesitates before saying, "How's Father Leonard this morning?"

Now it's my turn to hesitate. "Should I be talking to you about him? He has a lawyer now."

"Angela Jenkins is his lawyer, not your lawyer. I can't talk to him directly, but there's nothing to keep me from talking to you about him. Besides, I'm just asking how he's doing. You know, he is my parish priest."

"Okay, you're right." I sigh. "Not well at all."

"Has he talked to you?"

"Yes, but I know no more about why he was there than you do."

"Well," Helen says slowly, "I may be able to answer that."

"How?"

"Gladys Finklestein—my computer genius, remember?—was able to access Rachel Watson's phone and retrieve her text messages and call log. We don't have a report from the cell phone company about her other calls for the past month, yet. We won't be getting that for several days, but we do have a record of a call from Father Leonard's number to Rachel Watson at about 4:30 p.m."

"We already know about that," I say.

"The call," she continues, "lasted twenty minutes."

"What?" I say, unable to conceal my surprise. "He didn't tell us what they talked about, nor did he mention how long the call was."

"Considering the thirty text messages he sent her from about 1:00 p.m. onward, he probably called to keep her from leaving."

I almost drop my phone. "Thirty text messages? He mentioned nothing about texting her."

"From the messages, I'm not surprised."

"Well," I press, "what do they say?"

"I'd rather not tell you over the phone."

"You want me to come down to the station?"

She says nothing for a minute. "Tom, I shouldn't even be talking to you about this, much less showing you. But I thought you should know."

"Are you going to share these with his attorney?"

"Oh, yes, we're obligated to," Helen says. "I thought you should know for other reasons."

I let that sink in. "Okay."

"But not the station," she says. "How about lunch?"

"I don't think I will have time today, I've got noon mass and I'm meeting with Rebecca Myer to discuss funeral arrangements. Any idea when the body will be released?"

"I'm traveling to Baltimore tomorrow to meet with the state medical examiner; I'll know more then."

"Mind if I tag along? I've got to go by the Archdiocesan Office, anyway." That is a lie, but a small one. I just want to be there when the medical examiner tells Helen what they found.

"Sure, I'd enjoy the company," Helen says. "Anyway, why don't you come by my apartment later this afternoon? I'll show you the text messages. Unless you're scared to?"

"Why would I be scared?"

"I don't know. A priest, alone in a single woman's apartment. After everything with Father Leonard—"

"I think I can trust myself," I chuckle. "And you."

Helen says nothing for a moment. "Yes, Father Tom," she says, "you can trust me."

Thirteen

I stand with Rebecca Myer at the front of the church. She's looking around with slight wonder at the vaulted ceiling, the carved traditional marble altar holding the tabernacle behind the modern altar, six candles and a crucifix arranged along the front edge facing the congregation. To the left, a statue of the Virgin Mary; to the right, one of Saint Joseph holding the child Jesusa,; each statue with red votive candles flickering in the dim light. Stained glass windows down either side of the church cast a kaleidoscope of color, each window a scene from Jesus's life except for the one closest to the entrance to the sanctuary. That one portrays Saint Clare and is opposite the statue of the saint, with more votive candles arranged in front.

"You've been inside Saint Clare's before, of course," I say.

Still looking up, she nods her head. "Oh, yes, many times. The last time, I think, was my wedding. I may have been here at Christmas a couple of times since. I just forgot how breathtaking it is," she whispers. "So peaceful. I can't believe something so beautiful was built when the town was so small."

I smile and join her. "It was the Irish laborers' way of honoring the God who had helped them survive the potato famine and the passage across the Atlantic to Baltimore," I say. "Their pennies, and larger contributions from the townspeople, many of whom were themselves Catholic—Maryland was at the time one of the most Catholic states in the country—and many who were not." I look at her. "Your husband's great-great-grandfather, who was himself a devout Catholic, gave a large sum from what I understand."

"You can really feel a presence here," Rebecca whispers. "It's not like anything I've experienced anywhere else." She looks at me. "Is that God?"

I smile and nod. Turning towards the tabernacle, I say, "Remember, the Church teaches that God the Son, Jesus, is present in every tabernacle in every physical church around the world in the Eucharist. So yes, I would say the presence you feel is God."

"Mama brought Rachel and I when we were younger, but I'm not sure she really believes anything," Rebecca says. "She is a very practical woman, which makes her cold to many people. She taught Rachel and me that material things were important, the most important things in life. I guess that came from her growing up poor; from what she told me, her family didn't have much at all when she was little. She married Daddy, who's been successful in his business, so we've always been comfortable, but she wanted more for Rachel and me."

"More than Rachel becoming a nun?"

Rebecca laughs. "By the time Rachel told us that, we had stopped being surprised by her. Mama was never particularly close to Rachel, but after that . . . things were never the same."

She sighs. "I'll admit, Father Tom, I loved my sister but never really understood her in the last few years." She pauses. "We were twins, shared a womb for nine months, and were born only ten minutes apart—I'm the oldest, for what that's worth—but we were very different people."

"You look alike."

"On the outside, in many ways, we were the same," Rebecca says. "Inside, we were different. Rachel was smart but not particularly pretty, I'm pretty but not particularly smart—oh, I don't mean that as vain, it's what we'd tell each other."

"You grew up together, but I gather Rachel went away to high school?"

Rebecca nods. "We started out together at Myerton High. Right before our sophomore year, Mama decided that Rachel should go away for the rest of high school to a boarding school."

"Why did she do that?"

"She said it was because it would be better academically for Rachel. But there was another reason." She turns away from me to look at the altar.

"Where did she go?"

Rebecca laughs. "Well there, Father, is where, it gets funny. My 'Christmas and Easter' mother decided that the only place for Rebecca was an all-girls Catholic preparatory school in Wisconsin."

I raise my eyebrows. "Why in the world?"

Rebecca shakes her head. "Mama's said it was the worst decision she ever made, but at the time she went on and on about how prominent all the girls who went there were, how strong it was academically, how from there, Rachel could write her ticket into any Ivy League school she wanted."

"She didn't go to an Ivy League school, did she?"

"No. She wanted to come home, go to Myer. Mama wanted her to apply to a big-name school out of state. Instead, she went to Emmitsburg. We should have realized something was going on, but Rachel did a good job convincing Mama and Daddy that the only reason was because it had an excellent business school and she had won a scholarship—both of which were true." She sighs. "But the day of her graduation, she announced to us she was thinking about becoming a nun."

"And you all had no idea?"

"No, none. Mama was furious, ranted and raved during the entire dinner after graduation. Daddy said nothing—he usually says nothing. I was confused. Hurt that she hadn't told me. We had been close before she went away to school, despite our distinct personalities. I thought she could tell me anything. I guess she didn't feel the same way."

"Maybe she was afraid you'd tell your parents, or try to dissuade her."

Her laugh echoes off the walls. "Oh Father, you couldn't dissuade Rachel of anything once her mind was made up. And I wouldn't have tried. After I got over my hurt, I realized how I really felt."

"How did you feel?"

Rebecca looks at me, then the tabernacle. "Proud. And envious." She sighs quietly.

"She didn't enter religious life immediately, though. She went to work in Baltimore if I remember correctly."

Rebecca nods. "Yes, she worked there for a few years, then moved back here to take the job she had before becoming parish secretary at Saint Clare's."

"You became close again after she moved back to Myerton."

"Yes, yes, we did," she whispers.

We stand together quietly for a minute, then I say, "Win has seemed pretty upset by everything that's happened."

Rebecca's expression darkens. "Win's always been . . . protective of Rachel. He was that way in high school. They went out once or twice before Rachel went away."

"And you started dating him after your sister left?"

"Oh, Father, I had no interest in Win while he was dating my sister," Rebecca says. "But after Rachel left, Mama got it into her head that nothing would do except Win Myer and I would get together." She pauses. "And Mama usually gets what she wants."

"Except with Rachel."

"Yes, except with Rachel. Her announcing she was quitting her job to work at Saint Clare's because she wanted to become a nun was the last straw."

"Had she told you she was still considering it?"

"Yes, she had told me she was still thinking about it. I knew about her going to a convent near Emmitsburg for weekend retreats. We kept that from Mama. But it came as a surprise to me when she told Mama and Daddy. Mama was so upset. That meeting in your office was the first time in months they had even spoken."

"So you knew she was thinking about becoming a nun, but her email the day of her murder still surprised you?"

"The last I had heard, she was having second thoughts, that maybe she wasn't called to be a nun, that maybe God wanted something else from her. I remember her being confused for the last couple of months, distracted even, but excited at the same time."

"When did that start?"

"Shortly after she moved back to Myerton. I was glad to have her back. I had been lonely without her." She pauses. "Win's away a lot on business, and when he's home, he works a lot." She turns away, looking like she was contemplating the scene of the miracle of the Wedding at Cana, where Jesus turned water into wine.

"And after that, she began to express doubts?"

"Yes, like I say, she seemed confused, but also happy. It was very strange. I kept meaning to ask her about it. Then I received that email and I supposed whatever doubts she had were gone." She shakes her head. "Now, I guess I'll never know," she whispers.

I look down at her and place my hand on her shoulder. "Maybe someday."

She gives a sharp laugh. "Not likely, Father. I'm not winding up in the same place Rachel is, I'm afraid."

"You know, you can do something about that."

She looks up at me. "Maybe someday, Father. But for today," she continues, "tell me about my sister's funeral. Have you done many?"

"Actually," I say, "Rachel's will be my first."

"But you know how to do it, right? It's part of your training, isn't it? And you've been to other Catholic funerals?"

Slowly I turn to look towards the altar, focusing on the spot where the casket would lay.

"Only one," I whisper, "and I don't remember much."

***

In almost twenty years, I have forgotten that Helen is a terrible housekeeper. Her apartment is small, made smaller by the clutter scattered throughout the place. Almost every surface is covered with papers, books, and clothes, clean and dirty. I have no desire to go into the kitchen; I remember what a disaster it always was.

"Try to find yourself a seat," Helen says when she lets me in. "I haven't had time to clean."

"In the past year?" I say. She turns and gives me a look. "Sorry," I say with a grin.

"Hmm. You want something to drink? I have water and . . . maybe just water."

"I'm fine, thanks."

I pick up a stack of folders from a chair. Holding it in my hands, I look at Helen.

"Just put it anywhere," she says with a wave of her hand. "I'm going to change into something more comfortable." At my look, she laughs and says. "T-shirt and shorts, Tom, that's all I meant." She leaves the room with me still holding the folders.

Against the wall, there is a table that she apparently uses as a desk, so I place the folders on it. Over the desk is a large cork board, its surface covered with newspaper clippings and photographs, along with notes in her indecipherable handwriting. All have to do with a series of shootings in D.C. a few years ago. A couple of the articles have photographs of Helen, described as the lead detective.

Among the piles of folders and papers on the table is a framed portrait of a man. I pick it up and examine it closely. He's handsome, with curly brown hair and a winning smile. Dressed in a tuxedo, it must have been taken on his wedding day.

"Okay, that's better . . ." I hear Helen behind me, her voice trailing off. I turn to see her. She's not looking at me, but at the framed picture in my hand.

I hold it up. "John?"

She nods slowly, walking towards me.

"He looks like a nice guy," I say.

She swallows and smiles slightly. "He was," she says quietly. She takes the picture from me and looks at it, stroking it lightly with her finger. "This was taken on our wedding day. I loved him. I still do."

I nod. "I understand."

Helen looks at me. "I know," she says.

We stand looking at each for a few minutes in silence. Part of me wants to say something, but I'm not sure what. Another part of me wants to put my arms around her to comfort her obvious grief.

But another part of me—a big part—feels jealous of this man who had something I didn't—now, never will.

"Well," Helen says finally. "You didn't come over here for this. Here are the text messages between Father Leonard and Rachel." She walks to her bag and pulls out a folder. "You can take these, they're copies."

I take the folder. "Why are you giving them to me?"

She sighs. "Because I think you should know, for reasons other than the crime."

"What do they say?"

"Look for yourself."

I sit down in the chair I cleared and open the folder. Helen shoves a stack of laundry off the couch and sits opposite me. I read. The more I read, the more disturbed I become.

We sit in silence for the next several minutes. I reach the last of the text messages, the one where Father Leonard says, *I'm going to call you. Please answer*, and close the folder. I sit with the folder on my lap, leaning my head against the back of the chair, with my eyes closed.

Oh, Leonard, I muse. *What were you thinking?*

"Well?" Helen asks.

I look at her. "I admit it doesn't look good, but it doesn't mean he killed her."

"Perhaps not," she replies. "But it shows someone desperate, obsessed with seeing her, or at least talking to her. Her responses are those of a woman not too interested in either until the last couple."

"But he talked to her, he went over. She must have agreed to see him."

"Or, she told him not to come over, and he went to her place, anyway."

"There's no evidence of that!"

"Hey," she says, holding her hands up, "don't get mad at me. You're the one with the wayward priest. I'm just telling you how I see the texts, and how Brian will see them."

I plop them down on another stack of folders sitting on the coffee table. "Only if he's already decided Leonard's the murderer."

Helen hesitates. "He hasn't, but he definitely has decided that Father Leonard is the prime suspect."

I look at her. "What about you?"

"Me? It's still too early. We don't have the evidence reports back, and I haven't seen the post-mortem." She looks at me. "I'm just following the evidence, Tom. That's all I ever do."

I shake my head. "Well, what about that guy from her office?"

"Him? I'm looking into him." She stands and goes to her desk. Plucking a folder off a precarious pile, she opens it. "Name's Richard Strump. Turns out Rachel filed a police report on him for stalking her back in February. He was parked outside of her townhouse for hours. Officers arrived and told him to move along. He gave them some trouble, and he wound up in the county jail for the weekend." She looks up. "Apparently it wasn't the first time he's done something similar. According to the notes here, their company HR department had numerous harassment complaints filed against him. He kept his job—how, I don't know—but the arrest was jus,t too much. They let him go not long after."

"Well, there you go," I say. "She was responsible for him losing his job. Sounds like a motive to me?"

"Tom, they fired him in February. There are no other reports of harassment or stalking. You're saying he kept this anger against Rachel inside for months, then decided to kill her?"

"Revenge is a dish best served cold," I say.

"Don't quote Khan to me, Tom," she says.

"Okay, but are you going to look into him?"

"Yes, yes, I will. But it's not on the top of my list."

Later I'm in my car, thinking about Helen's last comment.

She's very busy, being the only detective in Myerton.

Maybe she could use some help.

Fourteen

"Hey, are you awake?"

I'm staring out the window of Helen's car as we travel I-70 towards Baltimore. Her voice startles me.

"Huh, what?" I say and turn to her.

She glances at me before returning to the road. "I asked if you were awake."

"Yeah, yeah, I'm awake," I say, stretching. "I've been awake the whole time."

"You haven't said a word since we left Myerton," Helen says.

"Sorry," I say, reaching for the to-go cup of coffee in her cup holder. We had stopped by The Perfect Cup on our way out of town. "I have a lot on my mind."

"Trying to figure out what to tell the Archbishop about Father Leonard when you see him, huh? What are you going to tell him?"

I shift in my seat, kicking aside the fast food wrappers covering the floorboard of her sedan. "I haven't decided yet. I haven't decided what it means."

"I would think it would be obvious," she says. "'Let me talk to you, I have a question to ask you.' 'I can't live the rest of my life without you, Rachel.' 'Please don't leave me again.' 'I want you Rachel, I'll give everything up for you.'" She pauses. "Except for coming out and saying, 'I'm leaving the priesthood to marry you,' it's clear what his intention was in going to Rachel's apartment."

"But he hasn't said that was why he was there," I say. "Okay, I'll grant you, he wanted to talk to her. He wanted to talk to her desperately. She had told her sister and her brother-in-law she was entering the convent. She was leaving the next morning."

"That's what she told Father Leonard, too," she says. At my glance she says, "We found an email to Father Leonard on her computer."

"We don't know that he saw it."

"You're ignoring the texts," she says with exasperation. "She said, 'Didn't you get my email? I've decided. It's for the best, Leonard.' He answered, 'You can't leave.'"

I sigh and nod. "I guess you're right. But none of that adds up to Leonard being guilty of her murder. In fact, it works against that theory."

"Angela Jenkins will argue that." She hesitates, then says, "Brian, however, is ready to have him arrested and charged."

"What?"

She nods. "He thinks the texts establish enough to have him arrested and charged with manslaughter, at least. I've persuaded him to wait until we get the autopsy report and other forensics back, but he's determined." She shakes her head. "No, Tom, I don't know why. I have to say, though, Father Leonard sure looks guilty."

"But you know him," I say. "He's too scared of his own shadow to murder anyone."

"Maybe plan to murder someone, but in the heat of the moment, overcome with desperation, who knows?"

"But what about someone else? What about Richard Strump? Have you asked him where he was at the time of her murder?"

"There's no evidence there was anyone else in the apartment."

"But Leonard—" I stop myself, realizing I was about to tell Helen what he had told me and his lawyer.

"But Leonard what?" she asks.

I hesitate. "I'm not sure I should tell you. It's something he said to me and his lawyer."

"Listen, Tom, I stuck my neck out showing you those texts. You owe me. What did Father Leonard say?"

I sigh and tell her Leonard's account of going into the dark apartment, feeling a presence, feeling suffocated, then waking up next to Rachel's body hours later.

Helen drives along contemplating what I just said. After a few minutes she says, "'A presence?' He said 'a presence?'"

"That's how he described it, a presence that suffocated him and caused him to black out. Maybe Strump killed her. Then when Leonard came in, Strump knocked him out?"

She shrugs. "Or Leonard could have blacked out after killing her, or he's lying about the whole thing." At my look, she says, "I'm saying what Brian will try to argue, Tom."

"What do you think?"

She shakes her head. "I just follow the evidence, Tom."

"And what does the evidence tell you?"

She thinks for a moment. "I don't have enough yet, but honestly," she sighs, "I don't think it looks good for him."

"But Helen—"

"Tom, I promise you, I will look into Strump, but for right now I think we should change the subject, don't you?" she says, cutting off further conversation.

"Okay, maybe we should." I look at her. Then I settle back in the seat.

We drive along, the silence thick between us.

***

The Archbishop leans back in his chair, his hands folded on his chest, and looks up at the ceiling of his office. I had spent thirty minutes or thereabouts telling him what I found out—or at least what I could. I couldn't share Rachel's confession, even with the Archbishop. But I told him about the text messages.

Finally, he speaks. "So Father McCoy broke his vow of celibacy."

I nod. "I believe there is evidence that he did."

"Am I right in saying there are things you cannot tell me?"

"Yes, Your Eminence."

He nods. "And you are right, you have no choice." He pauses and looks at me. "Father McCoy has not confessed?"

I shake my head. "Not as far as I know. He has said nothing to me about any of this. But he feels guilty. Inordinately so."

"His use of the discipline and cilice shows he's handling his own penance," the Archbishop says. "He has to know how spiritually dangerous it is to undergo those penances without proper direction."

"I don't think he cares," I say. "Frankly, I'm afraid of what he might do next."

He looks at me. "Do you think he might hurt himself?"

"With his state of mind, I wouldn't discount it."

The Archbishop sighs. "You must get him to talk to you, Tom, so you can counsel him. Before something worse happens."

"I'll try, sir."

He leans forward. "What about the investigation? How is Detective Parr handling things? Any problems?"

"As I told you, she's a professional. She's following the evidence." I pause. "The State Attorney is putting together his case against Father Leonard already. He doesn't want to wait for all the evidence."

"What's he like?"

I choose my words carefully. "He has personal reasons to act," I say. I explain to him about the election, about the political relationship between him and the Myer family.

"It also doesn't help that the attorney you retained for Father Leonard is his opponent in the upcoming election," I conclude.

The Archbishop grimaces. "Okay, I did not know that when I contacted her. Our lawyers gave me her name as a good defense attorney with no biases against the church. Her father was a Baptist preacher, apparently, so she's not hostile to the faith."

"She seems to be a talented lawyer, and I'm sure she'll represent Father Leonard well, but she has her own interests in the case besides merely seeing that justice is done."

"Everyone has ulterior motives, Father Tom, even priests," he says. "As long as her motives don't undermine Father McCoy having the best defense possible, I don't care what they are. I'm trusting you to keep an eye on her. If you think she isn't giving him the best defense possible, let me know."

"Be sure that I will."

"Good, good. Now," he says, "what to do with Father McCoy? Assuming he's not found guilty and sent to prison for murder." He sits back and drums his fingers on the desk. "He will need to spend time in penance and prayer."

"He'll need rest," I point out. "He's going through hell right now."

"A hell of his own making," the Archbishop says. "He must go through counseling, to see if he can return to his vows. But that means that Saint Clare's will be without a priest again."

We sit in silence for a long time. The question implicit in the Archbishops' statement floats between us.

Finally, I nod. "Yes, your Eminence."

The Archbishop smiles. "Good, good. We won't do anything until after this is over. In the meantime, I'll let Father Abbot know your return to the monastery is delayed indefinitely. Don't worry, I'll help him find another priest to serve the monastery."

I stand. "Thank you. I'm glad. I owe the Brothers a lot."

***

The Office of the Chief Medical Examiner is in a modern-looking building on West Baltimore Street in Baltimore. Unlike many jurisdictions around the country, they perform all autopsies in suspicious deaths in the state in one location. It's here that they transported Rachel Watson's body. Helen and I are here to see her, for me to arrange for her transport back to Myerton for her funeral, and Helen to receive the report of the forensic pathologist to confirm the cause of death.

"You were in there a while," Helen had said when I walked out of the Archbishop's office. She had waited for me in her car, eating a bacon, egg, and cheese croissant sandwich and washing it down with an iced coffee. She handed me a chicken biscuit when I got in the car.

"We had a lot to talk about," I had said.

Now we are standing in one of the examination rooms of the Medical Examiner's office. It's pretty much as portrayed in many TV police dramas, tile and stainless steel. The exam table, where the autopsies are performed, resembles the table in an operating room. Only here, the purpose is to find the truth instead of to heal. A body on the table is covered with a sheet.

The door opens, and a woman dressed in scrubs walks in. "Detective Parr?" she asks.

"Yes?"

"Hi, I'm Dr. Kashyap. I performed the post-mortem on Ms. Watson." She looks at me with confusion.

"I'm Father Tom Greer," I explain. "The family asked me to see to her release and return to Myerton."

"Ah," she says, nodding. "Do you want to wait outside while I go over the results with Detective Parr?"

"He can stay," Helen says before I can respond. "You're not squeamish, are you, Father?"

"No, no," I say with more certainty than I feel.

"Okay, suit yourself," Dr. Kashyap says. She walks to the table and pulls the sheet down, exposing Rachel Watson's lifeless body from the head to her waist. Modesty demands that I avert my eyes. There is no gore, just a carefully stitched y-incision across her upper torso and a thin slit in her stomach.

Opening the folder in her hands, she recites, "Watson, Rachel, white female, age 28, etc., etc." She proceeds with the time of the autopsy, the weight and condition of her organs, all very clinical.

Helen interrupts. "Do you have an approximate time of death?"

Referring to her notes, she says, "Between the stomach contents and the liver temperature taken at the scene, I estimate sometime between 6:00 pm and 8:00 pm Sunday night."

"Cause of death?" Helen asks.

"The victim had one wound," the doctor says. She points to the one in her stomach. "A sharp object entered the upper abdomen, penetrated the liver, and nicked the inferior vena cava. This is the cause of death. She exsanguinated because of a stab wound."

"Murder weapon?"

"A sharp knife like a kitchen knife."

That matches what they found near the body. Near Father Leonard.

"The sad thing is, they could have saved her," the doctor comments. At our looks, she explained, "The inferior vena cava has rather low pressure. Unless a stab wound is right into the inferior vena cava, any blood loss is relatively slow. Based on the wound, she could have lived for a half-hour, maybe forty-five minutes after being stabbed." She looks at Rachel. "If she had gotten to the hospital in time, it's likely she and her baby would have survived."

Helen and I look at the doctor. "What?" Helen asks.

"Her baby," the doctor repeats. "When she was murdered, Rachel Watson was about eight weeks pregnant."

Fifteen

"Okay," Helen says, "let's go over this again, Father McCoy."

We're sitting in the interrogation room at the Myerton Police station. Helen is across the table from Father McCoy and Angela Jenkins. I'm in a chair off to the side. She let me sit in as long as I was quiet. We have been here for about an hour, Helen asking questions, Father McCoy giving brief answers when he answered at all, his lawyer making notes on her legal pad and occasionally interjecting.

"My client," Jenkins is saying, "has already answered your questions, Detective. I don't see why you keep going over the same ground."

"Because, Ms. Jenkins, your client isn't telling the truth," Helen says.

"And you know that how?"

Helen hadn't mentioned the text messages up to this point. I notice her take a file folder from the bottom of the stack in front of her. She opens it and takes out a small stack of stapled pages.

"Because of these," she says, handing the papers to Father Leonard. He doesn't take them, but stares at a point behind Helen, staring at his reflection in the mirror. From where I'm sitting, I see his face. Anguish, pain, guilt—all etched in his expression.

"What's this?" Jenkins says, taking the papers and flipping through them.

"These are text messages your client sent the victim the afternoon before her murder," Helen says. "He sent dozens of messages and talked to her on the phone for about twenty minutes."

"He's already told you he talked to her," she said, tossing the papers on the table. "He told you he went to the apartment where he was attacked, was rendered unconscious, and woke up next to the body of the victim. He doesn't deny that. I'm wondering why you're still questioning my client when you should look for the person who was there before he was."

"We're looking into it, I assure you," Helen says, "but I want to know why he sent these messages."

"She was leaving," Father Leonard blurts, almost a whisper, his eyes still fixed on the mirror. "She told me she was leaving. I got an email saying she was leaving, I didn't get it right away, I didn't get access to my email until that afternoon."

"Father McCoy, don't—" Jenkins says, touching his arm.

"I tried to call," Leonard continues, ignoring her counsel. "She wouldn't answer. So I texted, and I said . . . well, you see what I said."

"What did you say to her on the phone?"

"I just wanted to see her, to talk to her, to have a chance to . . ." Father Leonard trails off.

"To have a chance to what?" Helen presses.

"To persuade her to, to ask her to . . ." Father Leonard slumps in his chair, staring at his folded hands, but says nothing else.

"If you have nothing else, Detective," Jenkins says, gathering her papers, "unless you will charge my client, then I think we're done here."

"Not quite, Ms. Jenkins, there is just one more thing," Helen says. She glances at me out of the corner of her eye. I lean forward slightly.

She takes another folder from the bottom of the stack and opens it in front of her. Quietly, she asks. "Father, did Rachel tell you she was pregnant?"

The question explodes in the room. Jenkins' eyes get big, and she jerks her head to look at Father Leonard. Father Leonard sits bolt upright, the anguish and pain replaced by shock and surprise.

"What? What? Pregnant? With a baby?" Father McCoy sputters, his voice raised. "What are you talking about? She said nothing to me about—I mean she mentioned nothing—I didn't know, I swear I didn't know."

"Father McCoy, please—" Jenkins says through gritted teeth, trying to get her client to shut up.

"She didn't tell you she was pregnant?"

"No, no, not a word! Oh, my Lord. Oh, my dear Lord! Oh, Blessed Mother!" he cries, slumps back in his chair with his hands over his face, and sobs. I stand up and move towards him. I kneel beside him and put an arm around his shoulders. He leans to me, still sobbing.

I look at Helen. She looks impassive, every inch the professional. "Detective," I say, "do you have everything you need right now? I think he's had enough, don't you?"

Helen nods slowly. "I think you're right. Father McCoy, you're free to go." She turns to Jenkins. "I'll want him back for more questions."

Jenkins nods. "You'd better be looking into his story, the person who was there in the apartment, the real killer, instead of targeting my client."

"I assure you we're looking at all possibilities," Helen says standing up. She looks at me and motions with her head.

I pat Father Leonard's shoulder. "I'll be with you in a few minutes, then we'll go back to the Rectory and get you something to eat." I stand and follow Helen into the hallway.

"Tom, you know how this looks, don't you?" she says.

"Oh, come on, Helen," I say, "you saw his reaction. He didn't know she was pregnant."

"He could be lying, you know. That could be an act for your benefit." Helen pauses. "Do you think she knew?"

"At eight weeks?" The times Joan was pregnant, she always knew by then. Unfortunately, soon after came miscarriages. Except for the last one.

"Yes," I say finally, "I think she would have known. Have you checked with her doctor?"

She shakes her head. "Not yet. I'll get the information and contact them as soon as possible." She crosses her arms and looked at me. "Wouldn't her being pregnant put the kibosh on her plans to enter the convent?"

I purse my lips and raise my eyebrows. "I hadn't thought of that. It would have, most definitely, at least put a wrench into the plans."

"I mean, she wouldn't have been planning to have an abortion, would she?"

"No, I don't see Rachel, from what I know about her, taking that route. Committing a mortal sin."

"But hadn't she already? Fornication is a mortal sin, after all."

I sigh. "And one sin often leads to another. So I admit it might be a possibility. More likely, though, she would have had the baby and put it up for adoption."

"But she couldn't do that in the convent, could she?"

I shake my head. "No, I don't believe convents come equipped with birthing rooms and midwives. She was up to something," I pause. "Maybe a call to the Mother Superior of the convent is in order."

"I'll take care of it," Helen says.

"Let me do that," I say. "It might be easier coming from me. They may not be very willing to talk to you." At her look, I say, "I promise I'll tell you what I find out. But I'll tell his lawyer as well."

She nods. "Fair enough."

At that moment, the door to the viewing room swings open and a very irritated Brian Dohrmann walks out.

"I've been in there waiting for you, Helen," he says. "What kept you?" He looks at me. "Oh, I see."

"I was just talking to Father Tom," Helen says.

"Hmm," Dohrmann says with scepticism. "Well? Why haven't you arrested him?"

"Because I'm not prepared to do that yet," she replies. "The forensic evidence is not back yet, we just got the post-mortem yesterday—"

"Yes, I heard of your little trip to Baltimore," he says, eyeing me with suspicion.

"I was there to arrange for Rachel's return to Myerton, on behalf of the family," I volunteer. "That's the only reason."

"Are you sure? That's the only reason? Or are you spying on the investigation?"

"Spying?" I laugh. "Brian, spying for who?"

"Are you serious? Do you think I'm an idiot?"

"Which question do you want me to answer first?" I say with a smile. Helen rolls her eyes.

Dohrmann opens his mouth, then shuts it quickly. He takes a deep breath. Turning to Helen, he says, "I just don't understand what you're waiting for?"

"Evidence," Helen says. "Probable cause. You know, a legal basis for an arrest?"

"I think you have enough, Helen. You have him finally admitting he came to the apartment to talk to her. You have those texts showing him desperately trying to contact the victim in the hours before her murder. You have the accusations against him. You have the fact that she was pregnant. It's clear to me, even if it isn't to you."

Helen's face hardens. Her eyes take on a dark hue, one I remember too well.

"He said he didn't know she was pregnant," I say, "and I'm not sure what you think all this adds up to."

"You wouldn't," Dohrmann spits. "So let me draw it out for you. Either he screwed her or he didn't, maybe she consented, maybe she was coerced. But it looks like he did. He wanted to see her, to talk to her about keeping quiet about his little indiscretion so it wouldn't ruin his career in the Church. Then she tells him he's pregnant, he's the father. He kills her to keep her quiet. Motive, means, opportunity."

"Very good, Brian," I say with a tight smile. "You should sell that story to Lifetime."

Dohrmann clenches his fists and makes a motion to me. I draw myself up. Helen steps between us and puts a hand on Brian's chest.

"Stop," she says. "Ignore him. Father Tom has a sarcastic streak. Don't let him goad you."

"You need to do your job," Dohrmann says to her. "I want you to arrest Father McCoy now! Now are you going to do it, or do I need to call the chief?"

The hand on his chest becomes a jabbing finger. "Listen," she shouts, causing two people in the hallway behind Dohrmann to stop and walk back in the direction they came from. "I don't care who you are! I don't care if you are the President of the United States! I don't care how many dates we've been on! You will never tell me how to do my job! And you will never threaten me again! Do we understand each other?"

Dohrmann looks shell-shocked. It is obvious he has never experienced Helen in full attack mode. I should sympathize with the poor man.

But I don't.

They stare at each other for a few minutes, not speaking. Father Leonard and Jenkins come out of the interrogation room. They stop and look at us standing in the hallway. From the look on Jenkins's face, it's clear that she heard at least part of Helen's explosion.

"If you will excuse me," I say to the two combatants, "I'm going to take Father Leonard back to the Rectory."

"Fine," Helen says, looking at Dohrmann.

"Fine," Dohrmann says, looking at Helen.

We're almost to the door of the police station when I hear footsteps approaching behind us.

"Wait one moment." We turn to see Helen and Dohrmann approaching us. She is holding a folder, looking serious. He has a look of triumph.

"What is it, Detective?" Jenkins asks.

Opening the folder, Helen says. "We just got the forensics report. The blood on your client's shirt matches Rachel Watson's."

"Well, that's not surprising; my client had no wounds on him."

"But he's never explained how he got her blood on his shirt," Dohrmann says.

"There's more," Helen continues. "The fingerprints on the murder weapon match Father McCoy's. There were no other prints on the knife. Just his." She closes the folder.

She inhales. "Father Leonard McCoy," she intones, "I'm placing you under arrest for the murder of Rachel Watson."

***

I burst through the door of the Rectory. I had left the police station as soon as they had taken Father Leonard into custody. He had said nothing as they led him away, not protesting his innocence, just a look of resignation on his face.

"It will be all right, Leonard," I said as they walked him down the hall.

"No," he mumbled, "it won't. It hasn't been all right for a while."

"Can I bring you anything?"

He stopped and looked at me. "My breviary and rosary, can you get those? They're on the table by my bed."

I looked at Helen, who nodded. "He can have them."

Anna hears me and emerges from the living room. "What is it, Tom?" she says at my frantic look. "What's wrong?"

"They've arrested Leonard," I say, "and I've got—"

"What do you mean, they've arrested Father Leonard?" Anna demands. "Why did they arrest him?"

"I don't have the time to explain, Anna," I say as I bound up the stairs to Leonard's room.

"But, Tom!" Anna shouts behind me.

"I'll explain later," I shout back. "Right now I've got to get something and get back to the jail."

I go into Father Leonard's room. The bed is unmade, and looks like someone had been tossing and turning in the night. He hadn't slept well. On the bed is the corded flagellum. The police have probably already discovered the cilice. No doubt Helen will ask about that, and no doubt Dohrmann will see that as evidence of guilt.

His breviary is on the nightstand. When I reach to pick it up, it slips out of my fingers and falls to the floor, face down, the pages splayed open. I pick it up by the spine. Several pieces of paper fall to the floor. Two are prayer cards, one of Saint John Vianney, the other of the Blessed Virgin. I pick them and the third card, which fell face down, off the floor. I stick the two cards back in the breviary and turn the other over. I stop and peer at it.

It's not a prayer card. It's a small, wallet-size photograph, the type typically part of school photo packets. This isn't a school photo, showing an awkwardly smiling adolescent Leonard McCoy. He's in the picture, but it was taken at a school dance. Leonard's dressed in a gray tuxedo, bow tie, and white starched shirt, his red hair bright in the faded color photograph. Standing next to him is a young girl, about sixteen or seventeen, wearing a pale green prom dress, her left arm bedecked with a wrist corsage. Her hair is up, yet still looks soft. She has the same look on her face as Leonard, one a mix of adolescent awkwardness and unbridled joy. It's the happiest moment of the happiest day of their young lives.

I look more closely at the girl. She's slightly pudgier in the photo, but there's no mistake.

I close my eyes and shake my head.

"Oh, Leonard," I whisper.

Sixteen

It's after normal visiting hours by the time I get back to the station. I called Helen on the way, letting her know I was on my way to see Father Leonard. She told me she would let the guards know I had permission to see him for a few minutes. I didn't tell her what I had just learned. I wanted to talk to Father Leonard first. He had to tell me the story himself, but what I knew explained so much.

The guard escorts me to the visiting room. After about ten minutes, the door opens, and the guard escorts Father Leonard in. He's not handcuffed or shackled, and he's still wearing the same clothes he had on.

Except he has no belt, and his shoes are missing the laces.

He sits in the chair in front of me, looking desolate. He sees the breviary on the table in front of me and I notice his eyes brighten.

"You brought it," he whispers. "Thank you." He reaches for it and pulls it across the table, clutching it to his chest. It's precious to him, that much is obvious.

Or rather, what's inside is.

"How are you doing? Are they treating you okay?"

"As well as can be expected, I suppose," he says, slumping against the back of the chair.

I look at him for a few minutes, saying nothing. He sits in silence, staring at a spot on the table.

"Is there anything you'd like to talk about?" I finally ask.

He raises his eyes to look at me. Slowly, he shakes his head. "No," he whispers.

"Leonard," I say gently, "I can't help you if you don't talk to me."

"My lawyer says not to talk to anyone."

"About the case," I say. "I'm not asking about the case. I'm asking if there is anything you need to tell me, anything you want to talk to me about, anything I need to know so I can help you."

"No one can help me," he mutters. "No one. I don't want help."

"Leonard—"

He cuts me off by standing up. "Thank you for the breviary," he says as the guard opens the door, having seen him move through the small window. "But I think I should go back to my cell." He turns around to walk to the door. He opens the breviary as he takes a couple of steps, then stops. The guard prods him forward, but Leonard stands in the room, his back to me, flipping through the pages.

I pull the small photograph out of my coat pocket. "Are you looking for this?" I say, placing it face-up in the middle of the table. Leonard turns and sees it. His shoulders slump, his head drops.

"Can you leave us for a little while longer?" I say to the guard. He looks at me, then at the pathetic figure standing before him, and nods. He walks out of the room and closes the door. Father Leonard and I are left alone in the cold grey room, the young priest standing motionless.

"Sit down, Leonard," I say. He does, still looking down, still slumping, the very expression of defeat. I slide the photograph towards him. For the first time in a while, he smiles and picks it up.

"That was a glorious night," he whispers. "She was so beautiful. The prettiest girl there."

"So that is Rachel Watson," I say. It's a statement, not a question, since I already know the answer.

Father Leonard nods. "Yes, that's Rachel. It was my school's dance—they didn't call it a prom, but that's what it was, our senior prom."

"Why don't you start at the beginning," I say.

He looks at me. "The beginning? That seems like a long time ago." He sighs and puts the photo down. Looking at the wall, he goes on, "It was my mother's idea, going to that school."

"The boys' school in Wisconsin."

He nods. "She always wanted me to be a priest, from the day I was born. I don't remember a time when she didn't say, 'Leonard, you will be a priest when you grow up.' She called me her Samuel, her offering to God." He smiled ruefully. "She loved Star Trek and the Lord. She may have named me after the doctor on the Enterprise, but there was no other career on offer. Apparently, I had been a difficult pregnancy, after years of her not being able to carry a child to term. So, she told me, one day she was kneeling in her parish church before the Tabernacle and she said if God would allow her to have a child, she would offer that child to his service." He opened his hands. "So my fate was sealed even before I was born."

"But you can't enter the priesthood because someone wants you to," I say. "It's a sacred calling; you have to receive it yourself."

"And I did," he replies. "The older I got, the more certain I became that I was to become a priest, just like my mother said. I loved the church—it was the only place I ever felt comfortable." He looks at me. "I was an awkward child. I didn't have many friends, I wasn't any good at sports. I'd rather spend my time in my room reading or praying than spending time with other people." He shakes his head. "I guess being alone wasn't good training for a parish priest."

"Relating to people is a necessary part of the job," I say.

"That's been the hardest part, the people," he says. "Anyway, I went to parochial school, served at the altar as soon as I could, spent every hour I wasn't at home or at school in the Church. It became my second home. My sanctuary." He swallows. "More so after my mother got sick."

I look at him. "What happened?" I ask quietly.

"Cancer," he says. "They diagnosed her when I was twelve. She fought it for two years, with multiple rounds of chemotherapy and radiation. But she lost." A tear flows down his cheeks. "On her deathbed, she made me promise I would follow God's call to the priesthood. So I did." He looks at the table. "I was fourteen."

"How did you wind up at the boarding school?"

"That had been arranged before my mother died," he says. "My father, well, he took her illness hard, drank—he was never violent, just sad. They both agreed I would go away to high school after she died, and from there, enter seminary. The high school was particularly for young men discerning the priesthood, almost like a minor seminary."

He sits back. "I wanted to go to the school. I was so hopeful. An entire school of boys like myself, committed to serving the Lord, looking forward to studying for the priesthood. I thought it would be round after round of study, prayer, spiritual discussions, everything I didn't have growing up."

I look at him. "It didn't work out that way, though."

"Things were no different," he says. "The boys, they were just like the ones I knew at home. Maybe even worse. There were still cliques they excluded me from, sports I couldn't play. They still teased me. They were all obsessed with girls and sex—two things I knew little to nothing about. Except for the ones obsessed with the other boys, there were more than a few there. So I wound up being more alone than I had been. I had no family, no friends, no one."

"So how did you meet Rachel?"

He brightens at her name. "Rachel," he repeats. "She was attending the all-girls school about five miles away. Monthly, the two schools would have socials, dances, get-togethers, carefully monitored, of course. Even though theoretically we were all on our way to seminary, the teachers thought it important that we be exposed to the opposite sex. The thinking was, I guess, that if we had calls to the priesthood, we'd have to know how to interact with women in our parishes, and if we weren't, we'd need to know how to talk to girls to get a wife later."

"Rachel was one of the girls, right?"

"Oh, yes," he says. "I still remember. It was a spring dance or something, Lent was over and it was Easter season, so the girls had decorated their gym in spring colors—you know, yellow and greens. It looked very bright and cheerful when we walked in. The dance was a required activity, so I had no choice but to go even though it was the last thing I wanted to do. So I sat in a chair in a corner while everyone else talked, laughed, and got to know each other."

He pauses, then his expression brightens. "Then I saw her. She was sitting on the other side of the gym, looking as miserable as I felt. She was slumped in the chair and her arms were crossed. She didn't want to be there and didn't want anyone to talk to her. I felt an immediate kinship with her. I must have spent half an hour summoning up the courage to walk across the room to talk to her, but finally that's what I did." He stopped and looked at the picture. "Maybe I shouldn't have. Maybe none of this would have happened."

"What happened next?" I press.

"I walked across the room and sat down next to her. I didn't know what to do next. I had spent so much time focusing on walking up to her, I didn't think about what I'd do once I had done that. So I just sat there like an idiot for a long time. Every so often, I'd turn to face her and open my mouth to say something, but nothing would come out. So I'd stay quiet. Finally, Rachel turned to me and said, 'If you're going to sit there, either say something or go get me a glass of punch.' She startled me, she had spoken so directly. But I got up and got her a glass of punch. After that, we started talking. By the end of the night, we were talking and laughing. It was the best night of my life up to that time."

He sits back in his chair and folds his arms across his chest. With a slight smile, he says, "After that, we'd spend time together at each dance. At some point, the teachers of both schools turned the monthly get-togethers into opportunities to teach ballroom dancing. So they taught us the waltz and other dances, along with manners and etiquette."

"Because you all needed to know how to get on in eighteenth-century Vienna," I quip. Father Leonard stares at me blankly. "Sorry, go on."

"She was my dance partner. We were actually not too bad, although we were both awkward and not in the least athletic. It didn't matter to either of us. I just enjoyed being with her, holding her close, I still remember what her hair smelled like. Neither of us had much experience dating, and we weren't dating."

"That went on for the next couple of years. We'd see each other at least once a month, and when the two schools had group field trips, we'd pair up. We were both still shy. I couldn't even hold her hand in public, only when we danced." He looks at me. "But I was soon in love with her. I didn't know it. But I was." He sighs. "Which just made things complicated."

"You know, Leonard, you weren't a priest yet," I point out. "You could have done some more serious discernment, talked to your spiritual director. Maybe—"

"No, that wasn't an option," he cries, shaking his head vigorously. "I couldn't disappoint my mother that way. I had promised her on her deathbed. No, I was still determined to become a priest. But Rachel, my feelings for her, confused me."

"Tell me about the photo," I say.

"It's exactly what it looks like. It was the last dance, one that honored the graduating seniors. Rachel and I both knew after that night, we wouldn't see each other again. She had another year at her school, and I—I was entering the seminary. Even though she was Catholic, she didn't fully understand. I think she felt the same way about me as I did about her. That night, that last night we spent together, oh, Tom, I've carried that memory with me for years. Just like I've carried that photograph. So I'd remember the last time I was truly happy." He stops and drops his head.

I look at him in silence for a few minutes. Finally, I said quietly, "Then she showed up at Saint Clare's."

His head jerks up, his eyes flashing. "I couldn't believe it when I saw her," he declares. "I mean, I hadn't seen her in so long, and I wasn't sure at first if it really was her, but there she was, sitting in the third row to the right of the altar. I was beginning my homily when I spotted her. I stopped in mid-sentence. I know everyone must have thought I was having a stroke or something. I don't remember the rest of that mass, I don't know how I got through my homily, and I'm not a hundred percent sure to this day that I didn't forget part of the prayers."

"After Mass, I hurried to the front of the church and scanned every face as people filed out, looking for her, not wanting to miss her. Part of me felt like a fool, but most of me was just so excited to see her again. Finally, I saw her. She was standing off beside one of the columns, waiting for the crowd to thin out. After what seemed like an eternity, we were left alone on the portico. We just stood there, looking at each other. Finally, we walked toward each other. We stopped about a foot from each other, neither of us knowing what to say. She spoke first. She said, 'Hi.' That's all she said. We stood there for the next thirty minutes talking. That's when I found out she had moved back to Myerton to take a job, and she was discerning a call to religious life. I told her how wonderful it was to see her, how happy I was about her consideration of a call."

Father Leonard stops and looks at his hands, which he rubs together. "She asked me to have lunch with her. That's brought me back to reality. I couldn't . . . I couldn't find myself in a situation like that. As strong as I felt, I kept thinking about what my mother would say. So I said no, that it was probably best if we just kept our relationship as pastor and parishioner." He takes a deep breath. "That's when it started."

"What started?" I ask.

Father Leonard spreads his hands. "She kept contacting me," he says. "She was there every Sunday, and sometimes during the week. Sitting on the front row, right where I could see her every time. She'd talk to me after mass, each time asking if I wanted to get lunch, dinner, coffee—each time, I said no. At one point, she asked me, 'What are you afraid of, Leonard?'"

"What were you afraid of?"

With plaintive eyes, he says, "Her. My feelings for her. Seeing her awakened inside me the memories of what it was like in high school, the feelings I had for her, that I had suppressed for so long."

"Leonard," I say, "you have a picture of her in your breviary. It doesn't seem to me you were suppressing your feelings."

He shrugs. "It was just a happy memory I didn't want to lose completely. So yes, I'd look at her picture every day. But it was safe. She was gone. I thought I'd never see her again."

"But you knew where she was from," I point out. "Didn't it occur to you when you were assigned here that you might run into her."

"I didn't think about it."

I look at him. I don't believe him.

"But," Father Leonard goes on, "I could take it, as long as I only saw her once or twice a week." He slumps in his chair. "Then we advertised for a parish secretary,"

"And she applied for the job."

"I just about had a stroke when her resume arrived at the Rectory," Leonard exclaims. "I was tempted to throw it away, but Anna had brought it to me, so she would have known. Besides Fern (last name), she was the only other applicant for the job. That's one reason I begged Anna to stay on."

He sits up in his chair. "I decided before the interview not to hire Rachel. The other applicant would be perfectly acceptable, I decided. It was better than the alternative." He sighs. "Then Winthrop Myer paid me a visit. He made it very clear to me that unless I hired Rachel, he would make no more donations to the parish. I know how sizable his donations are."

"He gave you a substantial one that day. What did you tell him?"

"I agreed to give Rachel the job," he says. "I couldn't stand up to him. I didn't want the parish to lose out because of my own weaknesses. It's not like she wasn't qualified."

"No," I admit. "Rachel's business training made her perfect for the position, if overqualified."

"I have to admit, it was great at first, seeing her every day. I tried to keep things professional. But quickly, I let my guard down. We'd work, she'd attend the noon mass, we'd pray the Rosary and Evening Prayer together before she went home. And we'd talk. We'd talk about the past, we'd talk about the Scriptures, about spiritual topics." He inhaled. "We'd discuss her call to religious life."

"Did you try to discourage her?"

He looks at his hands. He's twisting his fingers together quicker now. "Not actively. I don't think so. I don't know now. I think maybe at first, but then I saw how genuine her interest was." He shook his head. "I wasn't about to oppose God's call, no matter how much I may have wanted to."

I lean forward and place my hand on his. "What happened at the Memorial Day picnic?"

He closes his eyes and sighs. "That's when things fell apart. Things were so chaotic, so noisy, with all the children. I needed to get away, go somewhere quiet for a little while. So I walked off from everyone else. Rachel saw me and followed. She found me under a tree. She sat on the grass next to me. We sat quietly for a few minutes, when she turned to me and asked, 'Do you remember how to waltz, Leonard?' The next thing I knew, I was holding her, and we were waltzing. She was humming, we were moving together, and suddenly we were in high school again."

He clenches his eyes shut. "I don't know how it happened, but suddenly I kissed her. Just a quick kiss—we had never kissed before then, and honestly, I'd kissed no one before. She looked shocked, but not as shocked as I was. I began to apologize when she threw her arms around my neck and started kissing me. We stood there, kissing for what seemed like forever. She broke first. We stood there, our arms around each other, just looking into each other's eyes. Then I heard a rustling behind me and Miriam Conway calling my name. We quickly separated, but I could tell she had seen something. She told me it was time to bless the food. We walked back to the rest of the crowd and avoided each other the rest of the afternoon."

Father Leonard sits back in his chair and looks at a point behind me. "That night I was sitting in the rectory when she walked in. I stood, and we just looked at each other. Then . . ." He shook his head. "God help me, Tom, I broke my vows for the first time that night."

I nod. He is confirming what Rachel told me in the confessional. "That wasn't the only time, was it?" I say.

"I tried, Tom, I really tried!" he cries. "I even fired Rachel, told her we couldn't see each other again, but I couldn't stop thinking about her. I couldn't pray. I couldn't sleep."

"What about her call to religious life? What was she saying about that?"

"She was still determined to become a nun. After each time, we'd swear it wouldn't happen again, that we both needed to repent and go to confession, renewing our calls. And we'd do fine. But it happened twice after Memorial Day."

"Weren't you concerned that someone would see you, that they'd find out what was going on?"

He shakes his head. "I didn't care. It was only after the visit that I got worried."

I'm confused. "Visit? Who did you get a visit from?"

"Her brother-in-law."

I stare at him, amazed. "Winthrop Myer paid you a visit."

"He stopped by the Rectory, barged right in. He grabbed me by the shirt and pushed me against the wall. He said if I didn't stay away from Rachel, if I didn't keep my filthy priest hands off of her, he'd beat the crap out of me—he didn't say crap—and he called me all sorts of foul names. He called me a filthy pervert who shouldn't even look at someone as precious as Rachel."

"He must have seen you go into her apartment."

"Apparently, he did. You told me Mrs. Watson had asked him to spy on Rachel, right? He must have seen me go in one night and stay for a long time."

Win Myer had said nothing about visiting Father Leonard at the Rectory to confront him about Rachel.

"Well, after that I was more determined than ever to stay away from Rachel, to renew my commitment to my vow of celibacy, and recommit to my life as a priest." He slumps in his chair. "But so much had happened, and I couldn't stop thinking about her. So I began to think . . . ."

"You were reconsidering your priesthood, weren't you?"

He nods. "Yes. By the time the Archbishop received that letter, I was in turmoil. I was only going through the motions during Mass, during my prayers. I could barely eat or sleep. When the accusations were made, I panicked."

"You denied everything."

"Yes, I denied everything. I rationalized that I wasn't lying, that I never forced her to do anything. She was willing. More than willing." He stops talking and goes back to staring at his hands.

I lean forward and rest my chin on my hands. "Tell me about the day of her murder."

He sighs. "You already know."

"Why don't you tell me in your own words."

He swallows. "Okay, okay. You already know I left the monastery without telling anyone. I needed to get away. Believe it or not, I couldn't think there. I needed to decide once and for all what I was going to do. So I left and drove. I stopped for the night at a cheap motel near Thurmont, tried to get some sleep, but I couldn't. I left there about 9:00 a.m. the next morning and began driving again."

"When did you get her email?"

He shakes his head. "I don't remember exactly. I just remember getting it. I remember reading it. I remember screaming. I was going to lose her again."

"Her email told you she had decided to enter the convent," I say.

"The moment I read her email, I decided." He shuts his eyes tight. I say nothing.

"I decided," he whispers, "I decided that if I couldn't have her and remain a priest, then I could no longer be a priest." Then he was silent. The sentence hung in the air between us.

"You started texting her. You wanted to talk to her," I say.

"I had to tell her what I decided. I was going to ask . . . to ask her to marry me."

"What was your plan?"

"That we'd leave. That we'd just leave, that we'd find someone to marry us, that I'd so broken my vows that there would be no question of my being laicized."

"It's not automatic, you know," I point out. "It wouldn't have happened overnight."

"I didn't care about being a priest anymore," he shouts. "I didn't want to serve God, I didn't want to say Mass. I just wanted to be with her."

I sigh and look at her. "So what happened?"

"You know from the texts. She wouldn't see me at first, saying that she was determined to go away, that she had to go away."

I held up my hand. "Wait, what did she say?"

Father Leonard looks at me. "She said she had to go away."

She had to go away. I remember. That was exactly what she said in the texts. She hadn't mentioned the convent in the texts, only in the emails.

"She didn't mention the convent?" I mutter to myself.

"I became frantic," Father Leonard continues. "I sat in that overlook for hours, trying to get her to call me. Finally, she did."

"You talked to her for twenty minutes according to the call records."

"I had to persuade her not to leave. I told her I had decided that I loved her, that I wanted her to go away with me, to become my wife. She was confused, uncertain, said things were more complicated now, that she had something to tell me, but she wouldn't do it over the phone. She asked me to come to her place." He exhales slowly. "You know the rest."

We sit in silence for a few moments. Finally, I say, "She was going to tell you she was pregnant."

He nods. "I suppose she was. That must have been what she was getting at. That would have just made me more determined, knowing she was carrying my child. I wouldn't have let her leave me, take my child. I would have done anything to make sure that didn't happen."

I sit and think about what he has told me. On the one hand, it answers a lot of questions. About how Rachel became parish secretary in the first place. How their relationship blossomed so quickly into a sexual one. It never made sense to me that Leonard would break his vows with a woman he had known only a couple of months. But now, it makes sense. It was still wrong, but it has logic. Rachel just wasn't a woman; she was the woman Leonard had loved for years, the woman whose photograph he kept tucked in his breviary, the thing a priest keeps closest to him, looks at multiple times a day.

But there are other questions. Rachel was pregnant, so what about her call? Why mention going to the convent in the email but not in her texts? Was it just a shorthand she reverted to in answering Leonard, or was it something more? Was she really going to the convent? Or was she going somewhere else? Did anyone else know? Almost as important, why had Win Myer not mentioned his confrontation with Leonard at the Rectory?

"What should I do?" Leonard finally asks me.

"You know one thing you should do," I say, "need to do. We'll get to that in a minute. The other thing—you need to tell your lawyer. She'll tell you what you need to say to the police."

He nods. "I'll talk to her tomorrow. Can you be here?"

"Yes, I'll make the time." I sit back and look at him. "So are you ready now?" I ask.

He nods. "Yes Father, please."

Smiling, I take my prayer book and the small purple scapular from my pocket. I kiss it and place it over my shoulders. I look at Father Leonard across the table.

I say, "Let us begin this sacrament of God's mercy . . . "

Seventeen

A week later, I'm standing by the graveside of Rachel Watson, watching as they slowly lower her casket in the ground.

Standing with me are the members of her family. Her father stands with his arm around his wife. Mrs. Watson wears a black dress and is standing looking down at the casket. She's been dry-eyed the entire day, sitting stoically through the funeral mass and saying nothing during the graveside service. Mr. Watson stands quietly, every so often wiping a tear away. Rebecca, also in black, stands with her husband, a white handkerchief clasped in her hand, every so often wiping tears from her eyes. Her grief is in stark contrast to her mother's self-control. Win Myer looks desolate, a man bereft but using every ounce of strength to keep from showing it.

I say the final prayers and close my book. The Watsons and Win Myer turn and begin walking away. Rebecca stands by herself near the grave. I walk up to her and stand quietly. She's looking into the hole where her sister now lies. We stand like that for a few minutes.

"She's happy now, right, Father?" Rebecca says finally.

I nod. "Yes, I would say so. So would the Church."

"So she's in Heaven right now?"

I shrug. "Honestly, she's more likely in Purgatory. Most souls spend time in purgatory before entering heaven. The Church teaches that only the purest souls go straight to Heaven after they die."

"And in Purgatory, what is she doing?"

"She's being purified from the sins she committed on this earth, during this life. She's also probably praying for those she left behind. I can imagine she's praying for her killer."

Rebecca looks at me questioningly. "All the resentments and anger, they pale compared to what she's seeing now," I explain. "The souls in Purgatory are happy even though they are not in Heaven yet, because they can see where they are going."

"And Hell?" she asks. "What's there?"

"Eternal separation and punishment."

"Do you really believe that?"

I turn to look at her. "If I didn't believe in it all, I wouldn't be much use to anybody as a priest."

She nods, then walks away. I walk beside her towards the cars. The Watsons and Win Myer are standing by Myer's vehicle, waiting for Rebecca. My car is parked nearby.

"Are you coming to the house? That's where everyone is, for the after-funeral reception."

"I wasn't invited," I say. Looking at Win Myer, whose eyes are fixed on me, I say, "I'm not sure I'll be welcome."

"I'm inviting you. I want you there. Rachel would want you there. And as for Win . . ." She pauses. "As for Win, I'll make sure he's on his best behavior."

"He's taken your sister's death hard," I observe.

"Yes," she says coolly. "He has."

"Were they always close?"

"At one time, in high school. You know they dated before she went away."

"I remember you mentioning that. And then you two started dating?"

"That was mama's idea," she says. "She wanted me to marry Winthrop Myer from the time he first showed any interest."

"Interest in you, after Rachel left?"

She shakes her head. "Oh, no. Interest in her."

I stopped. "I don't understand."

Rachel smiled slightly. "Mama never thought much of Rachel and Win together, opposed them going out. She worked really hard to break them up, not that there was much to break up, really; they only went out a couple of times. That's one reason that they sent Rachel away to school, to get her away from Win."

"Did they see him as a bad influence or something?"

"No, I really don't know. Considering how she worked to push the two of us together, it couldn't be that. I've sometimes thought Mama didn't think Rachel was good enough for Winthrop Myer."

"And you were," I say.

She shrugs slightly. "I suppose. Anyway, Mama put us together and Win went along with it."

"But you two are married, so obviously he loves you."

"Really, Father, you think so?" She shakes her head. "I've always wondered. Win's always been so protective of Rachel, I've wondered . . . " She continues walking to the car.

I stand among the graves, watching her. Jealousy? Was she jealous of her sister, of the way Win felt about her? From Father Leonard's account of Win Myer's little visit to him, her husband had some powerful feelings about his sister-in-law. Was he just protective, like a brother? Or did Rebecca think there was more?

I feel the vibration of my phone in my pocket. It's Helen.

"Am I interrupting anything?" she asks.

"No, just finishing up Rachel Watson's funeral."

"Oh, I forgot that it was today. How did it go?"

"As well as funerals go, I guess. What's up?"

"I thought I'd let you know Brian is presenting Father McCoy's case to the grand jury tomorrow."

"No surprise about that," I say. "He's been wanting to do that since the day of the murder."

"What you need to know, Tom, is that he's asking the grand jury to indict him on first-degree murder."

I'm stunned. "What? On what basis? He believes Leonard went to Rachel's apartment intending to murder her?"

"Yes," she sighs. "I've tried pointing out to him that the evidence doesn't support any kind of planning, that everything points to a crime of passion, but he's got it fixed in his mind. He will argue that Father Leonard saw Rachel as a threat to his priesthood, that he killed her to cover up his behavior. That he knew she was pregnant and was afraid everyone would know what he did."

"It's not known that she was pregnant, is it?"

"No, we've kept that part out of the news so far, but it's only a matter of time before that little detail becomes public knowledge. I didn't even mention it to the family."

"Well, I have said nothing either. But Helen, Leonard claims he didn't know about the baby."

"What can I say, Tom, Brian will tell the grand jury he's lying."

"Does he really think the evidence supports first-degree murder? That he can get the grand jury to indict on that charge?"

"You've heard the cliche, a prosecutor can get a grand jury to indict a ham sandwich? Brian's good. He'll get the indictment, if for no other reason than to force Angela Jenkins into a plea deal."

"But Leonard's innocent, Helen."

"He may not be guilty, Tom, but he's hardly innocent in this. His statement proves that."

"But that's an issue for the Church to deal with," I say. "He broke his vow, perhaps the most serious vow a priest takes. It needs to be dealt with. But it doesn't make him a murderer."

"Perhaps, Tom," she replies.

I'm silent for a moment. "You think he's guilty, don't you?"

I hear her sigh. "Of premeditated murder, no, I really don't. But I think he killed her. All the evidence points to him."

"But there was someone else in the apartment before Leonard got there."

"We found no evidence of anyone in the apartment other than Father Leonard and Rachel."

"Have you even bothered to interview Richard Strump?"

She hesitates.

"You haven't, have you?" I say. "But Leonard said—"

"I know, he talked about a presence, about being suffocated, about passing out, then waking up hours later," she continued. "But I'm telling you, there's nothing to support that story. He made it up. Or is still confused or something. No Tom, what we have doesn't support his story." She pauses. "Besides, there is no one out there with a motive. Father Leonard's the only one. That's what Brian will tell the grand jury."

"Except Richard Strump. I don't understand why you haven't interviewed him."

"Because nothing points to anyone else, Tom!" she shouts into the phone. "I'm sorry, but the only one the evidence points to is Father Leonard McCoy. You may not like it, but that's the truth!"

We tell each other goodbye and I hang up. The Myers and the Watsons have driven off, leaving me alone at the cemetery. I look up the hill to my right and see the large maple tree shading a single headstone from the hot July sun.

Before I go to the Myers', there's a visit I need to make.

***

I arrive at the Myer Estate an hour later. Rebecca Myer greets me at the door.

"Thanks for coming, Father," she says as she closes the door behind me.

"Sorry I took so long, I had a stop to make first."

"Parish emergency?" she asks.

"No, I just had to see someone," I say.

She shows me into the dining room, where the table is spread with a variety of food. Fruit bowls, vegetable platters, a variety of cold cuts, and breads. I grab a plate and make myself a sandwich. I get a glass of water and go to find a quiet place to sit down for a few minutes.

The crowd is conversing quietly in small groups. In one of the armchairs sits Marjorie Watson. Edmund sits next to her on a folding chair. I walk up to the Watsons.

"Can I get you anything?" I ask.

"You've already done enough," Edmund Watson says, standing. He walks away.

"What are you doing here?" Marjorie Watson asks.

"Rebecca was good enough to invite me," I explain.

"Oh," she says. "I see. Well, that's okay, then." She sits back in her chair. Looking me in the eye, she says, "I suppose you're expecting to be paid?"

"Rebecca's handling the details," I say. I indicate the chair her husband vacated. She shrugs indifferently. I sit, balancing the plate on my lap.

"Your daughter's done an outstanding job keeping things together," I say.

"She's a wonderful daughter, a good wife to Win," Marjorie comments with a smile. "Always has been. She and Win are a great match. Best decision she ever made was to marry Winthrop Myer. I mean, just look around," she says, motioning at the surroundings. "She'd never have all of this otherwise."

"She told me that Rachel and Win dated in high school?" I ask, looking at her reaction.

She sits up and looks at me. "She told you that, did she? Well, it's true Win took Rachel out a couple of times, a school dance and one party at the country club. But it was never going to go anywhere."

"Oh, why is that?"

"Because Rachel, well, was Rachel," she says. "She just would never make a wife for Winthrop Myer. Someone else, maybe, but not him."

"Why not? I only met her twice, but Rachel seemed like a very nice, pleasant, intelligent young lady."

"Oh, she was all those things," she says, a slight smile playing on her lips. "But she had her head in the clouds, not an ounce of practicality about her. You know, Father, Win wanted to keep dating her, but Rachel—for reasons I will never understand—she turned him down. I asked her why, and she told me he wasn't what she was looking for." She looked around her. "Can you imagine? Unfortunately, poor Win couldn't let her go. I tried talking to him, but he still had his heart set on Rachel. Eventually, I made my decision."

"What decision was that?"

"To send Rachel away so that Win would forget about her, so he would give Rebecca a chance."

I look at her. So Rebecca's belief was true. The primary reason Rachel went away to high school was to get her away from Winthrop Myer.

"I wanted Win to fall for Rebecca," Marjorie continues. "Rebecca would make a good wife for Win, he just needed to see it. And he did, he did. It took a while, but," she waves her hand again, "he did."

We sit quietly for a moment as a tear falls down her cheek. "Tell me, Father," she whispers. "Did I do something wrong?"

I shake my head. "It's not for me to say. Do you think you did?"

Marjorie sighs. "I didn't think so at the time. For a long time, I convinced myself it was best for everyone. But Rachel came back from school changed. She always had a touch of melancholy about her, but she was sadder. The day of Rebecca's wedding, I found her crying in a closet. She didn't tell me why. I thought she had convinced herself that she'd never find a husband, that she'd be alone forever. Then she got this idea about becoming a nun." She shakes her head.

"How did she seem after that?"

Marjorie thinks for a moment. "She seemed happier, I'd say."

I smile. "That's because she had found someone she'd be with forever."

She looks at me uncomprehendingly. My plate's empty now, so I excuse myself to find a place to put it. I wander back into the dining room and place it on a small table along with others. Walking back to the main room, I pass the open door to Win Myers office. I peek inside.

Myer is sitting behind his desk, his head back, looking up at the ceiling, a drink in his hands. He's whispering something repeatedly. He's not seen me, so I take a step into the doorway and lean forward, straining to hear.

I can barely make it out, but he's repeating one word.

"Rachel. Rachel. Rachel."

Eighteen

The headline in the Myerton Gazette is straight and to the point.

PRIEST INDICTED FOR MURDER

The article states what I already know, that the county grand jury returned an indictment against Father Leonard McCoy, former priest of Saint Clare's Catholic Church in Myerton, for first-degree murder in the death of Rachel Watson. The reporter had called the previous day asking for a statement. I gave her none, having learned my lesson about talking to the press. The Archdiocese had no comment. Angela Jenkins was quoted in the paper, saying, "My client is being railroaded by an ambitious prosecutor who cares more about satisfying the wealthy and privileged than justice." The paper quotes Brian Dohrmann saying, "The grand jury heard the evidence, and I'm looking forward to getting justice for Rachel Watson."

I put the paper down when Anna places the plate containing a cheese omelet, bacon, and buttered wheat toast in front of me. She sets a jar of strawberry preserves on the table, then sits down with her coffee.

"I guess what they say about prosecutors is true," I comment.

"That they can get a grand jury to indict a ham sandwich? If Brian Dohrmann can persuade a grand jury that Father Leonard McCoy is a cold-blooded killer, then I hope I'm never ticketed for jaywalking. He'll give me the chair," Anna says as she drinks her coffee. "Well, what are you going to do about this?"

"I'll pray for him and the situation, but I know of nothing else I can do."

"Do you think he's guilty?"

I pick up a triangle of toast and slather on a spoonful of the strawberry preserves. I take a bite and chew while I consider her question.

"Well?" she presses.

I swallow. "I've tried to decide if I believe he's guilty. And I'll tell you, Anna, despite all the evidence, I still don't think he did it." I sigh. "But if I were on that jury and knew nothing else about him except what the State Attorney was telling me, the evidence he was showing me, I'd think he was guilty. Not first-degree murder, but that he was guilty of something."

"But he's not done anything he's been accused of, right?"

At my hesitation, Anna says, "Unless he is guilty of something. What?"

Since it was all going to come out soon anyway, I saw no reason not to tell her. So I told her what I could. About Father Leonard and Rachel, about their relationship, and about Rachel's pregnancy. As I tell the story, Anna looks more and more shocked and surprised.

"So that's everything, and I'd appreciate it if you keep it to yourself. It's going to all come out soon enough, but I'd like it to stay quiet for a while."

She nods and drinks her coffee. Anna sits quietly, looking out the window, processing the story I just told her.

"It doesn't add up to murder," she says. "If he loved her—and from what you've told me he did—he'd have no reason to kill her."

"According to Helen, the State Attorney is working on the theory that he used her, that she confronted him with the baby and demanded he take care of her, and he killed her to cover up evidence of his sin. So as not to damage his priesthood."

"Brian Dohrmann is an idiot," she says. "And to think I was going to vote for him. I must look at Father Leonard's lawyer more closely."

"I don't think he's an idiot," I say. "I think he wants a conviction so he can present it to the voters. You know, not afraid to stand up to a powerful institution like the Catholic Church."

"But afraid to say no to Winthrop Myer," she says, standing up and taking my plate and her cup to the sink.

Winthrop Myer. I think about him, sitting in his office at the house the day of Rachel Watson's funeral. Alone, in the dark, with a drink. Repeating her name over and over again. I remember Father Leonard's account of his meeting with Win Myer, how the man roughed the young priest up. I remember what Rebecca said about Win and Rachel dating in school, and what Marjorie Watson said about why she sent Rachel away.

For such an unassuming person, Rachel Watson had been the center of so many machinations, so many emotions, when she was alive. She was the one her mother wanted out of the way; she was the one who lost out to her sister; she was the one who had a brother-in-law with a deep interest in her; she was the one who led a young priest to break his vows and give up his calling. And, in death, she was the one who that same priest was accused of murdering.

The murder is connected to the relationships she had, as most murders are. I just don't know how.

"What are you going to do?" Anna says.

"Again, Anna, I don't know there's anything I can do."

As I say that, I think about Father Leonard's story of that night, the story the police discounted, about there being a presence in Rachel's apartment, about being suffocated and passing out, and waking up next to her dead body, his shirt covered in blood. The story the authorities discounted as a lie.

But the police had found no evidence of another person. The only evidence they found pointed to Father Leonard as being the only one at the apartment.

There was no forced entry, so Rachel was expecting someone. She let in the person who killed her. It was someone she knew. Father Leonard fell in that category. But so did several other people. Her sister, her mother, her brother-in-law, her father. But no one had said anything about being in her apartment that day. Had anyone seen anyone other than Leonard enter her apartment?

But why kill Rachel Watson at all? Who benefited?

There is only one person who benefited from her death. And he is sitting in jail at that moment.

I shake my head. There are so many questions about this murder, but the one thing I keep running into is that the person least likely to have committed this murder is the one who benefited the most.

Except he isn't the only one who had a motive. There was one other person, someone Helen hasn't bothered to interview. Richard Strump.

Something else bothers me. The day of her murder, Rachel Watson had sent Leonard, her sister, and her brother-in-law emails saying she had decided to go ahead and enter the convent. But she knew she was pregnant and couldn't enter the convent. Her bags were packed, so she was going somewhere. Leonard had told her he wanted them to run away together, so she was ready to go. But she was leaving Myerton before they even talked.

"So where was she going?" I say.

"What?" Anna says, startled.

"Sorry, I was just thinking out loud."

Had Rachel said anything to the Mother Superior at the convent? Had anyone asked her?

"Didn't you say Nate Rodriguez has that vlog now?"

"What? Yes, why?"

"I think I'll call him." To her quizzical look, I say. "There are just too many questions. I need to find some answers. Maybe Nate can help."

***

Nate must have broken the land-speed record getting to the Rectory, arriving about half an hour after I called him.

"I'm glad you called," he says as he quickly sets his recording equipment up. "I want to do a podcast on Father Leonard, but wanted to wait until after the trial. Then you called, and well, here I am."

"Thanks for coming so quickly, Nate." I pause and look at him as he finishes setting the microphones up to record. "We need to talk first."

"Sure, sure, okay," he says, sitting in a chair across from my desk, perched on the edge, expectantly.

"I don't believe Father Leonard is guilty," I say. "I have no evidence, but there are a lot of holes in the state's case. I need your help to look into this."

"Just call me Watson," he says with a grin, bouncing up and down in the chair like an excited toddler.

"We need to keep this quiet. We don't want to step on any toes."

His smile slowly fades. "So no interview."

"No interview, not yet. I need you to use your journalism skills to look into some things."

He sighs. "Okay, I'll be glad to help."

I take a sticky note and a pen. As I write, I say, "Rachel had a problem with one of her former co-workers harassing and stalking her. His name's Richard Strump. I need you to look into him." I hand him the sticky note.

"Richard Strump," he says. "You say he used to work with Rachel?"

"Apparently, he was arrested outside her townhouse back in February. He was fired a few weeks later for that and, apparently, harassing other women on the job."

"I can get a copy of the arrest report—they are public record," he says. "I'll find out where he lives."

"See if you can talk to him. And be careful."

Nate grins. "You know me, Father."

Yes, that's what worries me, I think.

"I also think you should interview Rachel Watson's neighbors, ask them if they saw or heard anything that night."

"Don't you think the police already questioned them?"

"Oh, I'm sure they did. But maybe they've remembered something since then."

"Okay, what else?"

"That's all for now, Nate," I say.

He nods. "I'll get right on it." He smiles sheepishly. "You know Father Tom, since I'm here, and I set everything up..."

I return the smile, but shake my head. "No, Nate, not now. If you'll excuse me." I stand and leave my office. I find Anna in the parish secretary's office, reorganizing the filing system.

"Anna," I say. "I have nothing on my schedule this afternoon after the Noon mass, do I?"

She stops and looks at the calendar on her desk. "No, you're clear all afternoon."

I nod. "Good. I've got a little trip out of town to make. I'll be back later tonight, so don't bother with dinner. I'll get something on the road."

"Where are you going?" she asks as I walk out of her office.

"To find out where Rachel Watson was going."

Nineteen

The young nun shows me into the small room. It's simply appointed, a couple of pictures of saints and the current pope on the wall, a statue of Our Lady in the corner. Two armchairs are in the center of the room, across from each other. The convent is semi-cloistered, so they allow visitors on a limited basis. I will not have to speak to the Mother Superior through a grill, but in this room set aside for the reception of visitors.

"Have a seat, Father," she says. "I'll go fetch Mother Evangeline."

I sit in one chair and look around for a few minutes. After only a short time, the door opens and the young nun returns, this time accompanied by an older nun clad in the traditional habit. She's physically imposing, about my height. I can tell nothing about her hair color, covered as it is. Her face is firm, but not intimidating. Her eyes are clear and focused, but soft and kind. She gives the impression of someone who has a great responsibility, but also one who is capable of great compassion.

"Bring us some lemonade, Sister, if you would please," she says to the young sister. She gives a slight bow and leaves the room. Mother Evangeline smiles as she approaches me.

"Father Greer," she says, inclining her head. "It is a pleasure to meet you."

"Thank you for meeting me on such short notice," I say. Mother Evangeline moves to her chair and sits. I resume my position across from her.

"I am still saddened by the news," she says. "The convent will pray the office of the dead for her soul. So sad, so tragic. And you say a young priest stands accused of her murder?"

"He's been arrested and indicted for the crime," I say. "I do not believe he did it."

"In my experience," she says grimly, "anyone is capable of anything, given sufficient motivation."

I consider what she says. "What can you tell me about Rachel Watson?"

She folds her hands and sits back in the chair. "I met Rachel a few years ago. She was working at a firm in Baltimore and came here for a women's retreat weekend. At the end of the weekend, she asked to speak to me. She said she had received a call from God that weekend to enter the religious life."

"What was your reaction?"

"I was pleased but wary." At my glance, she explains, "More young women than you would imagine come here for a weekend, find the experience attractive, and decide they're being called to this life. It's so different from the one they're living in the world. Most are in careers, have boyfriends, the like. Here, we are apart from the world. It attracts many who are tired, tired of what they experience out there. But it's fleeting. Many come, but few stay."

"What did you tell her?"

"I explained that we could lead her through discernment, but it was a long process before she could enter the convent as a postulant. There would be opportunities for discernment weekends, for spiritual direction, and I would have to work with her parish priest. She was attending a parish in Baltimore, so I got in touch with the priest. We went on from there." She stops and looks up as the young nun places a tray with a pitcher of lemonade and two glasses on the table between us, then watches as she leaves and closes the door.

She pours two glasses and takes one. "She attended each discernment weekend—we have them once a quarter—and she was the only one who did so consistently." She smiles. "I took that as a good sign, that she really had a call, that she was serious about discernment." She takes a sip and smacks her lips. "So good, so good," she mutters.

"Did she tell you she had decided to join?"

She shook her head. "No, as serious as she was, she kept putting off the decision. Then she moved back to her hometown. I took that as a sign she was getting things ready to make a move. She attended the Advent retreat here and told me she needed to get some things in order but she would get in touch after the first of the year about entering in the spring." She sat back. "But winter and spring came and went, and I heard nothing else from her."

"What did you think?"

"That she had changed her mind, like so many young women. I thought it most likely that she had met a young man and decided that she was called to the vocation of marriage instead of the religious life."

I think about what she says. That corresponds with her reuniting with Father Leonard and becoming the parish secretary.

"Then," she says, putting the now empty glass on the table, "one day, she called. She apologized for not getting in touch sooner, but explained that she had a crisis of faith, a reason to doubt her vocation. She assured me she was ready to enter the postulancy as soon as she settled her affairs at home." She looks at her hands. "There was something about her voice, her tone, which told me that her decision was a hasty one."

"What do you mean?" I ask.

"Father Tom, when you've been here as long as I have, you can tell just from talking to a young woman why she's contemplating this life. For some, a smaller percentage than I'd like, it's a genuine desire to follow God, to spend the rest of their lives in prayer and service. For most, they see it as an escape, a way of avoiding the pain in their own lives instead of dealing with it in the world head-on. It's not a bad motivation, mind you, but it's not the best." She sighs. "What part is a genuine call from God, and what part is avoidance, only the Lord knows."

The Mother Superior's words resonate with me. So much of what she says is familiar to me, to my circumstances, to the reasons I became a priest. I've struggled with the same question. Was I called? Or was I just avoiding pain? Was I doing that now?

"And Rachel?"

"Rachel, I sensed it was more the latter. I supposed there had been a nasty breakup with a young man; that was the usual reason."

"What are some other reasons you've seen?"

"Oh, there's a variety," she says with a smile. "Believe it or not, often it's a way to rebel against parents. It's funny, when I first entered the convent, so many young women rebelled by leaving the religious life and the Church of their childhood altogether. Now it's like they see the best way of rebelling against their parents is by embracing this life, and the stricter the life, the better. Ironic, isn't it? But then the Church has always been unfashionable and rebellious."

A desire to rebel. Against her parents, especially her mother, who had done so much to control her life. Was that the primary reason Rachel wanted to become a nun?

"When was this conversation?"

She looks to her side, as if trying to remember. "Let's see, I think it was just after Memorial Day."

Now it made sense. Memorial Day. The day of the picnic, and the beginning of everything.

"I thought everything was settled, or at least we began to prepare for her. I didn't hear from her again until two weeks before her death."

"She called you again?"

"Oh no, Father," she shakes her head. "She showed up here unannounced."

I lean forward. "Really? What happened?"

"It was just after Vespers when someone started ringing the doorbell. Not just once, but repeatedly. One sister went to answer and Rachel rushed in. She was hysterical, frankly sobbing, begging to see me. I'm surprised she had made it all the way here from Myerton without having an accident. I didn't see how she could have driven herself in that circumstance."

She stops and pours herself another glass of lemonade. I beg off when she offers me the pitcher. She sits back with her glass, tracing the rim with her finger.

"We finally got her calmed down," the Mother Superior continues, "gave her a good stiff brandy—we keep it for medicinal purposes, Father," she explains at my look of surprise. "After the brandy and some time, she could speak to me about why she was there. Since she had no suitcase, I knew it wasn't to stay."

"What did she tell you?" I ask, but already know the answer.

"Everything that you already know," she replies with a smile. "That she had begun a sexual relationship with the priest at Saint Clare's and had found out she was pregnant."

She put her glass down. "That changed everything. She couldn't enter the postulancy in that condition; as wonderful as children are, it's just not what we're equipped for. She knew that, said she still wanted to enter after the baby was born, and explained that she was planning on placing the child for adoption." She pauses. "I asked her if she had told the father. She said she hadn't, that she had no intention of doing so. That she was making plans to leave, take a job somewhere and have the baby quietly, then come back here and enter the postulancy. I had another suggestion."

"Which was?"

"Our order has a home for young unwed mothers in Virginia," she says. "It's one of the few in the country, though more are opening every year. I told her I could get her a place there, she could be cared for and the baby born there, and we would help coordinate the adoption. It would take a couple of weeks to arrange. She agreed to that. After we prayed together, I sent her on her way. She seemed more at peace."

"What did you say to her about telling Father McCoy?"

She gets a grim expression on her face. "I firmly advised her to tell the young man, that he had a right to know, if for no other reason than to understand the seriousness of his sin. But she was adamant that he not know; she said it would destroy him, that he was too good a priest to do that to." She shakes her head. "Though I have serious doubts about his goodness."

"It is a complicated situation," I say. "Father McCoy is a good man who made a serious mistake. But it wasn't done in haste. It was a culmination."

"Oh? In what way?"

I explain about their prior relationship, about Father Leonard's continued love for Rachel through the years of seminary and his early priesthood. She nods.

"I see. I did not know that." She sighs. "Attachments of the heart are the hardest to give up when you enter this life." A wistful expression passes over her face. "Yes, very hard," she whispers.

"As it turns out, it wasn't necessary," she says. "So sad, such a loss."

"I'm not sure what you mean?"

She looks at me. "The miscarriage. She called me a few days before her murder and told me she had lost the baby, and that after she recovered, she'd be at the convent to begin her postulancy."

I'm stunned. Before I can say anything, the convent bell tolls. The mother superior looks up. "Ah, that would be None," she says as she stands. I look at the time. It is just before 3:00 p.m.

"Would you care to join us before you leave, Father?"

I nod. "Yes, I would be happy to."

I follow Mother Superior from the room. My mind reels from what she just told me. A miscarriage? That was impossible. She was still pregnant at the time of her death; the autopsy showed that.

As I walk with Mother Superior to the chapel, a thought occurs to me, one that causes my blood to run cold.

"No," I whisper. "Not that."

"Excuse me, Father," Mother Superior asks.

"Sorry, I have one more question," I say quickly. She stops and turns. "You said she seemed like she was in no condition to drive. Did anyone see her leave?"

"I'd have to ask the sister who showed her out—oh, wait, here she is. Sister Dymphna," she stops a middle-aged nun. "You were with Rachel Watson when she left after her visit a couple of weeks ago, correct?"

"Yes, Mother Superior," she answers quietly.

"Did you see her walk to her car?"

"Yes. It was late at night and there's not a lot of light outside."

"Was anyone in the car with her?" I ask.

She looks at me, then the Mother Superior. The older woman nods, then the nun answers, "It was dark so I couldn't see very well." She stops to think, "Wait, that's odd."

"What sister?" Mother Superior asks.

"When Rachel got in the car, she got in on the passenger side."

"The passenger side, not the driver's side? Are you sure?" I ask.

She thinks for a moment, then nods her head. "Yes, quite sure. She got in her car on the passenger side."

***

I'm on my way back to Myerton, processing what I learned at the convent, when my phone rings. It's Nate.

"Hello?" I say.

"Father Tom," he whispers. "I found something. You need to come quick."

"Where are you? Why are you whispering?"

"Where am I? I'm outside Strump's house. You need to get here. I think I found out who killed Rachel Watson."

"I'll be there as soon as I can," I say before hanging up. I press the accelerator and look at the needle on my speedometer going past 75.

Twenty

"There was no one home," Nate whispers, "so I talked to his neighbors. That's when I found out."

We're sitting in his car, a mid-1990s Honda that has seen better days. The upholstery is worn, the paint has faded, and one of the back doors is held closed by a length of rope. Across the street is a small brick bungalow with a chain-link fence.

"You keep saying that," I say. "What did you find out?"

"His next-door neighbor," he points to a similar brick bungalow, "told me Strump is really quiet, doesn't talk to many people. Never had a problem until the other day."

"What happened the other day?"

"The fire."

I sigh. "What fire?"

"The one in the barrel in his backyard," Nate says. "He set it and then left. The neighbor was worried the fire would get out of control—you know we haven't had a lot of rain, and it's been hot, things are dry—so he doused the flames with his garden hose."

I shake my head. "Lots of people have burn barrels. It's not unusual."

"The neighbor said it was," Nate replies. "He'd never seen Strump do it before. So I got curious. What was he burning? So I looked."

"You went in his backyard? That's trespassing, Nate."

"But I found something. Come see it."

I look in his earnest and excited eyes. Then I look across the street. "Okay," I say against my better judgement. "But we need to do it quickly, before he comes back."

"He's been gone for hours," Nate says. "He must be out of town."

We sneak across the street and slowly open the gate. It squeaks on the rusting hinges. We pause and listen. Hearing no one, we walk into Strump's yard.

"It's around this way," Nate whispers. He pulls out his phone and uses the flashlight to illuminate our path. I follow him as we tip-toe through the grass around to the back of the house.

"There," he shows with his light. About twenty yards from the house is a metal barrel.

We walk to it and Nate shines his light inside.

"See? See?" he whispers excitedly.

I roll my eyes. "Nate, really? This is what you called me for?"

"What?" he says.

I shake my head and look down. The barrel is filled with porn magazines.

"You don't think this means something?"

"All this means," I whisper, "is that he was trying to get rid of his porn collection."

"But who pays money for porn magazines anymore when you can get it for free online?" Nate responds. I look at him. "Not that I would know, Father, I mean I've heard, not that I—"

"Calm down, Nate," I say, holding my hand up to stop him. I look down again and sigh. Then something catches my eye.

"Get me a stick or something," I whisper to Nate. Nate goes off and returns with a short garden trowel.

"Here," he says. "It's the only thing I could find."

"Shine your light right here," I say. With the trowel, I gently lift the charred magazine on top.

"Let me see your light," I say to Nate. Taking his light, I look at what's underneath. It's a photograph, printed out on photo paper from a color printer. The fire has singed the edges, and the water-stained part of the image, but I have no trouble making out who it is.

It's a photograph of Rachel Watson, outside of her apartment.

"Police, don't move!" Nate and I look at each other. A neighbor must have seen us and called the police.

"Raise your hands and turn, slowly," says the authoritative voice. We turn into the glare of flashlights. Squinting, I make out a figure pointing the light with one hand and a gun with another. Standing next to the one figure is another figure, also pointing a gun at us.

"We're not armed," I say.

"Father Tom?" My panic subsides as I recognize the voice.

"It's me, Dan," I say.

"Father Tom," Dan Conway says. "It's okay, Casey, I know him." Both officers holster their weapons and walk forward.

"We had a report of prowlers," Dan explains. "What are you two—hello Nate, how's your Uncle?—doing back here."

"Looking for evidence," Nate blurts.

"What?"

"He's right, Dan. We found something Detective Parr needs to see," I say, pointing at the barrel.

Dan shines his flashlight into the barrel. He whistles, then says, "Casey, get Detective Parr. Tell her she needs to get here ASAP with a crime scene team."

***

"Trespassing, Tom!" Helen shouts, three feet from me. Her fury flows over me like a hot wind from a raging wildfire. I did not expect her to be so angry. I thought when she arrived outside Strump's house that she'd take one look at what Nate and I found and she'd be—well, maybe not pleased, maybe not grateful, but certainly not furious.

But I took one look when she got out of her car and knew I was in for it. The resounding slam of her car door put the exclamation point on that.

"Trespassing," she repeats, "if not harassment."

Nate says, "He asked me to do it, Detective! It wasn't my idea!"

"You be quiet," she points to Nate. "I'm yelling at him now. I'll get to you." She turns back to me and opens her mouth to continue.

"Listen, Helen," I say, "I asked for Nate's help to look into Strump, to see if we could find anything that might tie him to Rachel's murder. Which we did. Aren't you even going to look?"

"And have a charge of an illegal search? No way, Tom. I already told you—"

"I know what you told me!" I shout. "I'm trying to help a good man who made a serious mistake avoid being tried for a crime he didn't commit! If you had been doing your job in the first place, interviewing Strump, instead of kowtowing to your ex-boyfriend, I wouldn't be standing here right now!"

She's staring at me, her mouth open, a fire growing in her eyes. I know I've gone too far, but I can't stop.

"Do you think I wanted to do this? Do you think I enjoy playing detective? Believe it or not, I don't! Not one little bit! I just want a quiet life, serving God's people as a priest, like every other man who wears the collar!" I take a deep breath. "But if justice demands I sneak around in the dark like Jessica Fletcher in a cassock, then I'll do it!"

I stop talking. I'm suddenly aware that the eyes of the other officers are on us. Helen's eyes have lost their fire, replaced by astonishment. I cannot remember a time in our past when I ever spoke to her this way.

"You're not wearing a cassock, Father," Nate mutters to me.

"Shut up, Nate!" Helen and I say in unison. We are staring at each other, like two opponents across a dueling field, each waiting for the other one to fire first.

Dan slinks up to us. "Excuse me, Detective Parr?"

"What is it, Officer Conway!" Helen snaps.

"Um, I think the owner of the house just got here."

Helen and I look at Dan, who is pointing past us. We turn to see an unassuming, rather portly man with thinning black hair, walking up the sidewalk from where he parked his green sedan.

"Officers," he says when he gets to us. He regards Nate and I with confusion.

"Richard Strump?" Helen asks.

"Yes," he says. He's fidgeting with his keys, shifting from one foot to another. "Is there a problem?"

"We found out what you were burning in your backyard," Nate blurts out.

"What?" he says, with panic in his voice. "What—what were you doing in my backyard?"

"Be quiet, Nate!" I hiss.

"These Officers found Father Greer and Mr. Rodriguez in your backyard," Helen explains. "Do you want to press charges for trespassing?"

"Press charge—no, no, that's okay. It's fine. No charges. Thank you." He moves to open his gate.

"One moment, Mr. Strump," Helen says. "Do you mind if I ask you a couple of questions?"

"Questions?" he asks nervously. "What questions?"

"Did you kill Rachel Watson?" Nate asks.

I grab Nate by the arm. "Come on, Nate, let's go!" I step towards my car when I hear Dan yell, "Hey! Hey!" I turn to see that Strump is running down the sidewalk. Not so much running, more plodding like an overweight Ewok. Dan takes off after him and has no trouble catching him. He brings Strump back to us.

"Do you want me to take him in?" Dan asks Helen.

"Why did you run, Mr. Strump?" Helen demands.

The portly man is wheezing. "I—I—whew, shouldn't have done that. I'm sorry." Strump bends over and grabs his knees. "Let me catch my breath."

"Why did you run?"

He looks up at Helen. "Why? I panicked."

"Obviously." She crosses her arms and looks down at the little man. "Would you care to tell me why?"

He stands up and sighs. "We better go inside." Strump looks at me. "Can the Father come?"

Helen looks at me. "If you'd like."

Helen, Strump, and I walk through the gate, leaving Nate and the other officers on the sidewalk. Stump unlocks the door and shows us inside.

"Pardon the mess," he says as we walk into the living room. It's only marginally cleaner than Helen's apartment. We find places to sit.

"After I heard about Rachel Watson," he begins, "I was expecting a visit."

"Why is that, Mr. Strump?"

"Because of my arrest," he says, looking at his hands. "Because of my stalking Rachel."

Helen reaches in her bag and pulls out her notebook and a pen. "That was back in February?"

He nods. "February 24," he whispers. "I'll always remember that date."

"Why is that, Mr. Strump?" I ask. I expect a non-verbal rebuke from Helen, but one does not come.

Strump looks down. "Because that's when I hit rock bottom," he whispers.

"You were fired from your job soon afterward," Helen continues, "because of your arrest?"

"That—and the other things," he says, still not looking at us. "There were several women at work that I—well, I mistreated them. I did things. Shameful things."

"Did you stalk them too, Richard?"

He nods. "But that was the only time I got caught."

"I bet that made you angry," Helen says. Strump looks up. "At Rachel. I mean, she had you arrested. She was responsible for you losing your job. That would have made anyone angry."

"I won't lie to you, Detective, Father, I was. Very angry. At her, at myself. For a couple of months, I didn't even leave the house. I did nothing to find another job." He exhales. "Then one day, I woke up and looked at my life. And faced the truth about myself. That's when the anger just vanished."

"What happened?" I ask.

"I admitted to myself that I had a problem," he says. "With women. With sex." He looks at his hands. "With porn."

"Ah," I say. "That's what you were burning."

"Yes," he responds. "I had gotten rid of my cable and had a friend put a blocker on my internet—he's the only one who has the password and gets a report every day about my internet usage—but I still had my collection of magazines." He swallows. "And the photographs I took."

"Photographs of Rachel," Helen says.

"Yes, Rachel, and other women. Mostly clothed. Some not." He pauses again, wipes a tear away.

"This is all very interesting, Mr. Strump," Helen says. "But I have to ask, where were you the night of Rachel Watson's murder?"

He puts his hand in his shirt pocket, takes a small disk out and tosses it on the coffee table in front of us.

I pick it up. "It's a sobriety chip," I say.

Strump nods. "Sex Addicts Anonymous. I got that Sunday. Three months of sexual sobriety." He looks at Helen. "The night of Rachel Watson's murder, Detective, I was at a meeting. I have about two dozen people who can tell you I was there from about 6:00 to 9:00 that night."

Twenty-One

"Are you satisfied now?"

We're standing at the end of the walkway leading to Strump's house. I look back at where we just left.

"You will check on his alibi, right?"

Helen puts her hands on her hips. "Of course I will, Tom. I mean, unless you'd like to do it for me? Hey, I have an idea, you do that and I'll say Mass this Sunday. How does that sound?"

"Listen, Helen, I—"

"No, you listen, Tom." She points her finger at me. "You have got to stop playing detective. One of these days, you will get hurt. You almost did last time."

"All I was doing—"

"I know what you were doing," she says. Her expression softens. "I know you were only trying to help Father Leonard, to find someone else—anyone else—who killed Rachel Watson." She touches my arm. "You need to face the fact that he did it."

I shake my head. "No, Helen, I can't believe that. He's not capable of murder. He loved her."

"People kill people they love all the time."

"He couldn't have done it."

"The evidence says otherwise."

"The evidence is wrong."

She sighs. "No, it's not, Tom," she says quietly. "The evidence points to him. It's the simplest explanation. Occam's Razor, remember? You taught me about that years ago."

I look at her.

"Anyway, just leave the detective work to me from now on, okay? I'm not always going to be there to get you out of a jam."

***

"Father Tom," Rebecca Myer says, "what a surprise."

It's the next afternoon. "I hope I'm not coming at an inconvenient time," I say as I step into the foyer of the Myer home. "And I apologize for not calling first, but I was out on my sick calls and was passing when I thought I'd stop in and see how you were doing."

She closes the door and stands with her arms crossed. "Fine, I suppose," she says. "It's still hard to believe, even though it's been, what, two weeks? It seems like only yesterday we got a visit from the police telling us that Rachel . . ." She trails off as tears well up. I hand her my handkerchief.

"Thank you," she says as she dabs her eyes. "Sorry about this."

"Not at all," I say.

"Grief is so strange, so unpredictable. I'll be going along with my day, and suddenly I'll see something small, or hear a snippet of music, and it all comes rushing back. Do you understand what I mean, Father?"

I nod. I'm intimately familiar with grief.

"Anyway, come in and sit down. Can I get you something?"

"No, I'm fine," I say as we enter the sitting room. Taking one of the armchairs, she perches on the edge of the sofa near me. "Is your husband home?"

"No, he's out of town on business for a couple of days. Continued problems with the wind farm project."

"And how is he doing?"

She sits back and looks out the window. "He thought a lot of Rachel," she says carefully, "cared about her a great deal. He's taken it hard. Harder than I remember him taking his parent's death."

I look at Rebecca. She is carefully choosing her words, and her voice is even. Her face betrays irritation.

"I must tell you, Rebecca, that I have a reason for coming here besides checking on you."

She smiles. "The whole 'just passing by' didn't seem likely, considering how far from a major road we are."

I return the smile. "I have a question."

"I hope I can answer. What is it, Father?"

I look her in the eye. "Did you drive Rachel to the convent one night about two weeks ago?"

Her smile disappears. She gets up from the couch and moves to the window. She stares out, not answering.

"You did, didn't you?"

She nods. "She was hysterical. I couldn't let her drive herself."

"Did she tell you why?"

"You mean, did she tell me she was pregnant with Father Leonard's child?" she says, spinning around. "Yes, yes, she told me. She told me everything that afternoon."

She paces. "She showed up unannounced, crying. Win was here, and knowing how he is about her, I took her through the house as quickly as I could to the back porch. I got her calmed down enough to tell me. She hadn't been feeling well for a couple of weeks, and her period was late. She went to the doctor, not having the courage to try a home pregnancy test, apparently. She got the news there. From what she told me, she ran out of the office as soon as the doctor said the words." She stopped and looked at Father Tom. "I was furious when she told me, not at her, but at him. I thought everything you hear about priests preying on members of their parish was true. That's what I was angry about."

"But she told you the story, didn't she?"

She gave a short laugh. "Oh, yes, as soon as I called him a bastard, she told me everything. About how they had met years earlier, but nothing happened. How she started attending Saint Clare's and was stunned to see him come in to do the service. About how they reconnected, how she took the parish secretary's job just to be near him." She paused. "She even told me about their first time." She shook her head and sat down. "I would have thought as educated as she was, she would have taken precautions, but I don't think it was something they planned."

"No, not from what I understand," I say.

Rebecca shoots me a glance. "I take it Father Leonard told you his side of the story."

I look at her, not indicating anything. "Oh, you can't tell me, can you," she says. Putting up her hands, she says, "Okay, I understand." She sits back on the couch.

"Why did she want to go to the convent that night?"

Rebecca shrugs. "I'm not sure. She just said she needed to go somewhere, that she'd be back the next day, probably. I could see she was in no condition to drive herself—I'm surprised she made it here from the doctor's office—and I knew Win had a meeting at the country club that evening so he wouldn't miss me. So I told him that Rachel and I were going out that evening and we'd be back later, then I drove her in my car. I didn't even know where we were going. I thought, honestly, she wanted me to take her to a clinic, you know . . . to take care of the problem." She looks down at her hands. "I'm ashamed for thinking that, but it crossed my mind."

"Did you suggest the possibility to her?"

"Oh, no," she shakes her head. "We had had more than one discussion about that, and I knew what her position was. I should have known that wouldn't be a possibility, but given the circumstances, I thought she might have decided to just get rid of the child."

"So I was a little surprised when we stopped at the convent. I had never been there before. She asked me to wait for her in the car while she went to talk to somebody. She practically ran to the front door, rang the bell several times before someone let her in. She was in there about an hour before she came out. I have to tell you, Father. The change was astounding. She was . . . calm, at peace, even happy."

"She told you what she and the Mother Superior had discussed."

"It seemed like an ideal solution. Go off to have the baby, put it up for adoption, then return and enter the convent—that frankly, I still didn't understand, but she was my sister and I loved her, still love her." A tear runs down her cheek. "So we drove back here, she got in her car, and went home."

"Did you tell anybody?"

"Absolutely not!" she exclaims. "Not Mama, not Win. She swore me to secrecy. We hatched a plan. It would take her a couple of weeks to get things arranged, but I would drive her to the maternity home when all the arrangements were made, under the guise of my going to a spa for a few days." She paused. "I was supposed to pick her up Monday morning."

"And the email about her entering the convent she sent you and Win?"

She smiles. "Clever, eh? That was the cover story. It would tamp down questions. And it was true, in a way. The maternity home is run by the order she's entering, and she would enter the convent after the baby was born."

I sit back and think about what she just said. "She called Mother Superior a couple of days before her death and told her she had miscarried. That was a lie. What was she going to do, Rebecca?"

Slowly, she says, "She called me on Wednesday, the Wednesday before her murder. She told me she had changed her mind about having the baby, that she didn't want to go through all that only to give the baby up. That she had to enter the convent as quickly as possible." She hesitates before saying. "She had made an appointment at a clinic in Hagerstown for Monday afternoon."

I close my eyes. To deal with the consequences of one sin, she decided to commit another. Something that happened too often.

"Did she tell you why she decided to have an abortion?" I ask.

Rebecca shakes her head. "No, and I didn't ask. I figured it was her decision. She was old enough, you know. So we made a slight change to our plans. I'd pick her up Monday morning, drive her to Hagerstown, she'd have the abortion, then we'd check in to a hotel for her to rest for a couple of days. Then I'd take her to the convent." She sniffles. "That's the last time I heard from her."

We sit in silence in the room. I hear movement behind me. "I thought I heard voices," Win Myer says jovially. "Rebecca, who—oh! What is he doing here?"

I stand and turn around, smiling. Win Myer is not.

"Hello, Win," I say. "I just came to—"

"He came to see how we were doing," Rebecca interjects. "Isn't that nice of Father Tom? I didn't expect you back so soon. How was your trip?"

"How are we doing? A damn sight better now that that monster will be when he gets what he deserves," he says, ignoring Rebecca's question. "I can't even believe you'd have the gall to show up here."

"I came," I say, my smile disappearing, "to see how you two were doing. Rachel was Rebecca's sister, and from what I understand, you cared deeply about her. Her death has been hard for both of you."

"What would you know about that?" he spits. "How would you possibly know about the pain of losing someone so precious, someone you cherished, someone—what Rebecca?"

I turn to see Rebecca shaking her head and motioning slightly at me. She must have heard my story.

"Win, stop," Rebecca says. "Father Tom—"

"He needs to understand the pain Father McCoy caused! You and your mother!" he cries. What he means, though, is apparent. He's referring to his own pain. Rebecca's face betrays her thoughts. She knows.

"Just let me know when he's gone," Win says, spinning around and stomping from the room. I turn back to Rebecca, who's watched him leave.

"Sorry about that, Father," Rebecca says. "He's taken Rachel's death hard."

"Well, you told me they were close."

"No, that's not true. They weren't close, at least Rachel wasn't close to Win. It's all Win."

"I'm not sure I follow."

"Oh, Win cared a lot more for Rachel than Rachel cared about him, in the last few years anyway," Rebecca explains. "I think our marriage upset her. I know she was upset the day of our wedding. After that, she kept her distance. Win, however . . ."

"You think he still loved her," I say.

"Think? I know he still loved her," she says. "He still loves her. Maybe not more than he loves me, though sometimes I wonder. I'd see it on his face every time he looked at her. I got used to it. But I trusted my sister."

I think how hard it would be to get used to someone I loved loving someone else more than me. The pain would have gotten unbearable. I look at Rebecca.

"And you didn't resent Rachel? Not even a little?"

"No, not at all."

"I'm sorry, Rebecca, but I find that a little hard to believe," I say.

"Why? It was Win, not her. She felt nothing about him anymore."

"But she was here," I say. "You'd be reminded every time you saw her that your husband loved her more than he loved you."

"No, I don't think—"

Pressing on, I continue, "No one would blame you if after a while you came to resent your sister's very presence." I pause. "And wanted to see her gone."

She looks at me, her mouth open, a protest dying on her lips. "What are you saying, Father Greer?" she asks coolly.

"Saying? Nothing. Just making an observation."

"I see," she whispers. She stands and walks toward the entrance to the room. "Thank you for stopping by Father, but I have things to do before dinner." She walks to the front door and opens it.

I stand in the foyer looking at her. "I'm sorry if I upset you," I say.

"Have a good evening, Father," Rebecca says. I incline my head and walk out.

Once in my car, I think for a moment before leaving. Then I get out and walk back to the house. An irritated Rebecca answers my knock.

"What is it, Father?" she says with exasperation.

"I just want to be clear," I say. "You didn't tell anyone about Rachel's pregnancy? Not your mother?"

"No, she made me swear not to."

"And you've said nothing to Win about it?"

"Win? Are you kidding? He would have gone crazy if I had told him. I can see him killing Father McCoy with his bare hands if he knew. You know, maybe I should have told Win. Then maybe my sister would still be alive!" She slams the door in my face.

On the drive back to Saint Clare's, I think about what I've learned that day. Rebecca had driven Rachel to the convent two weeks before her murder after finding out she was pregnant. At the convent, Rachel arranged with the Mother Superior to go to the Order's maternity home to have the baby and give it up for adoption. She had sworn her sister to secrecy, and Rebecca told me she had told no one. There were arrangements for Rebecca to drive Rachel to the home the Monday after her murder.. Then Rachel calls Rebecca to say the plan has changed, that she decided to have an abortion. Rebecca calls the Mother Superior and makes up a story about having a miscarriage, that she'd be at the convent the following week. Rebecca had no idea why Rachel changed her mind about carrying the baby to term. I couldn't figure that one out either. It was a secret that Rachel took with her.

"But was that the only secret?" I say out loud. Was there another? I had assumed—everybody had assumed—that Rachel's baby was Father Leonard's. But what if it wasn't?

I pull over. Rachel confessed to me about Father Leonard. But she hadn't mentioned the baby. She was already planning to have an abortion and didn't mention that. What else hadn't she told me?

And if Father Leonard wasn't the father of her baby, who was? There is one other possibility.

Winthrop Myer.

I shake my head. Rebecca said that Rachel had been careful to keep her distance from Win. But that wasn't entirely true. Rachel felt comfortable enough with Win to get him to persuade Father Leonard to hire her as church secretary. What if they were a lot closer than Rebecca knew? Or what if Rebecca suspected they were closer? Despite her protests, she had to resent her sister because of her husband's affection for her. It would have only been natural.

It is also a motive for murder.

I turn that thought over in my head. Rebecca could have killed her sister in a fit of passion, the jealousy and resentment she felt finally boiling over. Maybe she thought she and Win were going away together. Maybe she didn't believe that the baby was Father Leonard's, that the entire story was a cover. Maybe she became convinced that the baby was Win's, the product of an affair they had?

As much sense as it made, there were problems. Rebecca Myer is a slight, thin woman, a good four or five inches shorter than Father Leonard. I couldn't see how she could have subdued the bigger man, rendered him unconscious, and then staged the crime scene to frame the young priest.

"You're grasping at straws, Tom," I say, "that's what Helen will say."

I ponder all of this before dialing Helen's number.

"Tom," she says, "what's up?"

"Listen, I've learned some things you need to know. Things you need to look into. Things that bring Father Leonard's guilt into question."

"Damn it, Tom, really, you've got to stop playing detective!"

"I'm not playing detective," I protest. "I had questions, and I got some answers. I want you to follow up, since you're the professional."

"Well, what is it?"

"We've both been assuming that Father Leonard was the father of Rachel's baby."

She pauses. I can hear her thinking. "You're thinking maybe someone else?"

"Did they do a DNA test on the baby?"

"I assume they can, if they haven't," Helen replies. "We took DNA from Father Leonard at booking. Its standard procedure." She pauses. "All right, Tom, I'll ask them to run a DNA comparison to see if Father Leonard is the father or not. But it's all going to be moot in a few days, anyway."

"What do you mean?"

"I mean," Helen says, "that Brian and Angela Jenkins are talking about a plea deal for Father Leonard."

"A plea—but Jenkins has seemed so confident."

"Apparently, she's not as confident as you think she is. Nothing's settled yet, but in a few days Father Leonard's likely to plead guilty to the murder of Rachel Watson."

Twenty-Two

"It's the best deal under the circumstances, Father Leonard," Angela Jenkins says. "This way you won't spend the rest of your life in prison."

"Just the next twenty-five years," I say. "You'll be an old man by the time you get out."

"He'll be in his mid-fifties," Angela retorts. "That's not much older than you and I are. Besides, he'll be eligible for parole way before then, and I think it's a pretty good bet that he'll get out of prison after only a few years."

"Yeah, years he shouldn't have to spend, anyway."

"Look, Father," she says to me. "I don't know what you want me to do."

"I want you to defend an innocent man," I exclaim. "It's your job, isn't it?"

"It's my job to give my client the best defense possible, to represent his interest as well as I can," she jabs the table with her finger. "That's what I'm doing."

"You think you'll lose," I say.

She draws herself up before saying, "The state's evidence is damning. I think a jury would have a hard time finding reasonable doubt given the physical evidence and his own statements."

"I don't see how a reasonable jury will take his statements as a confession of guilt."

She opens up a folder on her desk. "The state will call Anna Luckgold to the stand. According to this, she told Detective Parr that a few days before Rachel Watson's death, he arrived back at the Rectory in an extremely agitated state after a visit to a parishioner."

I nodded. "Yes, I remember. That parishioner said something that rattled Father Leonard."

"'She asked me if I was still screwing that young secretary of mine,'" Jenkins read. She looked at me and Father Leonard, who stared at his hands. "Does that ring a bell?"

I sigh. "Yes, that's what he said, she said."

"Which prompted Father Leonard to say," Angela continues, "'She's ruined me, she's ruined me.'"

I look at Father Leonard, who still sits in his chair saying nothing.

"That combined with the fact that we now know he was intimate with Watson, that she was carrying his baby, gives him motive, according to the state. That Father Leonard here plotted her death as a way of covering up his behavior."

"It was consensual," I say, "Father Leonard didn't force himself on Rachel."

"We only have his word on that," she replies.

"She spoke to her sister."

"The state will say it's hearsay."

"We don't know for sure that Leonard was the father, anyway," I point out.

At that statement, Leonard jerks his head up. "What?"

"I know the police have requested a DNA comparison to confirm paternity," Jenkins says, "but it doesn't really matter if he's the father or not."

"What are you talking about, Tom? What is all this?" Leonard says, his voice frantic.

Jenkins pats the arm of her client. "Just calm down, Father." Leonard looks at her, then slumps back in his chair.

"It matters, Ms. Jenkins, because it gives other people motive," I say.

"There is no evidence of anyone else being in the apartment."

"You're afraid of the effect of losing on your chances in the election," I say, pointing at her for emphasis.

"Now look, Father," she says, slapping the table and standing up, leaning across the table, and glaring at me. "If I thought for a second we had a chance in hell of winning at trial, I'd do it. This has nothing to do with the election. This is not about me personally. This is about keeping him from spending the rest of his life in Jessup."

"But he's innocent," I plead.

"Oh, come on, Father! The innocent wind up in prison all the time! What makes him special is that he is one, a priest, and two, a white man. And plenty of the latter are innocent and behind bars."

"Stop, please, just stop," Father Leonard whispers. We almost don't hear him over our own argument. Both of us look at him.

He raises his head to look at us, an expression of resignation on his face. "I'll plead. I don't care." He closes his eyes and shakes his head. "It's what I deserve, after all I've done."

I sit down and grip his shoulder. "You didn't kill her, Leonard. Yes, you sinned. You broke your vows. But we can fix all that. You have got to stop punishing yourself."

"That's easy for you to say," he yells. His eyes have a dark expression, one I've never seen before in Father Leonard McCoy. "I carry this with me every day. I cannot get everything I've done, how I've betrayed the Church, God, my mother, out of my mind. And how do we know I didn't kill her? The fingerprints on the knife are mine. Maybe I blacked out after killing her and don't remember."

"Oh, Leonard, don't be ridiculous," I say. "You said—"

"I remember what I said, Tom. A presence. Being suffocated. Blacking out. Waking up next to her dead body, covered in her blood." He gasps. "The police say no one else was there. I probably imagined it all." He shakes his head. "There's just no sense in fighting it." He looks at his lawyer. "Tell them I'll take the plea. Let's get this over with."

Angela looks at me, then back at Leonard. "Okay, Father," she says, gathering up her papers. "I'll get in touch with the State Attorney. It will take a few days, and a court appearance. You must make a statement."

"Fine, fine, I'll say whatever they want me to say," he replies.

She leaves Leonard and I alone in the room. I look at him for several minutes. Finally, I say, "Leonard, I don't—"

"Tom, please," he says, looking at me with tears in his eyes. "Say nothing. It's done. It's my penance. Like she says, I won't be in prison for the rest of my life. When I get out, maybe then . . ." He returns to looking at his hands.

I look at him for a few more minutes, then stand. I pat his shoulder, then leave the pitiful figure alone in the gray room.

***

I'm alone in the Church, the only light coming through the stained glass windows, the votive candles burning in front of the shrines to Mary, Joseph, and Saint Clare, and the presence candle burning in front of the tabernacle. I've been kneeling on the bottom step below the altar since I returned from the meeting with Leonard and Angela Jenkins.

I look up at the cross, bearing the image of the suffering savior. God became man, perfect, sinless, who became sin for the entire world. Guiltless, allowing himself to be beaten, ridiculed, spit upon, and nailed to the rough wood for the guilty. A willing victim of the greatest injustice in all man's tortured history.

I close my eyes and think of Leonard, a man far from guiltless, far from sinless, who is about to plead guilty to a crime I know he didn't commit. And why? To punish himself for the sins he committed.

I shake my head. I pray for guidance.

An opening door disturbs the quiet of the church. Footsteps resound on the marble floors. I look up to see Winthrop Myer approaching.

"Your housekeeper said you'd be here," he says as he stops by me. I stand up.

I smile. "Anna's not my housekeeper, not officially anyway. She's my mother-in-law."

"Oh, I see," Win says. "That's why I came here. After you left, Rebecca told me about—well, I am embarrassed and angry with myself for what I said. I'm not a man who can admit easily when he's wrong, so it's taken me a few days to summon up the courage to come here. I apologize for what I said to you, Father Tom."

"It's all right, Win, no harm done."

"Thank you." He looks around. "I haven't been in Saint Clare's since the day of my wedding. It's beautiful here. Quiet. Peaceful."

"That's why I was here. I needed some peace."

"And then I showed up to disturb it," Win says. "I just wanted to come by and apologize. I'll let you get back to your prayers." He turns and walks away.

"Could you have been the father?" I ask.

He stops, but does not turn around.

I take a step towards him. "Could you have been the father of Rachel's baby?"

He spins around. I expect an angry retort. Instead, I am face to face with a man in agony. Tears are already streaming down his face.

"I don't know, Father," he croaks. "I don't know."

Win Myer collapses on the pew beside him, his body racked with sobs. I sit down beside him, my arm around him, holding him as he cries. He's saying things I can't understand.

We sit like that for a while. Finally, his sobs subside. He takes a deep breath. "Sorry, Father," he whispers, wiping the remaining tears away with his hand.

"It's okay," I say. "Do you want to tell me what happened?"

He's staring at the altar. "I haven't been to confession in—well, decades. I guess it's long past time." He turns to look at me. "How did you know?"

"I didn't," I say. "But you seem like a man who's been carrying an enormous burden of guilt for something more than just getting Rachel the job here."

"Yes," he says. He slowly shakes his head. "I am so ashamed. I've been ashamed of myself ever since it happened. You know I dated Rachel a bit in high school, before she left to go to that boarding school, before Rebecca and I got together."

"Rebecca and Marjorie told me that."

"I really liked Rachel in high school," he says. "I mean, she was just so different from the other girls. I was a Myer, the Big Man on Campus. Everyone treated me like I was something special. The girls—all the girls wanted to date me because I was a Myer and I had money, an expensive car, the whole works."

"But not Rachel."

He shakes his head. "Rachel saw me for who I really was and liked me for it. She didn't care about the money or the car. She just enjoyed being with me." He sighs. "It was so nice."

"Then she left and Marjorie put you and Rebecca together," I say.

"Yes. My mother wasn't much of a mother, but Marjorie—well, she really seemed to care for me. But for whatever reason, she didn't want me and Rachel together. So she sent her away. I was so upset when she left, but then I started dating Rebecca with Marjorie's encouragement." He closes his eyes. "Since they were twins, it was almost like I was still with Rachel. Sometimes I'd just imagine that Rebecca was Rachel. I remember one time I called Rebecca 'Rachel,' without thinking." He pauses. "She didn't like that very much."

"The day of the wedding, Rachel looked upset. Do you know why?"

"Yes," Win says. "I hadn't seen her very much over the years, just when she was at home for Christmas. But I still thought about her a lot. The day of our wedding, I saw her. And . . . and she was there, looking so beautiful in her bridesmaid's dress. I don't know what came over me, Father. I just started blabbering about how I still had feelings for her, that I felt about her in a way I didn't feel about her sister, that she only had to say the word and I'd ditch Rebecca and be hers."

"What was her reaction?"

"She was horrified, upset that I would say anything. She told me she would never betray her sister that way, that if I didn't want to marry Rebecca, it was up to me, but she'd have no part of it." He took a deep breath. "I was devastated. I decided to break it off with Rebecca, that I couldn't go through with our marriage, not feeling the way I did. So I went to Marjorie and told her. She . . . she talked sense into me. I pulled myself together and went through with it."

"So you just suppressed your feelings for Rachel?" I say.

"Yes," he says. "Or at least I tried. I think Rebecca suspected over the years how I really felt, but I did the best job I could to be a loving husband to her. I owed it to her. And Marjorie. Besides, Rachel was living in Baltimore and then there was that thing about her becoming a nun, so it wasn't too hard."

"But she moved back to Myerton. Didn't that make things more difficult for you?"

"She stayed away from us mostly, only seeing Rebecca at family occasions and alone. I never saw her alone until the day she came by to ask me to help her get the job at Saint Clare's." He smiled. "It was my first mistake."

"When did your second mistake happen?"

He takes another deep breath. "Memorial Day, that night," he whispers. "She came over here, visibly upset. She wanted to talk to Rebecca, but she was out of town on a girls' trip for a few days. I took her into my study and poured her a drink to steady her nerves." He pauses. "Rachel was a light-weight with alcohol. She told me what happened with Father Leonard."

"How did that make you feel?"

"Jealous, angry," he says. "That priest had something I never had, Rachel in his arms, in his bed. I—I couldn't stand it."

I look at him. "You raped her," I whisper.

"She was drunk!" he cries. "Practically passed out. She—she didn't resist."

"She was in no condition to," I say bitterly. "You committed a crime, Win, not just a sin."

"I loathed myself after it was over. I had imagined it so many times. It was nothing like I wanted it to be." He's crying again. "When she woke up the next morning and remembered what happened, she started screaming at me, yelling that she hated me, that she never wanted to lay eyes on me again. I begged her not to say anything, that it would destroy Rebecca and her Mama, pleading with her to keep it quiet."

"She agreed to do that?" I'm a little incredulous.

He nods. "Yes, she promised not to say anything. She just told me to stay away from her." He pauses. "And that's what I did. I never saw her alone again."

He bends over and puts his head in his hands. I consider what he just said to me.

"Do you think Rebecca suspected anything?"

"No," he says. "At least she never let on."

"Did you know Rachel was pregnant?"

"I overheard her telling Rebecca." He slumps and looks at me. "I was furious. I went to the Rectory, thinking I'd beat Father Leonard to death. But I just threatened him."

"The baby? Could you have been the father?"

He sighs. "It could have been mine. I don't know. Rebecca and I haven't had the best of luck having children ourselves. Turns out I'm the problem. Low motility." He shrugs. "The doctors said it would still be possible, just difficult."

I sigh and shake my head. "Win, did you get concerned that Rachel might tell someone?"

He sits up and looks at me. "If you're asking me did I kill her, no, Father, I didn't. I couldn't have." He paused. "I'm not even sure now how I can go on in a world without Rachel."

Twenty-Three

"I'm assigning you permanently to Saint Clare's, Father Tom."

The statement from the Archbishop delivered over the phone does not surprise me. After I told him about Father Leonard's plan to take a plea deal, it was inevitable.

"Yes, Archbishop."

"Have you seen him recently? How is he doing?"

"I haven't spoken to him in a couple of days," I say. "When I last saw him, he was . . . pitiful is the only word I can say."

"He sounds like a man guilty of something," he says.

"Oh, he's guilty of many things," I agree. "But not murder."

He pauses before saying. "Perhaps, perhaps."

"No, sir," I say, "no, he did not kill Rachel Watson."

"Your loyalty does you credit, Father, but I'd say on balance, if I were on a jury hearing the case . . ."

I sigh. "As I explained to you, he's pleading guilty so he won't spend the rest of his life in prison. But he's also doing it to continue performing penance."

"You've heard his confession," the Archbishop says. "Gave him his penance."

"Yes to both, Your Eminence," I say. "But he's not able to forgive himself, no matter how much absolution he's received."

The Archbishop sighs. "How unfortunate, how sad," he says. "Nothing he's done is unforgivable."

"Only by himself, sir," I say. "In doing what he's doing, he's allowing the actual killer to escape justice. If he won't help himself, I will."

"You're a good man, Father Tom," the Archbishop says. "As a priest, you can be a pain in my backside. But you're a good man."

"Thank you sir, I appreciate that."

I hang up and Anna walks into the office with a sandwich and a cola. "You haven't had lunch yet. I thought you'd be hungry."

"Thanks," I say, accepting the plate and glass. I take a bite and chew.

"So you're here permanently," she says, sitting across from the desk.

I nod and swallow. "Yes, at least as long as the Archbishop wants me here."

Anna looks at me. "Are you okay with this?"

"I don't really have a choice."

"You know what I mean," she says, leaning forward.

I nod. "Yes, I know." I sigh and take another bite of my sandwich. Swallowing, I say. "I'm tired. I've avoided this place long enough. God wants me here. So, I guess you all are stuck with me."

Anna smiles. "Well, I for one am glad."

"Thanks." I pause and look at her. "I need you to do something for me," I say slowly.

"Anything, if I can."

"Would you consider becoming my parish secretary and housekeeper?"

"I thought I already was," she exclaims. "I'll do it. I'll even move in here."

"You don't need to do that. I mean, you'll have to sell your house."

"I've been needing to downsize for years, I just haven't had a good excuse. But I'll keep the house, probably rent it out. There are always visiting professors or new hires at Myer College looking for places to live, and Myerton isn't flush with rental properties. Unless you don't want me?"

I laugh. "I'd appreciate the company."

She pauses. "Well, since I'm parish secretary, Miriam Conway still wants to have a nativity pageant."

I laugh. "Did she put you up to this?"

"No, absolutely not," she says. "I just think it would be a good idea. It'll get the parish a lot of positive attention which, frankly, after the last year we could use."

She's right. Saint Clare's has been the focus of two major criminal investigations since last summer.

"And," Anna continues, "it will give you a lot of goodwill among the young mothers who, let me be honest, carry a lot of weight in the parish. You'll want them on your side."

I nod. "I'll call Miriam as soon as I can."

At that moment, my phone rings. "It's Helen," I say.

Anna says, "I suspect you have a few things to talk about." She stands up and leaves my office, shutting the door behind her. I look at the closed door, wondering how much she's figured out about Helen and me.

I answer the call. "Did I catch you at a bad time?" Helen asks on the other end. "I know how busy you probably are."

"No, I was just talking to Anna about a few things."

"Have you eaten? I thought we could grab a bite."

I look at the remnants of the sandwich. "Ack, you caught me just as I finished. How about coffee?"

"The Perfect Cup? Sure, sounds good to me." Helen pauses. "I have something to discuss with you."

***

The young waitress brings us our order at the table along the sidewalk, me an iced coffee in recognition of the time of year, Helen a chicken salad on croissant with a sweet tea.

"I hope you don't mind," she says before tucking into the sandwich. "I haven't eaten since breakfast," she explains with a mouthful of food.

"No, I ate earlier," I say. "Busy?"

She nods before swallowing, washing the sandwich down with a gulp of tea. "A couple of cases. No murders, thankfully. You know, this was a quiet town before you came back. Since then, two murders. All associated with Saint Clare's."

I laugh. "Are you saying I'm responsible?"

She smiles. "If I were a more suspicious person, I'd have to wonder. But it's just a coincidence. Probably."

"Well, you'll have more opportunities to find out." At her look I say, "I've been assigned to Saint Clare's permanently, or as permanent as any assignment in the Church is, as long as the Archbishop wants me here."

She sits back. "So you're staying this time? No monastery?"

I shake my head. "No, no monastery. I will be a parish priest here."

Helen cocks her head to one side. "How do you feel about that?"

"Anna asked me the same question." I sit quietly for a moment. "Contented. Satisfied that this is where I belong. Where God wants me to be."

We look at each other across the table for a minute, our eyes fixed on each other. A breeze carries the faint scent of vanilla from her hair across the table, tickling my nose, triggering memories of past moments together. I see the sun shining off her raven-black hair, which brings out the azure blue of her eyes. They're deep pools. I remember a time when I could lose myself in those eyes.

Suddenly, Helen turns her attention back to her sandwich. I sit back and say, "So what did you want to talk to me about?"

She swallows her food, takes another drink of tea, wipes her mouth with her napkin. Helen folds it carefully, then absentmindedly twists it in her hands. "I have something to tell you. And something to ask you."

"Okay. What is it?"

She clears her throat and looks me in the eye. "Do you ever miss it?"

This is not what I was expecting. "Do I miss what?"

"It," she says without explanation. "You know, the thing as a priest you can't have, or at least shouldn't have."

At my quizzical look, she says, "Oh, come on, Tom, you know what I'm talking about."

I smile slightly and say, "Helen, I don't understand what you're getting at."

"Oh, you, you're just being difficult," she says with exasperation. Leaning across the table, she says with a low voice. "Sex. Intimacy. You know." She sits back to wait for my answer.

"What prompted this?" I ask.

She shrugs. "Father Leonard. Rachel. The whole situation. Two people who knew each other years ago, finding each other again. It's clear Father Leonard carried the memory of Rachel and his feelings with him for years. They meet again, and one thing leads to another." She pauses. "For both of them, it was new. But you know what it's like to be intimate with another person. You were married to Joan. I was married to John. Before them, while we never—well, we were intimate in other ways. I just want to know if you miss it at all?"

I smile slightly. "Do I miss physical intimacy? No, not really. Sometimes, though, I miss the other."

At her questioning look, I explain, "Just having someone to come home to, to talk to, to share experiences with. That's the real sacrifice of celibacy, at least it is for me. The physical part. You can take a cold shower, pray a rosary, do many things when you're tempted. But there's nothing you can do when loneliness comes." I sigh. "And being a priest can be very, very lonely."

Helen smiles. "I thought you like being alone?"

I look up. "Now that I'm alone most of the time," I say, "not so much."

"So you get tempted?"

"I am still a man, Helen. That didn't change the day they ordained me."

She looks at me and whispers, "Do I tempt you, Tom?"

I look at her. The silence is heavy between us for a moment. I clear my throat. "Honestly?" I say quietly. "Do you really want to know?"

She stares at me for a moment, obviously struggling between two possible answers to my question, then nods.

I take a deep breath. "Sometimes, when the sun hits your hair just right or I allow myself more than a brief glance at what you're wearing or we're talking and I can see your eyes—I remember us together. Am I tempted? In a way. Not to break my vows, but to allow myself to get closer than I should. Again, the loneliness is the worst part of this job."

Helen nods. "I understand that."

"So," I say, "what about you? Do I tempt you?"

Helen takes a sudden interest in her iced tea, Avoiding my gaze, she says, "That's why I asked to see you. To tell you—" She straightens her shoulders and looks at me. "To tell you I can't do this anymore."

"Do what anymore?" I ask, feeling my stomach knot up.

She waves her arm between us. "This. Whatever this is."

"We're just friends, Helen. There hasn't been anything even remotely—"

"I know that," she says quietly. "That's what makes it so hard for me."

I look at her and shake my head. "I—what are you saying, Helen?"

She sighs. "For years, I didn't miss it. John's death and my grief, my missing him pushed out any thoughts or desires. But over time, you remember what it was like—sex, yes, but everything else you were talking about too." She looks at her plate. "I'm still hungry."

Helen signals the waitress and orders a cinnamon roll. I ask for a chocolate doughnut.

"Last year, after you came back," she continues, "the feelings of loneliness got stronger. I remembered what our life together was like. Oh, it wasn't perfect, and the way it ended was awful, but we had a lot of good times." She looked at me. "Here you were, suddenly back in my life. But you were . . ."

"I was unavailable" I say.

She nods. "I thought the fact that you were a priest would deter me. It wasn't like I would try seducing you away from the Church, get you to break your vows. I know you too well. But I found myself thinking about you more and more. And the more I thought about you, the more unhappy I got."

"Why are you unhappy?"

Helen gets a slight smile. "I'm an only child, remember? When they find out, people always ask me if I got whatever I wanted. I said yes, but only because I'm very picky about what I want. But when I want something, nothing else will satisfy me. Do you see what I'm saying?"

I'm at a loss. "No, I really don't."

"Tom," she says with exasperation, "I'm unhappy because I can't have you. Because there can never be an us. Because that's what I realize I want. Us." She pauses as she wipes a tear from her eye. "And that's something that can never be."

I sit in front of this woman I used to love—am I really thinking in the past tense—who's just admitted that she wants me. "Helen—I—I—I don't know what to say."

She takes a deep breath. "There's nothing you can say. You're a priest. We both know what that means. But I—I can't do it anymore."

I just look at her as she says, "I was already thinking about what to do, but I wasn't certain you'd be staying. Now that I know, my mind's made up."

"What are you going to do?" I ask quietly. But in my heart, I know the answer.

"Tom, I'm leaving Myerton. I've received a job offer from the police department in a town about the size of Myerton near where I grew up in Nebraska. My aunt and uncle are still alive, but they're getting on in years, so—"

"Helen," I say quickly, "look, you don't have to leave. We can stop spending time together—I mean, you want me to stop playing detective anyway. No more lunches or coffees together. I'll only see you at Mass, or you can go back to attending Mass in Frostburg. You don't have to uproot your entire life just because of me."

"But I'm not, my dear Tom," Helen whispers. "I'm doing it for me. Be-cause—because I'm scared what might happen if I stay."

We lapse into an uncomfortable silence. My mind is turning, the lover and priest arguing loudly.

You know this is best, Tom, for both of you, the priest says.

You can't lose her again, Tom, the lover says.

I clear my throat and say, "Helen, I—"

"Oh, good, there you are." I turn to see an excited Nate Rodriguez bouncing up the sidewalk towards us. Excited is Nate's natural state, so it doesn't surprise me, but today he seems particularly exuberant.

"Hi, Nate, what is it?"

With a grin from ear to ear, he stops next to us. "I did it, Father Tom. I really did it."

"What d'you do now, Nate?" Helen asks, a weary tone in her voice.

Looking at her, he says triumphantly, "I found a witness."

"A witness? You found someone?" I ask.

As he nods vigorously, still grinning, Helen says, "Wait, what? Tom, you asked Nate to find a witness to Rachel Watson's murder? Skulking around Richard Strump's backyard wasn't enough for you?"

"I had to do something, Helen, you had—"

"Great, just great. Thanks a lot."

"Let's just hear him out, Helen. Nate, what did you find?"

"Like I just said. A witness. The next-door neighbor. Actually, not right next door. His place is a few doors down from Rachel Watson's townhouse. But he has a clear view of her place. I was there. You can see the front of her place real clear. The crime scene tape is kind of falling off, Detective."

Helen is about to say something when I put my hand up. "A neighbor, you say?"

"Uh-huh."

"We interviewed the entire neighborhood already, Nate," Helen says. "No one saw anything."

"But you didn't interview the guy I found."

"How do you know that?" I ask.

"Because," Nate says triumphantly. "He left town the night of the murder and just got back two days ago."

Helen's mouth drops open. "Damn," she whispers as she gets up and grabs her tote bag. "Nate—well, I guess I have to say good work. Send me the name and address to the Father's phone."

"Right," Nate says, pulling his phone out of his messenger bag.

"What?" I say, surprised by the sudden turn of events. "Why my phone?"

She looks at me, a slight smile appearing on her face. "You are coming with me, aren't you?"

Twenty-Four

"Look, I already told the nervous kid," says the voice from under the 1973 Ford Mustang, "I know nothing about that girl's murder. I didn't even know anything about it until I got back from my business trip two days ago. Darn oil plug rusted." The man scoots out from under the car, his face and hands covered with grease spots and dirt.

"Mr. Walkin," Helen says. "Any information you can give will help."

"You may help keep an innocent man from going to prison," I say.

"Huh, you talking about that young priest? I heard he got the girl knocked up. Priests shouldn't do that, you know?"

"Please, sir, can you tell us what you saw that night?" Helen gets out her notepad.

Walkin stands up and walks over to his tool bench. We're standing in his garage, the Mustang on jack stands, the air hot and heavy with the smell of motor oil mingled with sweat. It's almost overpowering. A trickle of sweat rolls down my spine. Black clericals are not what you really want to be wearing in the summer, and it's not even that hot today.

"Look, all I know is what I told the kid."

"Well, tell me now."

Walkin looks at Helen. "Listen, I was in a hurry that night, so I only caught glimpses of stuff. And the only reason I noticed was because it was so strange."

"What was strange?" I ask. Helen shoots me her standard 'be quiet' look.

"The people," he explains. "Rachel was a quiet girl, I guess I should say young woman, she was closer to thirty, I guess. She didn't get visitors. She'd come and go, we'd exchange good mornings or afternoons or evenings when we'd see each other. But she kept to herself. And like I say, she didn't have visitors."

"That night was different?"

"Yeah. I was in a hurry to get packed and get out of town. I was taking a red-eye out of Dulles to Seattle. I was going to leave earlier, but stuff came up. It takes a couple of hours to get there, you know, and my flight was leaving at 11:00, so I was cutting it close. So I was throwing things in the car, running in and out of the house. I remember looking toward her place when I saw someone go inside."

"Go inside? Did they knock or just let themselves in?" Helen asks.

"I didn't see her knock, but she could have."

"Her?" I say. "It was a woman. Are you sure?" Helen glares at me again.

"Yeah, I'm sure. I may be older, but I can still tell a man from a woman, even though that's difficult these days."

"Can you describe her?"

"A woman, she was wearing a dress, I don't remember the color. Could have been blue. Or red. Maybe yellow."

"How tall was she?"

Walkin thinks. "About your height. She was a little thinner, not as chunky as you."

I stifle a snort. Helen's jaw clinches.

"Did you see her leave?"

He shakes his head. "No. She could have, I guess, I was in and out, she could have left when I was inside."

"Did she drive herself? Did someone drive her?" Helen asks.

He shrugs. "Didn't notice. Like I say, I was trying to get packed. I didn't notice anything else until the guy showed up."

Helen and I look at each other. "What guy?"

"Tall guy. Even at a distance, with these eyes, I could see his red hair. But that's not what got my attention." Pointing to the entrance to the parking area, he says, "He must have taken that turn at about twenty. You could hear his tires squeal. He sped in here into a parking space and jumped out of the car practically before the car stopped moving. Not even sure he turned the engine off."

"And you're sure he had red hair," Helen asks.

"Yeah, I'm sure. Bright red hair. Almost didn't look real. But you couldn't miss it."

"Did you see him leave?"

"Like I told ya, I didn't see anything else. After he went inside—"

"Did he knock?" I ask, ignoring Helen's eye roll.

"Knock? Maybe. Yeah, I think he did. He knocked and rang the doorbell, like he couldn't wait to get inside." He paused. "You know, I think I'd seen him there before, coming out. One morning."

Helen and I look at each other. "How long ago was that?"

"Maybe a month, maybe more. Don't really remember."

Helen makes notes in her notebook. "So he knocked and rang the doorbell?"

"Yeah, then the door opened and he went inside."

"Did you see someone let him in?"

"No, didn't see that."

"About what time was all this," Helen asks.

"Let's see," he thinks. "I finished loading the car and pulled out not long after that so, maybe 7:00?"

"7:00? Are you sure?" I ask with excitement.

"6:45, 7, 7:15 no later than that."

"And you didn't see anyone leave after the man went inside? And no one else went into the townhouse?"

"Like I say, not while I was here."

Helen thanks Walkin, who grabs a socket wrench and scoots back under the car. We walk out of the garage. I turn to Helen and say, "Did you hear—"

"Shush, Tom, let's wait until we get in the car," she says with a hushed tone.

We get in her car and she lays her head back on the headrest, hands gripping the steering wheel, her eyes closed.

"An eyewitness we missed," she says. "I can't believe it."

I say nothing for a moment. Finally, she sits up and starts the car to let the air conditioner cool the stuffy interior.

"Did you hear what he said? He says someone got to Rachel's townhouse before Father Leonard did. A woman."

"A woman. So he was telling the truth." She sighs. "Two murder cases in a row and I get it wrong. What am I doing in this job, anyway?"

I put my hand on her shoulder. She jerks her head to look at it, and I remove it quickly. "Listen, you said it yourself. You had the physical evidence. It pointed to Leonard." I pause. "And you were under pressure from Brian."

"I'm a professional, Tom," she snaps. "I don't allow outside pressure to keep me from doing my job. No, I let myself ignore any other possibility once the forensics came in. Father Leonard killed that girl to hide his sin, I thought. That made the most sense." She stops. "Maybe I was blinded by my feelings. I think I still have problems with the Church, the way they've done things, because of John's experience."

I nod, remembering her late husband's abuse at the hands of his priest as a young person. "Understandable. So do I."

She stares out the window in silence for a few minutes. "This case just stirred everything back up, colored my judgment."

"You did a good job, from what I could see, standing up to Brian's rush to charge Father Leonard."

"I did it because I didn't want Brian to think he could run over me because of our past relationship," she says, turning back to me. "I ignored my gut, my sense that despite everything, some things didn't make sense. I didn't follow up on the initial interviews, I didn't recheck the neighborhood. If I had—"

"Walkin got back just a few days ago," I point out. "You could have still missed him."

"Why are you doing this, Tom?"

I smile. "Undeserved guilt is something I know a little about. I don't want to see you beat yourself up."

She looks at me, then nods. "Okay, so we have a witness that brings the entire case against Father Leonard into question. We have an unknown woman entering Rachel Watson's apartment before Father Leonard. How long before did he say?"

"I don't think he did. So it could have been an hour, it could have been fifteen minutes."

"But she was still there when Father Leonard arrived, which means there was someone in the apartment we missed." She closes her eyes. "And what description do we have? A woman, about my height, wearing a dress. That only describes, say, almost every woman in the area."

I turn from Helen and look out the window. "What is it?" she asks.

"It also describes one woman I can think of," I say. "And she also had a motive, the most ancient motive of all."

"And that is?"

I look at Helen. "Jealousy."

***

The lights are on at the Myer house when we arrive.

"Now, listen," Helen says before we get out of her car. "Don't say anything, Tom."

"I won't say a word," I raise my hand to swear.

"That's what you always say. I can interrogate a suspect without your help, you know? I've been doing this job for a long time."

"I know all that," I say. "So, is she a suspect?"

"You're the reason we're here, Tom! What do you think?"

I didn't want to think what I had been thinking. But there was only one woman I could think of who had motive to murder Rachel Watson, whose appearance at her door wouldn't surprise her.

A few moments after Helen knocks, Win Myer opens the door. "Detective," he says pleasantly to Helen. Looking at me with a slight scowl, he says, "Father."

"I hope we're not interrupting," Helen says. "May we come in?"

"Well, we're just finishing up dinner, about to have coffee and dessert in the library. Would you care to join us?"

"That's very gracious of you," Helen says, "but we don't want to trouble you." I look at Helen, but she stills me with a glance out of the corner of her eye.

"No trouble, it's just family. Rebecca, myself, her mom and dad." He shows us into the library. I walk to the wall with the photographs, looking again at their wedding pictures. There is Rachel, looking dour. Win, his smile patently fake. But this time, I look at Rebecca.

Her smile is genuine. Happy, a joyful bride on her wedding day. The happiest day of her life.

"Detective," I hear Edmund Watson say. "I don't see why you're here. You arrested the guy who murdered Rachel. What point is there in your showing up and interrupting our evening?"

"Some new information has come to light," Helen says. "New information that could cast some doubt on things."

"What? Are you saying that the priest is innocent?" Marjorie Watson asks.

"I'm saying, Ms. Watson, that the information needs to be investigated, just to make sure there hasn't been a miscarriage of justice."

"What information is that?" Win Myer asks. He's entered the room with a drink in his hand.

Helen turns to face him. "Information that places someone in addition to Father McCoy at Rachel's townhouse at the time of the murder." She turns, walks up to Rebecca Myer, and looks down at her. Rebecca looks up at Helen, a look of surprise on her face.

"What? So Father McCoy was telling the truth?"

"We'll get to that in a minute, Ms. Myer." Helen takes out her notebook. "But first, did you tell Father Greer you were to meet Rachel at her apartment on Monday morning?"

Rebecca looks at me. I avoid her gaze. I had tread very close to the line of what I could tell Helen. But I only told her enough. Helen had filled in the rest, or at least the rest to complete the basic picture.

"Yes, I was supposed to meet Rachel on Monday morning."

"Oh, what are you talking about, Rebecca?" Marjorie asks impatiently.

"I was supposed to meet Rachel at her apartment and drive her somewhere," Rebecca says to her mother.

"What? You told me you were going to a spa," Win says.

"That was a cover story to explain where I was going."

"And where were you going, Ms. Myer?" Helen asks, her pen poised above her notebook.

She hesitates before saying, "I was going to drive her to Hagerstown. To an abortion clinic."

Helen sits down in a chair. "I see."

"I know. I lied to you," Rebecca says. "It didn't seem a big deal, that it had nothing to do with her murder. The email? It was all part of the cover."

"So she really wasn't leaving to go to the convent?" Helen says. "You and she were going to Hagerstown so she could have an abortion."

Rebecca nods. "From there, I would take her to the convent after she rested for a few days."

"She had told you," Helen says, "that Father McCoy was the father."

"Yes, who else could it have been?" Rebecca asks.

I look over at Win, who has become white as a sheet.

Helen looks at her for a moment. "Tell me, Ms. Myer," she continues. "What was your relationship with your sister like?"

"My relationship with Rachel?" Rebecca asks, confused.

"Really, Detective, why all these questions? Get to the point!" Win Myer says, his speech a little slurred since he's downing his second or third drink of the night.

"I will in a moment, Mr. Myer," Helen says over her shoulder. "Please don't interrupt."

During this, I'm scanning the wall of photographs. I settle on the one of Win in Afghanistan. Next to it is the group photo of his platoon, a smiling Win Myer standing on the end.

"Well, Rebecca," Helen asks quietly.

"I loved my sister—love my sister, detective," Rebecca says. "She was my best friend, despite our differences. Even after she said she wanted to become a nun, I didn't understand it, but," shooting a glance at her mother, "I didn't reject her."

"I didn't reject her," Marjorie protests. "I shared my opinion with her, that it made little sense for a well-brought up, educated woman. She rejected me."

"Anyway," Helen says, "there were no problems between you two?"

"Only the usual between siblings," she replies.

Helen makes a note in her book, then appears to read something. Looking back up, she says, "Didn't Rachel and your husband date in high school."

Rebecca is about to answer when Win says, "That was only a couple of times. After she went away, Rebecca and I started dating then fell in love. We're married, you know."

"But you've always had a lot of affection for Rachel, haven't you?" Helen asks. I have said nothing to Helen about my conversation with Win. She drew her own conclusions from the little I said.

"Not that it's any of your business, but yes. I've always looked at Rachel as the sister I never had. I've felt, well, like a brother. Protective."

"Oh, that's a bunch of crap and you know it," Rebecca suddenly screams at Win. "Brother! Only if you had incest in mind!"

"Really, Rebecca, calm yourself," Marjorie says.

"Oh, shut up, Mama! Just shut up! I'm just so sick of you and him and your little scheming! You got him involved with this whole thing, getting him to spy on Rachel and Father McCoy!"

"That was only after Win came to me with his concerns," Marjorie says. "I agreed with them and he volunteered."

"You have him wrapped around your little finger," Rebecca continues, in full heat now. "And you're wrapped around his. Seems like everyone is tied to everyone else in this family except me!"

She stands up and strides toward Win. "And you! Don't give me that big brother crap! You never got over her! She was the one you always wanted, not me! The only reason you dated me was because of her!" she points to Marjorie. "God, the only reason you married me was so you could call her Mama and stay close to Rachel!"

Helen and I are looking at this spectacle when Helen says, "Would you care to elaborate on that, Ms. Myer?"

She turns to Helen and takes a few deep breaths. "We started dating in high school after they sent Rachel away to boarding school," she begins. "Mama pushed it. After Rachel left, Win would come over to the house, began spending a lot of time with us." She paused. "I thought at first that he wanted to spend time with me. But he always seemed happiest around Mama. And over time, I came to realize he wanted me for two reasons. One, because of Mama. And two, so he'd always be close to Rachel, even if only as a brother-in-law." She looked at Win. "That must have made it easier to stand me, huh, since we were twins and I looked like her."

"Now, Rebecca, don't be—" Win says.

"Don't. You. Dare. Call. Me. Ridiculous," Rebecca says firmly. "You really think I've been fooled all this time? The only reason I never said anything was because I was certain Rachel would never betray me by having an affair with you. Even though I knew you'd jump at the chance if she ever gave you the slightest hint of interest."

"Were you certain, Ms. Myer?" Helen asks.

Rebecca turns, a questioning look on her face. "I'm not sure what—"

"Did it ever cross your mind that Rachel's baby might not be Father Mc-Coy's after all?"

Rebecca glances at me, no doubt remembering a similar question from me.

"She told me it was his baby," Rebecca says, walking back towards Helen.

"But did you believe her? Or did you, deep down, worry that it might be your husband's?"

"No," she shakes her head.

"You were already jealous," Helen presses. "Did you think your worst fears had been realized, that your sister and your husband—"

"No, no, not at all! I trusted Rachel!"

"But maybe she betrayed that trust," Helen continues. "Maybe that drove you to do something about it?"

Rebecca stares at Helen, her mouth open, shocked.

Helen stands up and looks Rebecca in the face. "We found a new witness, who saw someone matching your general description entering Rachel's apartment before Father McCoy arrived. Before her murder." She looks at Rebecca, letting the force of her words settle in. "What do you say about that?"

"I wasn't there," Rebecca whispers. "It wasn't me."

"If it wasn't you, Ms. Myer, then who could it have been?"

Helen's question floats in the room's silence. I look at the family, torn by their own emotions. I wait for something to rip the tension.

"It was me," Marjorie Watson says. She stands up and looks at Helen.

"It was me, Detective. I was there. I killed my daughter. I framed the Father."

Twenty-Five

The next few minutes are chaotic. Helen stands, looking confused. Rebecca Myer screams and collapses on the couch in tears. Edmund Watson stands next to his wife, talking in her ear, saying, "What are you talking about, Marjorie? What in the world are you talking about? What nonsense is this?" Marjorie Watson for her part stands stock still, staring into space, her jawline firm.

"Well," Helen whispers to me when she walks to where I am standing. "This is a fine mess."

"What are you going to do now?"

"Do? Do? I'm going to listen to what she has to say," Helen says. "Either she's covering for the daughter or she's telling the truth. We can check to see if Rebecca has an alibi. In the meantime, Tom, let me do my job. And keep your mouth shut. Just sit over there, will you please?" She indicates an armchair in the corner. I nod and go sit down.

By the time Helen returns to the family, things have calmed down somewhat. Edmund's sitting down, still looking confused. Win has taken a seat, slumping either from intoxication or resignation. Rebecca is sitting on the couch, her hands folded in her lap, her head down, her shoulders moving slightly, showing she's still crying.

"Have a seat, Mrs. Watson," Helen says, indicating a chair. Marjorie sits on the edge of the chair, stiff, head held high.

"You can ask your questions," Marjorie says, "But I've already confessed. I did it."

"One thing at a time, Mrs. Watson," Helen says, turning to a fresh page in her notebook. "So why don't you tell me what happened?"

She pauses a moment before speaking. "I got a call from Win about 3:00," she begins. "He was upset. He told me about the email, about Rachel's plan to enter the convent. He knew she hadn't told me, but he thought I should know. And he was right. I'm her mother. I should know these things."

Turning to Win Myer, Helen says, "You said you hadn't read the email."

Win avoids her look, taking another sip of his drink.

Turning back to Marjorie, Helen asks, "What did you do?"

"At first, nothing," Marjorie says. "I just stewed. I was angry that she hadn't told me." She pauses. "The more I thought about it that afternoon, the more upset I got. The more determined to put a stop to it before she ruined her life. So I went over there."

"Did she know you were coming?" Helen asks.

Marjorie shakes her head. "We hadn't spoken since the meeting with Father Greer."

"The meeting where you admitted sending the anonymous letter to the Archbishop," I say from the corner.

"Father Greer," Helen says, looking at me. "Please do not interrupt again or you will have to leave."

I hold up my hands. "Sorry, Detective. I won't say a word."

Helen glares at me, then turns to Marjorie. "Is what Father Greer says true?"

"Oh, yes, I sent the letter."

"Did you witness everything you described in the letter?" Helen asks.

"Why is that important?"

"I just want to get a complete picture," Helen replies. "Did you see what you described in the letter?"

"Well, no, not in so many words," she says hesitantly.

"Where did you get the information?"

"Well . . . well from Win mostly," she says. Helen turns to look at Win Myer, slumped in the chair.

"And how did he come into possession of it?"

"He grew suspicious of Father McCoy after Rachel started working at the parish," Marjorie replies. "He told me he felt guilty about getting her the job. He began looking into things, just to make sure nothing bad was going on. Then he found out about their carrying on at the Memorial Day picnic."

I look at the two of them. Win is looking down at his drink.

"So the day of her murder," Helen continues, "you went over there to—"

"To talk some sense into my daughter, or try one last time," Marjorie says. "I showed up and knocked. She answered right away. I could tell she was expecting someone else."

She was. Rachel had opened the door expecting Father Leonard. But instead, it was her mother.

"How did she react to seeing you?"

"As soon as she saw it was me, she got all angry. She demanded to know what I was doing there. I told her it was to talk her out of throwing her life away. She asked me what business it was of mine. I told her it was because I was her mother. She laughed at me, saying it had been years since I had acted like a mother to her. She was just mean and spiteful, ungrateful for everything I had given her."

"You had treated her badly for years, Mama," Rebecca says. "What did you expect?"

"I did not mistreat her! Was I firm? Yes. She had no idea what was best for her." She shakes her head. "I tried to talk some sense into her. I told her she'd be throwing her life away if she went to that place. I said, if you want to be religious, fine, but you can do it in a quiet, respectful way, a way that won't make people think there's something wrong with you. I mean, you see what I mean, detective?"

She exhales. "Then she told me she wasn't going into the convent right away. I was happy, relieved. For a minute."

"Then she told you why," Helen says.

"I can't believe she had done something so stupid, getting pregnant, something only a lower-class piece of trash would do these days, with all the birth control that's available. Isn't sex considered a sin, Father? I guess they just ignored that one. Then she told me she was going to have an abortion."

She sighs. "I thought I had a chance. I told her she couldn't go into a convent, not having done that. That she needed to forget about it, come to her senses."

Marjorie's tone strikes me as odd. She is describing a very emotional scene in an almost emotionless way.

"Then she went crazy," she continues. "She ran into the kitchen and grabbed a knife. She ran at me with it, screaming at me to get out, to leave her alone."

"Were you scared?"

"No, not really. Surprised more than anything else. I told her to put the knife down. She lunged. I moved out of the way and grabbed her arm, trying to get the knife away from her. We struggled. Suddenly, she cried out. We both looked down. There was blood coming from her stomach. She'd been stabbed in the struggle."

Helen has stopped writing at this point. "She stabbed herself," she repeats. "In the belly."

"Yes, in the stomach. I let go of the knife. She slid to the floor, then fell over. She was dead."

That couldn't have been true, I think.

"Did you try to help her, or call for help?" Helen asks.

"I was going to call someone," Marjorie says, "when there was a knock at the door, then the doorbell."

"Father McCoy."

Marjorie nods. "He was outside. I looked at Rachel, then realized the opportunity."

"Opportunity?"

She exhales. "To pay him back for what he did to her."

I sit up and open my mouth, about to say something. Helen turns to look at me. I slump back in my seat, closing my mouth.

"You framed Father McCoy for murder because he had gotten your daughter pregnant? Is that what you're telling us?"

Marjorie nods. "Yes, that's what I'm saying."

Helen shakes her head and sighs. "What happened next?"

"I grabbed something off the coffee table, something heavy, I think it was a vase or something, I don't remember. I heard him open the door, and he called her name as he walked up the stairs. It was dark in the living room, so he couldn't see me. When he got to the top of the stairs, I snuck up behind him and cracked him across the head with the vase. Fortunately, it didn't break, but he went down hard. He was still alive but knocked out. I grabbed him and dragged him near Rachel's body. I smeared some blood on his clothes, then took the knife and wiped the handle clean, fingerprints, you know. I placed the knife in his hand to make sure the handle would show his prints, then tossed it on the floor between him and Rachel. Then, I wiped down any surface I might have touched. I wiped the vase clean, placed it back on the coffee table. Then I got out the vacuum cleaner and vacuumed the whole place. I took the bag with me when I left. Later, I burned it in the grill out back. Along with the clothes I was wearing. They had Rachel's blood on them."

"What did you do then?" Helen asks quietly.

"Detective, what do you think I did? I went home. I snuck in the back way and stripped my clothes off in the laundry room. I had just done laundry so there was a housedress I could throw on. I bundled my clothes and put them at the bottom of the hamper. I was going to wash them, but it occurred to me that the blood might not come out. So I burned them as soon as I got an opportunity."

Helen finishes writing. She looks at Marjorie Watson for several minutes. Win's eyes are closed. I can't tell if he is asleep or thinking. Edmund looks dull. Rebecca is staring out the window, resting her chin on her balled-up fists.

"That's my story, Detective Parr," Marjorie says. "That's my confession. I killed Rachel. I framed Father McCoy. There, you have it. Arrest me."

Helen stands up and takes her phone out of her purse. "This is Detective Parr," she says when someone answers. "Send a car out to the Myer home. We're taking someone into custody. Call the chief and let him know I need to see him as soon as possible." She pauses, then adds, "Call the State Attorney. He should be in the office today." She hangs up her phone and says, "Ms. Watson, you must come down to the station to make a formal statement. But right now I'm arresting you for obstruction."

"What?" she says. "But I killed Rachel. I told you that."

"You say you were there when she died," Helen says. "Your story points to a tragic accident. But you deliberately set about to frame an innocent man and send him to prison for the rest of his life for murder. It was cold, it was calculating, and it hindered my investigation. I may not charge you with murder or anything else in Rachel's death, but I sure as hell will see you go to prison for that!" She grabs her bag and pushes past the woman, heading to the entrance to the room. There, she turns. "Coming, Father?" she yells.

Quickly, I get up and trot to catch up with her. She's outside in the driveway by the time I do so, standing with her hands on her hips, looking into the sky, a stream of muttered profanities flowing freely from her lips. I stand warily to one side while she does this.

Finally, she stops and turns to me. "Have you ever heard of anything like that in your life?"

"Honestly, no," I say. 'What she said—what everyone said—was just remarkable."

"Bat-crap crazy if you ask me. I mean, I feel sorry for Rachel and Rebecca, with a mother and father like that. And Win, he's no prize, I'm surprised Rebecca's put up with it for all these years."

"Probably her mother's influence," I say. "Though it's clear that Rebecca is her favorite." I point back at the house. "Do you think it's a good idea to leave Marjorie Watson alone?"

"What's she going to do? High-tail it out the back door, scamper across the tennis courts, vault over the property wall? She gave up her story freely. She almost seemed proud of herself. Proud. And the story she told about how Rachel died?" She shakes her head. "I've had serial killers express more emotion when they described killing their victims. Cold. Absolutely cold."

I nod. "Yes. She confessed freely." I turn and look at the house.

"What is it, Tom?" Helen asks wearily.

"What do you mean?" I say, turning back to her.

"I mean, there's something. What is it? Just tell me. I'm too tired to pull it out of you."

I furrow my brow and approach her. "Didn't that whole scene strike you as . . . odd?"

"The bunch of them are odd," Helen exclaims. "The story is odd, a mother coolly describing the death of her daughter practically in her arms, then how she framed a priest—a priest, for heaven's sake!"

"But her account, what she said happened, the way she said it. There is something about it that doesn't sit right with me."

"Oh, for goodness' sake, Tom."

"For example," I press. "She said her daughter pulled a knife on her and was killed in the struggle. But that would have been completely out of character for Rachel."

"People do strange things when they're angry," she replies.

"She describes a struggle with the murder weapon. Wouldn't that usually leave both of them cut? Were any cuts or wounds on Marjorie's hands? Did the medical examiner find any on Rachel's hands?"

"Tom, please—"

"And," I point at the house, "she says she cracked Father Leonard across the skull with a vase, and that she knocked him out."

"Okay?"

"Marjorie Watson is a good foot shorter than Father Leonard," I say. "Also, a heavy object like she described would have left a big bump, maybe even a gash. But the doctors found nothing." I pause. "And then there's—"

"No, stop," Helen says, raising her hand. "Just stop. Tom, I don't know what you want. We have someone saying they framed Father Leonard. That alone sets him free."

"But her confession doesn't fit all the facts, Helen." I shake my head. "No, there's something wrong with this whole thing."

"Dammit Tom! Stop playing Father Brown and listen to me. You said you never believed that Father Leonard killed Rachel Watson. Well, we've just had someone exonerate Father Leonard. Maybe it doesn't fit the evidence perfectly, but it's enough to call the entire case against him into question. Maybe Rachel died exactly as Marjorie Watson says, maybe she didn't. But I know this. I have a confession to obstruction, and I have a confession to at least an accidental death, at most a negligent homicide. I'll take the win. You should too, you know. Another innocent man walks free, Tom, thanks to you."

Her phone rings. She digs through her bag and pulls it out. Looking at the number, she sighs. "And now I have to tell the State Attorney he will have to go into court and move to quash an indictment." She shakes her head, then answers. "Brian, sorry to bother you, but there's something you need to know." She walks off to where I cannot hear her.

I'm left standing alone by her car in the driveway. A few minutes later, a police car pulls in. Dan Conway gets out, nods his head at me, then walks toward Helen. Helen hangs up, says something to Dan, and they walk together to the house. A few minutes later they emerge, Marjorie Watson walking between the two of them. Edmund follows behind them, telling his wife he will call their lawyer, not to say anything else, while Marjorie tells him to keep quiet. Rebecca stands in the doorway, watching the police taking the woman responsible for her sister's death away, a look of confusion and disbelief on her face.

Someone is missing. I look around. Finally, I see Win. Instead of standing behind his wife, comforting her as I would expect a husband to—as I would have in the same circumstance—he's by himself in the library, looking at the scene through the window.

He catches sight of me, then turns quickly away.

Dan helps Marjorie Watson into the back of his car, then closes the door. He drives off. Helen walks up to me.

"I need to go to the station, but I can drop you off at the Rectory first."

"Thanks." I look back at the house. "Give me a minute," I say, and walk to Rebecca.

"Are you okay?" I ask.

She stares past me for a moment. Then she looks at me. "I don't know," she whispers. "I really don't know." Tears flow, then sobs. She collapses against my chest, painful wails torn from the depths of her soul floating into the early summer evening.

I say a quick prayer and pat her head. Through the open doorway I can see Win Myer. At my glance, he turns and walks off.

Twenty-Six

After a few minutes of sobbing, Rebecca calms down enough to give me the name of a friend we can call to come over to be with her. I have no confidence she'll get any support or comfort from her husband. The woman arrives about fifteen minutes after I call, then Helen and I leave.

"Brian wasn't happy?" I say to her as we drive.

"He wasn't unhappy," Helen says. "He accepted the facts. That we had got it wrong."

She drives along in silence. We continue that way until we get to the Rectory.

"Thanks for the lift," I say.

"I couldn't have you walk home in the dark, now could I? I'll let you know when Father Leonard's hearing will be."

I watch her drive off, then walk into the Rectory and head into the living room. I collapse on the couch, then lean over so I'm laying on it. I close my eyes. I could fall asleep right here.

"Tom? Is that you?" I open my eyes and sit up. "Where have you been, Tom?" Anna says. "You've been gone for hours. You were having coffee with Helen, and then I expected you back."

"Things happened," I say, wiping my hand across my face. "I could use a drink."

"I'll get you a coke."

"Put some rum in it, will you," I say. She stops and looks at me. I never drink anything harder than beer. Unless under stress. And today, I'm under stress.

"You'll understand when I explain what's happened."

I'm astonished that Anna sits through the entire story without saying a word, almost without moving. She looks for all the world like a little girl sitting around a campfire listening to a ghost story.

"So, they will release Father Leonard in a few days," I finish. I've drunk the rum and coke and I'm feeling relaxed. Not drunk, just relaxed.

Anna shakes her head and sighs. "No wonder you started drinking," she mutters. "That's some story Marjorie told."

223

I nod. "It is some story, all right."

Anna's eyes narrow. "You don't believe it, do you?"

"Not all of it, no," I say. "The part about Marjorie framing Father Mc-Coy? Yeah, that I believe. She's calculating enough to do that. She schemed to have her favored daughter marry into the richest family in town, she plotted to get her other daughter out of the way. I'm sure she did all that she said, smearing Leonard with Rachel's blood, wiping the fingerprints, even vacuuming the apartment to remove any traces of evidence. All that I can see her doing." I stop talking.

"But the other part of her story?" Anna asks,

"It's too, I don't know, too something," I say, my exhausted mind groping for the right word. "Some parts just don't make sense to me."

Anna rests her chin on her hands. "What does Helen think?"

"Helen's just thankful that an innocent man's not going to prison," I say. "She believes Marjorie is telling the truth. I don't think she believes some details of the story, but the whole—yeah, she buys it."

"Then why don't you? She's the detective, not you. Solving crimes, catching criminals, that's her job." Anna stands up. "Maybe you should stop thinking about this, just be thankful Father Leonard's been exonerated. Let the police worry about the other. You need to settle down."

"Well, I'm not going anywhere," I say with a sweep of my arms.

"That's not what I'm talking about," she replies as she takes a step forward. "I mean Helen. Neither of you has said anything, but I'm no fool. Maybe someday you'll feel comfortable enough to tell me y'all's story, I know there's one, and I'm dying to hear it. I will not go crazy and scream at you if you tell me, no matter what it is."

I look at her. "You're right. I'm sorry. I'll tell you about Helen, but not tonight. I'm too tired."

"I've waited this long," she says. "But whatever feelings you have for Helen, you need to deal with them and put them away. Father Leonard's situation should be warning enough for you."

I nod and sigh. "Right again, Anna. But it's not going to be a problem. She's leaving Myerton."

"What? Where is she going?"

"Nebraska. A police department in a town near where she grew up."

"When is she leaving?"

I shake my head. "I don't know."

Anna looks at me, stunned by the news. Her face softens, she leans over and gives me a kiss on the cheek. "I'm sorry, son," she says, then leaves me alone.

I look at the fireplace. "So am I, Anna," I whisper. "So am I."

***

It's about 2:30 a.m. in the morning when I wake up with a start. A dream. Another dream about the night of Joan's murder. Finding her killer and unburdening myself of the guilt I'd carried for ten years hadn't stopped the dreams entirely. But this one differed from all the others.

In every other dream, it had been Joan laying dead in my arms, just as it had been the night of the murder. In every other dream, Randy Earl had stood over me, pointing the gun at my head.

Tonight, Helen lay dead in my arms. Tonight, a shadowy figure pointed the gun to my head. I woke up when it pulled the trigger.

I swing my legs over the edge of the bed and run my hand through my hair, making a note that I'm in desperate need for a haircut. I haven't had one since going to the monastery. I realize I'm hungry, remembering I hadn't had dinner the evening before. So much had happened, I forgot to eat.

I pull on my robe and go down to the kitchen. In the fridge, I find half a cold roasted chicken. I take the whole platter, get a glass of water, and walk into the sitting room where the television is. I click it on and flip through the four hundred channels. Finally, I come across an old war movie, black and white. Spies behind enemy lines, trying to break into Nazi headquarters or something like that. I tear off a chicken leg and eat.

Father Leonard's getting out of jail. He's not going to prison. He didn't murder Rachel Watson. But there's still everything else he did. All of that will have to be dealt with. An idea comes to me, one that would solve several problems at the same time. I must call the Archbishop in the morning to tell him they will release Father Leonard and to run my idea past him.

Then there's Helen. She didn't say it in so many words, but she's leaving because she still has feelings for me. After all these years, my coming back awakened something in her. She wants there to be an "us." And that's something I can never give her.

But what are my feelings for her? I shake my head and take another bite of chicken. Any feelings I have for Helen don't matter.

On screen, a group of paratroopers is sneaking through the woods outside of some Nazi headquarters. I don't know why they're there. Either to kidnap someone, kill someone, steal something, or blow something up. In a war movie, the options to explain a group sneaking through the woods at night are limited.

My mind wanders to Marjorie Watson. The methodical way she framed Father Leonard. The depths of evil to which human beings can descend will never cease to amaze me. All for vengeance. All because—

I stop chewing. Why did she go to such lengths to frame Leonard? Simple vengeance for his relationship with her daughter? Did she care that much, did it enrage her so much that she would even vacuum Rachel's apartment to remove any trace of herself? Her presence in the apartment could be explained well enough. She was Rachel's mother. It would have made sense that she would be there. And according to her account, Rachel's death was a tragic accident, brought about by her own actions. Why cover up what wasn't even murder to begin with?

But what if it wasn't just vengeance? What if it wasn't really an accident? Her entire story bothered me. It just made little sense to me.

What if she wasn't covering up for herself?

What if she was trying to protect someone?

On screen, the paratroopers stop at the edge of the woods, and time the guards as they patrol back and forth across the entrance to the facility.

If she was trying to protect someone else, then her entire story was a lie. Or at least the part about how Rachel died. But who would she go to such lengths to protect?

One paratrooper is sneaking up behind a guard, who has stopped walking and has his back to the woods. Why is his back turned? He wouldn't do that in real life. Any threat would come from the woods, not the building. I shake my head. I'm trying to make fiction logical. Real life never is. Why should fiction?

I tear off some breast meat from the carcass. As I chew, I turn the question over in my mind. Who would Marjorie care about that much, to create an entire story that implicated her in not one but two crimes?

The paratrooper has stopped about two feet behind the guard, who is still standing with his back to the woods. Either the guard is deaf, or the big paratrooper has the deft footing of a ballet dancer, because the guard doesn't hear the threat coming out of the dark.

It would have to be someone with a motive to murder Rachel. That was a very limited list. One, Father Leonard, was already eliminated thanks to Marjorie's story. It's ironic that it happened that way; she helped the man she wanted so badly to frame.

The paratrooper moves forward slightly.

Rebecca was jealous of her sister. Jealous of her husband's feelings for her sister. Was she fearful that Rachel's baby was Win's, that she had proof of her worst fears coming true? Was Marjorie trying to protect her daughter, keep her from being arrested on suspicion of murder?

Finally, the paratrooper leaps, grabs the hapless German guard around the neck. The guard struggles, unable to cry out because of the muscular arm constricting his windpipe. I expect the paratrooper to pull out his knife, to finish the soldier off. Instead, he keeps his grip. Gradually, the guard stops struggling, loses consciousness. The paratrooper gently lowers him to the ground, then cuts the wire fencing around the facility.

I pick up my glass and bring it to my lips.

Then I stop. I sit on the edge of the couch.

Someone out of the darkness, suffocating someone to unconsciousness.

I stand up and start pacing. Father Leonard insisted there was a presence in the townhouse when he arrived. Marjorie says she was there. She says she came up behind him and clocked him on the back of the head with a heavy vase. But Leonard said he was suffocated unconscious. From behind. By the unknown presence.

One thing I know. Marjorie Watson is physically incapable of doing that. She's too short, for one. For another, she doesn't have the strength to do it.

So who would be tall enough and strong enough to grab him around the neck and hold him as he struggled long enough to render him unconscious?

And who would know how to do that without killing him?

I look at the screen. The paratroopers are following their leader through the wire.

Someone would have to have training in how to subdue someone quickly and quietly.

Someone like a Green Beret.

I dash up the stairs to my room and grab my phone off the nightstand. I find Helen's number. I'm about the press dial when I stop.

It's 2:30 a.m. in the morning. Do I really want to wake her up over a hunch? I sit on the edge of the bed looking at the phone. I send a quick text, then get up and get dressed.

***

I question my sanity as I sit outside the Myer house. It's 3:30 am, and the place is dark.

"So what's your plan now, Tom?" I say to myself. "Brilliant idea, coming here in the middle of the night. What did you think you would do?"

I have no idea. When I left the Rectory I had a vague idea of confronting Win Myer with my suspicions, to try to get him to admit to the murder of Rachel Watson. The more I drove, however, the more I realized what a crazy idea that was on several levels.

First, I have no evidence. Second, if Win Myer is a murderer, then he's shown he has no problem killing. Third, no one knows where I am. My text to Helen was short and to the point, but "I know who did it ... call me" would give her no idea where to look if I go missing.

In all, not one of my more brilliant ideas.

But here I am, sitting in my fifteen-year-old car outside the Myer house, which looks much more foreboding in the dark than it does in the daylight. Which is saying a lot, because it looks very foreboding in the daylight.

A line from a Star Trek episode comes to mind. "We are committed," Captain Kirk said, which prompted Scotty to ask, "Aye, but to what?"

"To what indeed, Scotty?" I ask myself out loud.

I square my shoulders and cross myself. "Saint Michael the Archangel," I mutter, "defend us fools in battle . . ." Which is not exactly how the prayer goes, I know, but under the circumstances, I need the prince of the heavenly host to know exactly who he needs to defend tonight.

I take a deep breath and get out of the car. I walk up to the door.

Instead of knocking or ringing the doorbell, I try the doorknob. It turns. I push the door open slowly, trying to keep it from squeaking on the hinges.

I stand in the open doorway, peering into the darkened interior. Dark except for a light coming from under a closed door.

The door to Win Myer's office.

I stand there for a few minutes not knowing what to do. Then, I do the dumbest thing possible.

I enter a dark, creepy house in the middle of the night. At this point, I can hear Saint Michael throw down his sword and shield and say, "That's it, I can't help this stupid priest."

Anyone who has seen any number of horror films knows that the number one rule is you never enter a dark and creepy house. It's the rule that uncounted teenagers break in every movie. It's how they wind up as corpses.

And here I am, walking unannounced and uninvited into the house of someone I believe is a murderer.

I tip-toe across the polished wood floor of the entrance, trying my best not to make a sound, alert for the sound of anyone in the room with me. I don't hear anyone, so I continue toward Win Myer's office. I don't hear anyone inside.

I get to the door and reach for the handle. I hesitate, then grip it. I turn the knob and slowly push the door open. I look inside.

The office is empty.

I take two steps away from the room. But I can't go any further. Something is blocking my escape.

A presence in the dark.

The next moment, a powerful arm grabs me around the neck. I grab at the arm, clawing at it, trying to extricate myself from its grasp. I kick, my shoes contacting shins.

"Shh, quiet, quiet," a voice whispers in my ear. I smell alcohol. "Don't struggle. Don't struggle. Struggling will only make it worse."

The light coming from the office gets dimmer and dimmer. Darkness begins to envelope me. I hear a voice say, "It will be all right, Tom."

I recognize the voice.

I whisper, "Joan."

Then blackness.

***

Light is streaming through the windows when I wake up. My entire body is sore. I cough, my throat hurts. I rub it to bring it some relief. I probably have a bruised neck, I think.

I look around, unsure where I am at first. Some kind of brick building, the windows dusted over with age and neglect. The entire place is dusty, covered in cobwebs. I hear the scurrying of tiny feet behind a rusted piece of equipment, looking for all the world like an old steam engine or turbine. The large flywheel is connected by a now-rotted belt to a smaller piece of equipment, from which wires run to the wall.

I slowly get to my feet. I'm unsteady and my head hurts. I stagger to the window and look out.

Across a grassy expanse, I see the rear of the Myer house. I seem to be on the edge of the woods. I turn to look at the equipment in the room with me.

The power house. I'm in the power house, the one that Thomas Edison himself built.

Win Myer. He must have brought me here after knocking me out. Put me in a place where I wouldn't be found for a while, knowing it would be hours before I woke up. Giving him enough time.

But time to do what? I rub the back of my neck, running the possibilities through my mind.

Time to turn himself in, to keep his mother-in-law from being punished for his crimes? No, he would have spoken up during Marjorie's confession if he had any real idea of taking responsibility for what he did. Time to leave Myerton, to run where the law might not find him? He has enough money to do that. But why run if no one suspected him? There is no evidence—I have no evidence, just a hunch. There is no one who knew the whole truth who could accuse him. Or would accuse him. Marjorie knows the truth, and she will go to prison to protect her son-in-law. Father Leonard couldn't identify him. Rachel Watson is dead.

Everyone who can accuse Win Myer of murder is dead, couldn't or wouldn't.

I stop my pacing. I'm wrong. There is one person who knows the truth. One person who can accuse him.

Win Myer.

"Oh, no," I whisper. "Dear Lord, no, not that."

I'm still a little unsteady as I make my way to the door. The hinges have rusted, so it's a little difficult to pull open. I manage to do so, and squint as the light pours in.

I plod across the huge back lawn, making my way with uncertain steps up the slight slope towards the house. It's hot, and I'm soon sweating under the exertion.

I stop about halfway and bend over to catch my breath. From the direction of the house, I hear someone calling my name.

I look up. It's Helen.

I knew she'd find me.

Focusing on her, I continue my slow trek up the hill. She sees my struggle and hurries down the grass towards me. I topple over when she grabs me.

"I've got you, come on, let's get you inside." To a nearby officer, she yells, "Get the paramedics, now!"

"How did you know where to find me?" I gasp.

"I didn't know you were here, not until I saw your car in the driveway," she says. We get to the patio and she takes me inside. The cool air hits me, reviving me some. She helps me to a chair.

"What do you mean, you didn't know I was here?"

"Tom, you sent me a text message at 2:30 this morning that only said. 'I know who did it... call me.' How was I going to figure out where you were from that? I mean, it's not like you said, 'I'm going over to the Myer house where I may be killed.'"

"You didn't ping my cell phone?"

"Frankly, I was about to have Gladys do just that—you have really got to stop confronting murderers on your own, Tom. I'm not always going to be here to save you."

"You didn't this time," I say, rubbing the back of my neck.

She ignores my comment. "Like I said, when Anna called me to say you missed 8:00 Mass—why don't you just stop doing it, I think you miss most of the time—and you weren't in the Rectory, I knew you had done something stupid. I was going to try to locate you when we got a call from Rebecca Myer."

I stop and look at Helen. "Win Myer's dead, isn't he?"

Helen nods. "She found him in his office. He shot himself in the head. She didn't hear the gunshot. It's a big house and their room is on the far end from his office." She pauses. "He left a note. Not so much a note as an essay. It's five pages long."

"What did he say? Did he confess?"

Just then the paramedics come. Helen stands by, concerned, while they check me out. Blood pressure, respiration, ask me to follow their finger with my eyes, check for any injuries.

"How is he?" Helen asks.

"He looks okay, blood pressure, respiration, O2 levels, heart rate all look normal," one medic says. "But we should take him to the hospital to have him checked out."

Helen's about to respond when I say, "I'm not going anywhere, not right now."

She looks at me but, noticing my determination, says, "Fine, Tom. Fine." To the paramedics she says, "Just wait outside." They gather their equipment and leave us alone.

"What did the note say?"

"It would be easier to tell you what the note didn't say," she said. "Like I say, it goes on for five pages. Some of it reads like he was drunk; it rambles, and the handwriting is almost illegible. But the gist of it is he went over to Rachel's a little after 6:00 p.m.. He said he wanted to try one last time to talk her out of going to the convent. According to the note, he had been stalking her off and on since she got back to Myerton. He's been obsessed with her since high school. The note goes on about how much he loved her, how he always loved her." Helen sighs. "The whole thing is a weird combination of creepy and pitiful."

"So he went over to Rachel's."

"She told him she wasn't going to the convent," Helen continues. "She told Myer that Father Leonard was on his way, that they were going to run away together. He was leaving the priesthood, and they were going to marry and raise their child together."

"But she wasn't going to do that," I say.

"I know," Helen says. "But that's what he said in the note. He broke down, apparently, and told her how much he loved her, how he had always loved her, and begged her not to go. He told her if she stayed, he'd divorce Rebecca so they could be together, he'd be the child's father. According to note, she rejected the idea, said she could never do that to her sister, and besides any feelings she once had were gone. She loved Leonard and wanted to be with him." Helen paused. "He said he decided that if he couldn't have her, then no one could, though he also said he didn't mean to kill her."

"He stabbed her in the stomach to kill the baby," I said.

"He said that's all he wanted to do. He said he didn't mean to kill her."

I shake my head, imagining the scene. The look of shock on Rachel's face, a desperate and desolate Win Myer watching as she sinks to the floor, blood pouring from her belly.

"Where does Marjorie Watson come into this?"

"He says he called her," Helen says. "He didn't know what to do, so he called Marjorie. She got there around 6:45 p.m. and was helping him figure out what to do when Father Leonard arrived. He rendered Father Leonard unconscious, then framed him the way Marjorie claims. Myer said he forced her to help him."

"Why did he kill himself?" I ask. "Guilt?" I think of our conversation in the church, and his last words to me.

"The note doesn't give a reason," Helen says. "After the rambling confession, it just stops. Like I say, it looks like he had been drinking. There's an empty scotch bottle and glass next to him, along with the gun in his hand."

She puts her hands on her hips. "Now, will you go to the hospital?"

I shake my head and try to stand up. I reach out to Helen for help. "Where's Rebecca Watson? I should go see her."

"Why?"

"Because it's my job, Helen!" I exclaim. "I'm a priest! She's hurting. Her sister is dead, her mother confessed to a crime, her husband just killed himself after confessing to murder, and her father doesn't seem like he knows what planet he's on half the time. She needs someone, and right now I'm the one who's here. She needs comfort. You have demanded that I let you do your job. Now I'm demanding you let me do mine. Now, are you going to help me up and tell me where she is?"

Helen opens her mouth to say something, then shakes her head. "Fine, Tom," she says as she helps me to my feet. "You've gotten more stubborn the older you've gotten. You can talk to her for a few minutes, but then you're going to the hospital."

The surrounding room tilts a little as I get to my feet. I'm still unsteady and it takes a minute for me to get my footing. I nod and say, "All right. Might be a good idea."

"She's in the living room," Helen says as we walk down the corridor from the entrance to the patio. On the way to the living room, we pass Win Myer's office. The door is open. Crime scene technicians are taking photographs, noting the position of everything in the room. Win's body hasn't been moved yet.

"Wait," I say to Helen. "Take me to him."

"Tom," Helen sighs.

"My job, Helen. Please."

She helps me into the room. Helen signals to the technicians to stop what they are doing. I make it the last few steps to his desk on my own.

He's slumped across the desk, the gun in his right hand. The empty scotch bottle and glass sit in mute testimony to the pain he was trying to numb, to the courage he was trying to summon, to take the last desperate step of taking his own life. There's a pencil cup to his left, spilled over at some point.

I shake my head. I say a prayer for his soul and make the sign of the cross over his lifeless body. I sway a little. Helen is at my side to keep me from keeling over or touching anything in the crime scene.

"Come on," she whispers. "There's nothing else you can do."

I nod. Win Myer is beyond anyone's help now.

We get to the living room. Rebecca Myer is sitting on the sofa, looking out the window, her hair disheveled, wearing a bathrobe and slippers.

I step into the room. "Rebecca," I say quietly. She doesn't acknowledge me.

"May I sit with you for a few minutes?" I ask. At first, there's no response. Then a slight nod.

I walk across the library and sit down. Her hair is damp, and I'm hit with a familiar smell.

Vanilla.

For several minutes, she doesn't speak. Through the open door, I can hear the movement and the murmur of the police and the crime scene techs as they go about their job.

"I'm sorry," Rebecca whispers. "I'm sorry Win hurt you."

"I'll be fine," I tell her. "No permanent damage done."

"I'm surprised he didn't kill you. He's killed before, you know. First in Afghanistan in the Army. He used to tell me when he was drunk. He'd cry over it, cry like a baby. I'd cradle him in my arms." She takes a ragged breath. "He'd only ever let me touch him when he was drunk."

I listen quietly to her, touching her shoulder.

"He killed my sister," she gasps, tears returning. "He killed her because he couldn't have her, because she wouldn't have him. I always knew, I always knew, Father. I was right, you know."

"I'm so sorry."

"I always knew he wanted Rachel. But I knew Rachel would never betray me." She pauses. "Maybe if she had betrayed me, Rachel would still be alive. I'd be alone, devastated, angry with her, and never be able to forgive her. But she'd still be alive."

"You mustn't think that way."

"And Mama," she went on. "She tried to protect Win by confessing to the crime."

"Looks to me like she confessed to protect you," I say quietly, stroking her shoulder, trying to comfort her.

"No, no, I know her. She was concerned Detective Parr would get to Win. She couldn't have that, not her golden child. If it was just me, I might be in jail. She'd have let me go."

"I've seen her with you, she favored you. She sent Rachel away so you could have Win instead of Rachel."

Rebecca shakes her head. "She favored me because I was with Win." She gives a short laugh. "She couldn't have him herself. Maybe I should have worried about her instead of Rachel. Given half a chance, Mama would have slept with Win, I know."

She sighs. She goes back to staring out the window. "He killed my sister. He wanted her. And he killed her."

"He wanted Rachel instead of you," I whisper. "That's why you killed him, isn't it?"

Rebecca turns to me. "How do you know?"

"For one, your hair is wet. You told the police you came downstairs and saw the body, then called them. Shooting him at such close range would have made a mess. You had to take a shower to clean up. Am I right?"

She nods. "Anything else?"

"The gun. It's in his right hand. Win's left-handed, isn't he?"

She gives a short laugh. "Yes. I can't believe I forgot that. I guess in the shock."

"Why don't you tell me what happened?"

"A confession, Father?"

"An unburdening."

She looks at me, then nods. "I woke up, and he still wasn't in bed. The sun was coming up, so I went downstairs to look for him. I found him in his office. He had passed out drunk, I saw the empty bottle and the glass from the doorway. I went to wake him up, help him upstairs to finish sleeping it off—it wouldn't have been the first time. It was only when I got to the desk that I saw the gun. And the note."

"You read it."

"The entire thing. It was like, like every fear I had set in black and white. It was all there, his confession to murdering Rachel mixed in with his declarations of love for her, saying he had always loved her, always wanted her." She pauses. "It was all there. I had proof that what I had always suspected was true. And to top it all off, he had killed her."

I say nothing, just a prayer in my mind for this poor woman.

"He said in the note he couldn't live with himself, that he wanted to die," she continues. "So he had every intention of killing himself. I guess he passed out drunk before he could pull the trigger. The gun looked like it had fallen out of his hand when he slumped over."

"Out of his left hand," I say.

With a tight smile, she says. "Yes, out of his left hand. I remember little of what happened next. I think I just stood there looking at him, stood there for a long time. I thought what a pitiful excuse of a man he was, what a coward, to kill an innocent woman, to allow Mama to lie for him instead of taking responsibility, to lie to me for years, saying he loved me when he didn't."

"You got angry."

"I did, Father Greer. The more I looked at him, the angrier I got. Finally, I decided that if he wanted to kill himself, I'd help him. I picked the gun up off the desk and put the barrel to his head. But I couldn't pull the trigger. God help me, I couldn't do it. I mean, even after everything, even if he didn't love me, I still loved him. I thought once he sobered up, I'd get him to turn himself in, and somehow we'd get through everything."

She shudders. "I had just moved the gun away when he stirred. I leaned over and shook him slightly. 'Win,' I whispered in his ear." She closed her eyes. "He said . . . " She cries again.

"He said Rachel," I finish quietly.

She nods and collapses against me, sobbing. I hold her for a long time, her body wracked with sobs. Finally, I see Helen standing in the doorway. I look at her, then back at Rebecca. She's calmer, sobs replaced by quiet tears rolling down her cheek.

"I need to go, Rebecca. But I think you know what you need to do," I say to her. She looks at me, then nods slowly.

I get to my feet. I'm steadier now, the room not tilting as much. I make my way across the room to Helen.

"What did she say?" she asks as I pass her.

I stop and look back at the figure on the sofa. She's looking out the window again.

"She'll tell you," I whisper. "I can't, remember?"

Twenty-Seven

The crowd of reporters shouts questions as Father Leonard and Angela Jenkins walk out of the courthouse. I'm standing a short distance away, watching the spectacle unfold.

"Father, how does it feel to be free?"

"What are your feelings about Win Myer?"

"Are you going to stay in the priesthood?"

"Where are you going after this?"

"People, people, please," Jenkins says, motioning to the crowd to quiet down. The shouts give way to murmurs, which finally give way to silence. "Father McCoy is extremely pleased that the State Attorney moved to quash the indictment and the judge accepted it. Neither gentleman had much choice given that the actual perpetrator of this horrendous crime gave a full confession in writing before his own death."

Reporters ask questions again, but Jenkins goes on. "It's a good day for justice, it's a good day for the people of Myerton. But it's a reminder of the great responsibility officers of the court have to look at the evidence without prejudice, without trying to put their thumbs on the scale of justice to benefit the rich and powerful at the expense of the weak. That's what Brian Dohrmann did in this case. Fortunately, thanks to the hard work and the personal integrity of a few people, a miscarriage of justice was averted. Now let me get the good Father back to his parish where he can rest. Thank you."

Jenkins takes Father Leonard, looking as confused as ever, by the arm and forces her way through the press of reporters. They haven't seen me yet, and since I'm partially hidden behind a tree, I'm certain no one will see me.

"Hiding from someone?" I jump. Helen has snuck up behind me.

"Just the baying hounds of the press," I say.

"What? You want to deny the representatives of the fourth estate a chance to ask you questions?" she says with a smile.

"In a word, yes," I say.

"Don't blame you," Helen says. Her eyes follow Jenkins and Father Leonard to the attorney's car. "What will happen to him?"

"Father Leonard," I say, "has some work to do."

"What do you mean?"

"Prayer, thought, he needs to decide if he wants to stay a priest or not. You don't think that's work? Trust me, it's work."

"He's not staying here, so where is he going?"

"I've talked to the Archbishop about that," I say. "I suggested he spend several months at Our Lady of the Mount. It's perfect. They need a priest to provide the sacraments, Leonard needs a place where he can pray and heal." I pause. "The monastery is the perfect place for that."

Helen is looking at Angela Jenkins as she gets into her car. "Leave it to her to turn it into a political speech," she mutters. "Brian'll hit the roof when he sees it."

"How is he doing?"

She shrugs. "I don't know. I haven't seen him today."

The crowd of reporters having dispersed, we emerge from my hiding place and walk towards the sidewalk.

"What are you thinking about?" Helen asks.

"Swords."

She stops. I turn to her. "You know how Scripture describes the Word of God?"

"Ah, wait, don't tell me—"

"As sharper than a two-edged sword. Soldiers used a two-edged sword in battle. Do you know why the sword had two-edges?"

She shakes her head. "It can cut if swung down or if brought up," I explain. "Either way, it can kill."

"And you were thinking about swords because?"

"I was thinking about how love is like a two-edged sword. It has such power to bring people together. It brings hope. It brings life into the world. It's wonderful. It's one of the three theological virtues. God is love. The entire Church rests on Love. Love has so much power for good." I shake my head. "It also has so much power for evil."

At Helen's questioning look, I go on. "Look at all that's happened. Father Leonard loved Rachel. The love he felt led him into sin, into breaking his vow of celibacy. Rachel loved Leonard. Her love led her to question her call to the religious life. Win Myer loved Rachel, a love which was perverted into obsession, which is why he killed her. Marjorie Watson loved her son-in-law, which led her to dispose of one daughter and betray another. Rebecca Watson loved Win, but couldn't live with him not loving her, so she killed him. So love can create. It can also destroy."

Helen sighs. "You always were the life of the party, you know that?"

I laugh. "It's just the musings of a cynical priest, Helen."

Looking at her watch, she says. "I'm hungry. How about lunch?"

Just then her phone rings. Helen rolls her eyes and fishes the phone out of her bag.

"Yes, Dan, what is it?" She listens. "Well, it took them long enough, but why . . . What!" Helen's eyes get big. "Say that again? You're sure of the time?" She listens as Dan Conway tells her something. She looks at me. "Contact the bank. I want the surveillance footage yesterday." She listens and smiles. "Good job, Dan, you've earned your pay for the week. We'll be right there." She hangs up.

"Come on, Tom, we have a problem," Helen says over her shoulder as she strides off.

I trot to catch up with her. "Wait, what's going on, Helen?"

She turns around. "We finally got Rachel Watson's bank records. It's standard practice in any investigation, but it took the bank a long time to get them together. Apparently, they just changed computer systems and they've had problems." She inhales. "She made an ATM withdrawal from the branch near her townhouse at 6:42 p.m. on the night of her murder. So the person Walkin saw entering Rachel's townhouse was Rachel."

I look at her, wide-eyed. "But that means she couldn't have been in her apartment when Marjorie Watson says she got there. She couldn't have been in there when Win Myer says he killed her."

"And," Helen says slowly, "no one else entered the townhouse before Father Leonard."

I'm feeling sick to my stomach. "Oh, my dear Lord," I whisper.

Helen nods. "Yes Tom. I'm sorry, but you've been wrong all along."

Twenty-Eight

"I was taking a nap in my cell," Marjorie Watson says. "I don't know why you'd drag me out to ask me more questions. I confessed days ago. You have Win's note. You've already released Father Leonard."

"We've had some additional evidence," Helen says. "This shouldn't take too long if you're honest with us now."

"Why is he even here?" she points to me. "The last thing I need is a priest."

"Never mind why he's here," Helen replies. "I have two things to show you." She opens the folder in her hands.

"This," Helen says as she lays a piece of paper on the table in front of Marjorie, "is a listing of all Rebecca's financial transactions in the last week of her life." She points to a line at the bottom of the page. "This is the last one. An ATM withdrawal for $600. We assume that was to pay for the abortion in Hagerstown."

Marjorie shrugs. "So?"

"Look," Helen says. Marjorie leans forward to read where Helen's finger has stopped. She squints, then looks up at us with surprise.

"But, but, that's—" she sputters.

I nod. "Yes. The last withdrawal she ever made was at 6:42 p.m. on the night of her murder. Around the same time you claim you arrived at her townhouse. And after the time Win Myer claimed in his suicide note that he killed her."

She's wide-eyed, her mouth slightly open as Helen places a photograph in front of her. "This is from the ATM surveillance camera. It's Rachel. Look at the time stamp." She sits back and crosses her arms.

Marjorie picks up the photograph. Still looking at it, she sits back in her chair, tears beginning to well up. "She didn't do it," she whispers.

I lean forward. "You thought Rebecca had killed her sister, didn't you?"

Biting her lip, she nods. "The detective seemed so sure," she whispers. She shakes her head as the tears flow down her cheek. "I couldn't, I couldn't see her go to prison. I'd already lost one daughter."

"So you made up the entire story," Helen says, "because you wanted to draw attention away from Rebecca."

"Yes," she says.

"You'd confess to a crime you didn't commit, go to prison?" I say.

"You're not a mother, Father Tom," she says. "Despite what Rebecca and Rachel thought, I love my daughters. I'd do anything for them. I've done everything for them. Oh, I know how I come across. I'm not a snuggly mommy type, I never was. I wanted my girls to be strong and independent, but I wanted them to be secure. When Rachel showed no interest in Win Myer in high school, I put Rebecca and him together. Sending Rachel away may have been a mistake, but I did it out of love." She sighs. "I know it makes little sense, but that's all I've ever done."

"Out of his love for you, Win confessed in his suicide note. He was covering for you. He knew you were trying to take suspicion off Rebecca. Plus, he felt guilty over . . . other things," I say.

"Did you go to Rachel's townhouse that night?" Helen asks.

She shakes her head. "No. At the time of her murder, I was home. I don't remember what I was doing. Edmund was out with some colleagues of his. So I have no alibi."

Helen shakes her head. Pointing to the picture, she says. "Rachel provided you with an alibi." She stands up. "I must talk to the State Attorney, but you'll be free in a few days. You should call your lawyer. I'll arrange for that."

We start at the door when Marjorie asks, "So Father Leonard killed my daughter?" She fixes me with a glare. "So, you are responsible, Father Greer, for Rachel's death. If you had just listened to me, she might be alive today."

I glance at her but say nothing. Helen opens the door and we step into the hallway. Helen tells the officer to take Marjorie back to her cell.

We walk together down the hallway to her office. She drops into her desk chair and places her head on her arms.

"Where's Father Leonard right now?" she asks.

"He's probably at the Rectory," I say.

She looks weary when she sits up. Grabbing the receiver of her desk phone, she presses some buttons. "This is Detective Parr," she says to the person who answers. "Send a car to the Saint Clare's Rectory and get Father

Leonard." She pauses. "I don't care what they tell him, just bring him here!" She slams the receiver down and looks at me. "What?"

I'm looking to one side, staring at a spot on the wall. "Huh? Oh, I was just thinking. You were right. And as much as it pains me to say it, Brian was right. Leonard did it. He fooled me." I pause. "Apparently, I'm a very gullible person."

Helen smiles. "You think the best of people, that's one reason I fell in love with you."

I look at her. "I've become more cynical. I should have clung to that this time. Then I might have seen through Leonard's deceptions."

"Excuse me, Chief." I turn to see Gladys Finklestein in Helen's doorway. "This just came in for you." She rolls in and hands an envelope to Helen.

"Thanks, Gladys," Helen says.

"No problem, Chief," Gladys replies. Turning to me she smiles. "Hi, Father Tom," she says, slightly breathlessly.

"Hello, Gladys," I reply. "How are you doing?"

"Me? Oh, I am much better now. It's been a while since I've seen you."

"You haven't been at Mass, I've noticed."

She actually bats her eyelashes and plays with a strand of her blue hair. "So, you've missed me?" she asks. "Because I've sure missed you."

"Gladys!" Helen says.

The young woman jumps. "Huh? Oh, yeah. OK. I'll just go back to my office." She starts to the door and turns around slightly. With a coquettish grin, she purrs, "Bye, Father."

Looking after her as she leaves, I say, "You weren't kidding about her."

Helen doesn't answer me. Instead, she says, "These are the results of the DNA test on Rachel's baby. It's definite. Father Leonard was the father."

Before I can answer, her phone rings. "Yes?" she answers. Looking at me, she says. "What do you mean there's no one at the Rectory?"

I pull my phone out and dial Anna. After a few rings, she answers. "Hello," she says. In the background I hear other people and the pinging of cash registers.

"Anna, where's Father Leonard?"

"Father Leonard? Why are you asking? You know where he is."

"What do you mean?"

"When he got back to the rectory, he told me you told him to go to Our Lady of the Mount immediately. He packed his things and left about half an hour after he got back. I've been wondering where you've been."

I look at Helen. "Thanks, Anna." I hang up.

"He's gone," I say, "But I know where he is."

Twenty-Nine

Helen calls the state police and asks them to go to Our Lady of the Mount to detain Father Leonard.

"I want to talk to him," I say.

"Tom, this is a police matter. Besides, what makes you think he'll say anything to you now? He's either not spoken or lied this whole time."

"Because he's carrying a tremendous burden," I say. "He has to be getting tired. He needs to tell someone. Besides, I need to know why."

"He can tell me when I arrest him."

"That's not what I mean."

We look at each other. "If you hear his confession," Helen says slowly, "you won't be able to tell me what he said."

I nod. "That's true. I'll try to get him to agree to confess to you for his crimes, but there are no guarantees." I pause. "But he's at the end of his rope. Otherwise, he wouldn't have left Saint Clare's so abruptly."

"I don't know, Tom," Helen shakes her head. "I'd rather you spoke to him after I took him into custody and interviewed him."

"You've interviewed him before," I point out, "and you got very little. And none of the truth. So you won't be any further behind than you were."

Helen sighs, then nods. "Okay, when we take him into custody, I'll allow you fifteen minutes. After that, I'm taking over. Sound good?"

I nod. "Sounds great."

"It's not like I need his confirmation of what we already know," Helen says. "The physical evidence really points to him. Brian got an indictment once. He'll get another one. It would just be easier all around if he confessed."

"Easier for Brian, don't you mean?"

"Don't start Tom, not now. For me, too. I mean, I'm the one who followed your word. That it was Rebecca the neighbor saw go into Rachel's townhouse. I'm the one who bought Marjorie Watson's story. And then there was Win's note."

I nod. "But I so wanted to believe Leonard was innocent. He just doesn't seem like the type to murder someone."

"Take it from me, Tom," Helen says, patting my arm. "Most murderers are like that. They're not perpetually mean. They look perfectly normal on the outside, and most of the time, they are. But something pushes them into thinking they have no other choice but to take a human life."

"People always have a choice."

She shrugs. "Maybe they just can't see it. Or maybe they see the choice as an impossible one."

***

I consider what Helen said to me as we drive to the monastery. It's dark by the time we turn off the main road onto the long gravel drive. Outside of Brother Martin's cabin are two Maryland State Police cars, their occupants speaking to Brother Martin by the light of the headlights.

Helen parks and gets out. I fumble with my seatbelt and follow her.

"Troopers," she says. "What's going on?"

A Latina trooper says, "Detective, the suspect was not in his cabin. This gentleman," she indicates the elderly monk, "refuses to let us into the main building."

Looking at me, Brother Martin says. "I've explained to these officers, it's the great silence. We cannot disturb the brothers."

"It's important, Brother Martin," I say. "We need to find Father Leonard. Do you have any idea where he is?"

He shakes his head. "No. He got here right after Vespers and asked for the same retreat cabin he had last time. I hadn't been expecting him and explained that the cabin hadn't been cleaned after the last retreatant. He insisted it was no problem. He practically demanded the cabin." Brother Martin looked grim. "Such a different man than last time. I should have known something was wrong. But I knew he had been under a strain, so I ignored my concerns."

"And that's the last you saw him?"

"Yes," Brother Martin replies.

"We need to find him, Brother Martin," Helen says. "Can you please let us search inside the building?"

"I'm sorry Detective," he shakes his head. "We cannot break the great silence. Besides, I strongly doubt he's there."

"Why is that?" Helen asks.

"Because they lock the door from the inside, and I'm the only one outside with a key."

Helen and I look at Brother Martin. "Since when did the brothers begin locking the door?" I ask.

"Right after you left this last time, we had an intruder in the middle of the night. Got to the chapel and tried to take off with the candlesticks. Fortunately, Brother Bartholemew heard him and subdued the man."

I smile. Brother Bartholemew is a former defensive tackle for the Baltimore Ravens.

"Brother Bartholemew," Brother Martin explains to Helen, "suffers from insomnia."

"So if he's not in the main building," Helen says, looking around, "where is he?"

"We were just about to call in a search team with dogs, get a helicopter with infrared and night vision," says the other State Trooper.

While they're talking, I'm looking in a familiar direction.

"That won't be necessary," I say quietly. "I think I know where he is."

***

I'm right.

Father Leonard is on his knees before the statue of Our Lady in the Grotto. The moonlight brightly illuminates the statues of both Mary and Saint Bernadette. I can make out Leonard on the ground between Bernadette and the statue. He's muttering loud enough so I can hear him. He's saying the sorrowful mysteries of the Rosary.

I try to tiptoe up to him, but I step on and break a small branch. Father Leonard jumps up with a cry, spinning around.

"Who—who's there," he stammers. "The police? Have you come for me? I didn't mean to do it!"

I approach carefully, not wanting to spook the already fragile Father. "It's me, Leonard," I say.

"Oh," Father Leonard says with a sigh of relief. "Father Tom. I thought—"

Walking closer, I say, "You're right, Leonard. The police are here. They know what you did, Leonard. They know you murdered Rachel."

Father Leonard's mood changes. He advances toward me, his fists clenched. In a moment, he's transformed from a pitiful lamb to a raging bull, his breathing heavy. He turns and stomps off a few feet. "Stupid girl," he mutters. "Just like my mother warned me about."

"What did your mother warn you about?"

He spins around, extending his hands. "Women, Father Tom! Surely you understand what they're like!"

I shake my head and sit down on one of the rough-hewn benches stretched before the Grotto. "Why don't you tell me? What did your mother tell you about them?"

He paces like a caged animal, stricken, wounded, looking for an escape. Only instead of running, Father Leonard is looking for something else. Understanding.

"She warned me, she warned me all about them," he says. "How they were sent by Satan to tempt me, to distract me from my calling. 'The devil has the power to take on a pleasing shape,' she'd say, every time a girl showed any interest in me. I had a friend in kindergarten. She had pigtails and green eyes. I can't remember her name, but she was my only friend. One day, my mother came to pick me up from school. I walked up to her holding my friend's hand and said she was my girlfriend." He paused and shuddered. "I was smiling until I saw the look on my mother's face. She yanked me away from my friend and practically threw me in the car." He looked down at his feet. "When she got me home, she used one of my father's belts on me. She yelled at me the whole time, saying the devil sent all girls to take me away from my calling, that I needed to stay away from them."

"My God," I whisper.

"She kept me home after that," Father Leonard says. He stops his pacing and looks at me. "She was right. That's what women are for us, aren't they? Tempting us, testing us constantly, wanting to take us from serving the Lord to serving their fleshly needs."

"She didn't keep you home the entire time, did she? You went to Mass, you saw girls your own age there?"

"I stayed away from them," Father Leonard says. "After Mass, we'd go straight to the car and go home. I'd spend the rest of the day meditating on the mass readings or studying." He brightens up. "I taught myself Greek and Latin that way. It's amazing what you can do when you're not distracted."

"But surely you were friends with boys? She couldn't object to that?"

"Oh, she said they were just as bad, worse. She said they'd either try to show me indecent pictures of girls to tempt me to defile myself, or they were little perverts who'd try to turn me into a pervert." He sighed. "Besides, it's not like anyone wanted to play with me, anyway. I was the weird boy with the science-fiction name and the strange mother. So they stayed away from me."

"I don't understand, Leonard," I say. "If she was so concerned, so protective, why did she want you sent away to a boarding school for high school?"

He smiles and sits down opposite me. "She thought it would be okay. She was concerned that after she died, there would be no one to protect me—my father really didn't care, you see. Besides, a rather strict and traditional order ran the school, and since it was all boys, she told me it would keep me free from temptations. She was wrong."

"That's when you met Rachel."

"Yes," his face brightens for a moment, then darkens. "Every time I saw her, every dance, I just felt the temptation so strongly. I'd go back to my room and do penance. I kept thinking I had disappointed my mother."

I look at Father Leonard. "You were afraid of disappointing your dead mother by seeing Rachel?"

"I knew she was already disappointed," he whines. "I knew she could see everything I was doing. I'd hear her voice, her warning voice, in my head every day. I even felt the marks on my back from years ago. I had been so careful, but I found myself drawn to Rachel. I—I couldn't help myself."

"You were young, Leonard," I say. "You're still young. This life we have, it's hard, it's a discipline. It's not for everyone. Maybe you were finding . . ."

"No, no, don't say it!" He cries, shaking his head vigorously. "No, I'm a priest. I was always meant to be a priest. My mother told me she promised God I would be a priest."

Father Leonard plops down on the bench in front of me. In the dim light, I can see his shoulders sagging. He's defeated, exhausted. But there is still more he needs to say.

"So you graduated high school, went away to Seminary," I say quietly. "You kept Rachel's photograph."

"I wanted to forget about her," he whispers. "But I couldn't. She . . . she had a hold on me. Every time I looked at her picture, I'd feel happy." He drops his head. "Then I'd hear my mother's voice telling me to tear the picture up. But I couldn't. I knew that disappointed her."

"The day of her murder," I say, "Did you really plan on asking her to marry you? Did you really plan on leaving the priesthood?"

"Yes!" he screams. "Yes! I was content to stay a priest until I got her email saying she was going away. I saw that, and I realized I didn't want her to go. The only way I could think to get her to stay was . . . to give up everything for her." He pauses. "To disappoint my mother for her."

I put my hand on his shoulder. "So you went to her apartment, told her what you had planned, and asked her to marry you. What happened?"

He stands up with a jerk, his fists clenching. "She said no," Leonard says through gritted teeth. "After everything I had done, after everything I was prepared to do, she said no, she was going to the convent. We needed to forget about each other, I needed to renew my call." He's breathing heavily. "I—I just couldn't believe it. After everything. I thought she was different. But my mother was right. Satan had used Rachel to pull me away from God."

"Did she tell you she was pregnant?"

Even in the dim light, I can see the rage in his eyes. "That made it worse! Not only was she a tool of Satan, she was going to murder an innocent."

"You couldn't let it happen, could you?"

"No!" The pitiful expression is gone, replaced with a maniacal one. "No, I couldn't let her do that to an innocent child. I had to deliver her soul from hell before she could condemn herself. Don't you see, Father? I saved her from committing a grave sin!"

I look him steadily in the eyes. "You stabbed her."

"Yes! Yes! I had to! She left me no choice!"

"But she didn't die right away."

He shakes his head. "No. She lay on the floor gasping, looking at me with her eyes wide. I held her, stroked her hair, told her it would be all right, that she had a chance to repent of her sins. I said the prayers for the dying and gave her absolution. I had just made the sign of the cross when she breathed her last."

"Then you sat with her dead body for hours," I whisper. "You concocted a story, then called me, pretended not to remember anything, said a presence suffocated you in her townhouse?"

He nodded. "I think I knew it wouldn't work. I knew God was punishing me for turning my back on Him and on my calling. I deserved to go to prison." Then he smiled. "Then when Marjorie, then Win, confessed to her murder—even to framing me—I could see it all. God was showing his approval. He had forgiven me for everything, allowing me a second chance."

I shake my head. "No, Leonard. We found out that Rachel got to her townhouse just before you did. That the only person who could have killed her was you. Besides, you just confessed to the crime."

"Only to you, only to you," he says. "And you can't tell anyone!"

"He may not be able to," Helen says as she walks into the clearing from the woods. "But I can. Father Leonard McCoy, you're under arrest for the murder of Rachel Watson."

He jumps up as she approaches. "But you eavesdropped on my confession to Father Tom!" he cries. "You can't say anything either! You'll be excommunicated!"

"But I wasn't hearing your confession, Leonard," I say slowly.

Father Leonard looks down at me, wild-eyed. "What? Yes, you did! You asked me—"

I shake my head. "No, I said nothing about hearing your confession."

"He's right, Father Leonard. We have the entire conversation on tape."

Father Leonard looks at her, then at me, then collapses onto the bench. He turns and looks up at the statue of Our Lady bathed in the moonlight. He lowers his head and sobs.

Epilogue

The headline of the Myerton Gazette says it all.

Saint Clare's Priest Arrested, Charged with Murder

I don't read the article, since I already know what it says. Much of it is just a summary of the press conference at the Police Station earlier that morning, and quotes pulled from the statement of State Attorney Brian Dohrmann. That contained a defense of the state's original case against Father Leonard, criticism of the defense attorney, and what I thought was a gratuitous slap at the Catholic Church.

Anna comes into the office with a cup of coffee. "Did you read it?" I say as I take the mug from her.

"I read it," she says, sitting down. "I still can't believe it."

I shake my head. "Neither can I. I can't believe I was so wrong."

"It's not your fault, Tom."

"He had me completely fooled. I really thought he was innocent, I believed his entire story."

"He had us all fooled. No one I know thought he was guilty."

"I was so quick to judge the Myers and the Watsons. I just knew one of them had something to do with it."

"From what you've told me, Marjorie Watson thought so, too."

I shake my head. "But the only member of the family guilty of murder was Rebecca. Because of her jealousy."

Anna sits back. "What will happen to her?"

"I don't know," I reply. "I guess she'll be indicted for murder. I understand Angela Jenkins has signed on as her defense attorney."

She raises her eyebrows. "I guess her disdain for the Myer family has its limits."

I shrug. "My calendar is clear today, isn't it?"

Anna nods her head. "You had two meetings today. I rescheduled them for next week. I figured you'd be busy."

"Thanks. I want to go see Father Leonard, spend some time with him."

"How was he when you left?"

I consider her question. "Calm. Surprisingly so. I heard his confession—for real, this time—and granted him absolution."

Anna cocks her head to one side. "You almost crossed a line with him at the monastery, didn't you?"

I grimace. "I got right on the line. But he never asked me to hear his confession then, he just started talking. I used, shall we say, prudential judgement? But I will take it up with my confessor when I see him."

"Well, speaking of confessions," Anna says, sitting back. "You've still never told me the story about you and Helen."

I smile and place the now empty coffee mug on my desk. "All right, all right," I say. "The fact of the matter is that years ago, Helen and I—"

My phone rings. "Speak of the devil," I say when I see the number. Answering, I say, "Hi, I was just talking about you."

"Tom," Helen says, a solemn tone in her voice. "You need to come down to the jail."

The blood drains from my face. "What's wrong, Helen?"

"It's Father Leonard," she says. "A guard found him in his cell." She pauses. "He's dead, Tom. He hanged himself with torn strips of his shirt."

I hang up the phone without saying a word. Anna looks at me with concern. "Tom? What is it?"

I look at her. I've lost the ability to speak. Without a word, I get up and walk out of my office, Anna calling after me. I walk from the Rectory to the church.

The church is quiet, the morning sun streaming through the stained glass, the votive candles flickering. I cross to the center of the sanctuary and kneel on the bottom step. I look up at the tabernacle. Tears form in my eyes.

Taking my rosary, I pray for the souls of the dead.

The End

About the Author

Susan Mathis was born in and grew up in an extremely small town in Alachua County, Florida where her family has lived for more than 100 years. When Susan was still very young, James (J.R) Mathis was born in a somewhat bigger small town about 100 miles south of where she lived. Within a decade, James' small town would become part of Orlando, the biggest tourist destination in the United States. He was not amused. That is how, while Susan was running barefoot, swimming in lakes full of alligators and feeding chickens, James was sitting in his bedroom reading books faster than his father could bring them home from the library.

Were James and Susan to write their love story, it would definitely be an enemies-to-lovers trope. They met in the library where he was working. He found her demands for books that he had to pull and bring to her so unreasonable that he actually turned her into the head librarian. She in turn was so anxious to drive him away that when some friends secretly set them up she laid out an entire speech about how miserable her life was (she is typically very upbeat). Little did she suspect that he had a passionate attraction to misery and they were married just over a year later.

Fast forward 26 years, three children, four grandchildren and 20 years of James working for the Federal government. He was diagnosed with a highly treatable but still very scary form of cancer. As so often happens, this brush with mortality inspired him to do something he'd always wanted to do, write a novel. After the publication of the second Father Tom Mystery, Susan joined him as coauthor. As far as the Mathises are concerned, writing together is the most fun a couple can have sitting at a computer.

Read more at https://www.facebook.com/groups/J.R.MathisAuthor/.

Printed in the USA
CPSIA information can be obtained
at www.ICGtesting.com
LVHW040208080424
776725LV00018B/77

9 781393 951155